HERE FOR YOU

HERE FOR YOU

Praise for D. Jackson Leigh

Unbridled

"A hot, steamy, erotic romance mystery with edge, exciting twists and turns, great characters and an unforgettable story that I was completely invested in. It was difficult to put the book down and I thoroughly enjoyed the whole experience of reading it!"
—*LESBIReviewed*

Blades of Bluegrass

"Both lead characters, Britt and Teddy, were well developed and likeable. I also really enjoyed the supporting characters, like E.B., and the warm, familiar atmosphere the author managed to create at Story Hill Farm."—*Melina Bickard, Librarian, Waterloo Library (UK)*

Ordinary Is Perfect

"There's something incredibly charming about this small town romance, which features a vet with PTSD and a workaholic marketing guru as a fish out of water in the quiet town. But it's the details of this novel that make it shine."—*Pink Heart Society*

Take a Chance

"I really enjoyed the character dynamic with this book of two very strong independent women who aren't looking for love but fall for the one they already love…The chemistry and dynamic between these two is fantastic and becomes even more intense when their sexual desires take over."—*Les Rêveur*

Dragon Horse War

"Leigh writes with an emotion that she in turn gives to the characters, allowing us insight into their personalities and their very souls. Filled with fantastic imagery and the down-to-earth flaws that are sometimes the characters' greatest strengths, this first *Dragon Horse War* is a story not to be missed. The writing is flawless, the story, breath-taking—and this is only the beginning."—*Lambda Literary Review*

"The premise is original, the fantasy element is gripping but relevant to our times, the characters come to life, and the writing is phenomenal. It's the author's best work to date and I could not put it down."—*Melina Bickard, Librarian, Waterloo Library (UK)*

"Already an accomplished author of many romances, Leigh takes on fantasy and comes up aces…So, even if fantasy isn't quite your thing, you should give this a try. Leigh's backdrop is a world you already recognize with some slight differences, and the characters are marvelous. There's a villain, a love story, and…ah yes, 'thar be dragons.'"—*Out in Print: Queer Book Reviews*

"This book is great for those that like romance with a hint of fantasy and adventure."—*The Lesbrary*

"Skin Walkers" in *Women of the Dark Streets*

"When love persists through many lifetimes, there is always the potential magic of reunion. Climactically resplendent!"—*Rainbow Book Reviews*

Swelter

"I don't think there is a single book D. Jackson Leigh has written that I don't like…I recommend this book if you want a nice romance mixed with a little suspense."—*Kris Johnson, Texas Library Association*

"This book is a great mix of romance, action, angst, and emotional drama…The first half of the book focuses on the budding relationship between the two women, and the gradual revealing of secrets. The second half ramps up the action side of things…There were some good sexy scenes, and also an appropriate amount of angst and introspection by both women as feelings more than just the physical started to surface."—*Rainbow Book Reviews*

Call Me Softly

"*Call Me Softly* is a thrilling and enthralling novel of love, lies, intrigue, and Southern charm."—*Bibliophilic Book Blog*

By the Author

Romance

Call Me Softly

Touch Me Gently

Hold Me Forever

Swelter

Take a Chance

Ordinary Is Perfect

Blades of Bluegrass

Unbridled

Forever Comes in Threes

Here for You

Cherokee Falls Series

Bareback

Long Shot

Every Second Counts

Dragon Horse War Trilogy

The Calling

Tracker and the Spy

Seer and the Shield

Short story collection

Riding Passion

Visit us at www.boldstrokesbooks.com

HERE FOR YOU

by

D. Jackson Leigh

2023

HERE FOR YOU

ISBN 13: 978-1-63679-299-6

This Trade Paperback Original Is Published By
Bold Strokes Books, Inc.
P.O. Box 249
Valley Falls, NY 12185

First Edition: July 2023

Credits

Editor: Shelley Thrasher
Production Design: Stacia Seaman
Cover Design by Tammy Seidick

This book is dedicated to my family and friends, past and present, who stood by me or just called for a conversation during my 2022 year of fighting breast cancer. Thankfully, I've been pronounced clear, but the support I received made a huge difference in keeping my spirits up while my energy was so low. You were here for me. I love you all.

FOREWORD

If any of you are fans of barrel racing or participate in the sport, please note this story is a work of fiction.

While researching for this book, I realized barrel racing involves a confusing web of different organizations, levels of expertise, and rodeo circuits. Several times I failed to find answers to my questions about the rules, so I had to go with a common-sense answer.

Also, I fashioned Lacey Bishop's hop from rodeo to rodeo to fit the timeline required to unfold this story, exercising the right of a fiction writer to manipulate which towns held rodeos and when. Please forgive this type of inaccuracy if you live in one of those towns and they don't host a rodeo, or maybe hold it during a different time of year.

If you can forgive any discrepancies between facts and my fictional story, please sit back and enjoy the ride.

D. Jackson Leigh

CHAPTER ONE

The sun beat down on the chute leading into the outdoor dirt arena, warmed by an unseasonable heat wave, as Lacey Bishop mentally reviewed the cloverleaf pattern she would ride around the barrels one more time. When she adjusted her hat low on her forehead, sweat trickled past her temple and along her jaw.

Lacey's buckskin mare, Denver, was a competitor, pumped and primed for the reckless sprints and spins around the three barrels before an all-out, homestretch gallop past the timer. So, she let Denver work herself into an adrenaline rush, turning her in a small circle to contain the horse's excitement and loosen muscles needed to make the hairpin, near-full-speed turns. She ignored the frowns of other riders whose horses were agitated by Denver's twirling wind-up as they waited their turn.

One more twirl as her name was announced, and she clapped her calves against Denver's flanks to rocket them past the arena's electronic timer. Clods of the soft dirt flew around them as she shifted her weight to help Denver keep her footing when she dug into the first turn. Tight and perfect. Lacey tightened her legs and pressed the balls of her feet against the wide stirrups to stretch over the mare's neck for a low, aerodynamic gallop to a point about six feet to the right of the second barrel, then eased back in the saddle to slow their pace as they hit the turn's pocket and cut sharp enough that her leg barely brushed the other side of the barrel without tipping it. She focused on the crucial third barrel. Too many racers, eager for the mad dash to the finish line, cut the last turn short. Knocking the barrel over would add a devastating five-second penalty to their time. She sat back to slow for a clean turn, then shifted her hundred and twenty pounds forward over Denver's withers—stretching over her neck like a flat-race jockey—for the final sprint to trip the timer.

The announcer's voice boomed over the speakers. "Fourteen-point-three-eight seconds! Lacey Bishop takes the lead in her final run."

Lacey and Denver shot through the chute and onto the adjacent warm-up area, where they finally slowed, and she guided her mare into a figure-eight pattern to gear down to a cooling walk. They had made it around once when the announcer's voice boomed over the arena again.

"Our final contestant is Brittney Abbott, riding Dash of Charm, now in second place." This competition awarded the win to the fastest run, rather than a cumulative time from the contestants' three runs. So, Brittney needed to run only a hundredth of a second faster to regain first place, even though her earlier times weren't that fast.

"Brittney can beat that time, no problem," one rider said loud enough to ensure Lacey heard as she and Denver returned to watch Brittney's run.

"Go, Brittney," another said.

"You've got this, Brittney," a third yelled. Several of the group of other contestants near the chute cast furtive glances at Lacey, but she sat tall in the saddle and ignored them.

Brittney was pretty, feminine, and wealthy. They either were her friend or aspired to be so they would be included in the parties Brittney threw in her hotel suite each time she won an event.

Lacey would always be an outsider. She lived in her horse trailer/camper and showered at truck stops or campgrounds that allowed horses. She ignored the other riders as much as they avoided her. Her solitary life didn't bother her, but she hated how they whispered anytime she was near. And she resented that they all were cheering for Brittney to snatch this win from her.

Well, not all.

A tall, dark-haired woman shook her head and pushed away from the metal rails of the arena enclosure where she'd been watching the action. She turned toward the parking lot but paused and looked up as she neared Lacey.

"Congratulations on your win," she said, running her gaze over Denver before locking it with Lacey's.

Captured by the woman's smile and blue eyes, Lacey nodded until her brain could engage. She cleared her throat. "Final scores aren't in yet."

The woman shrugged. "She's going to blow it."

Lacey finally tore her attention from the woman and stood in her stirrups in time to see Brittney round the second barrel and head for the third. Her trajectory was a scant foot too wide, but Brittney overcompensated, and her boot scraped against the barrel mid-turn. She whipped her horse down the homestretch, on target to stop the timer at fourteen-point-three-six, but the barrel teetered on its left edge and toppled a second before Brittney and Dash tripped the timer.

The cheers went abruptly silent, replaced by a few groans as a five-second penalty changed her time to nineteen-point-three-six. Dash shied away when Brittney sprang from the saddle and kicked at the chute's rails while yelling a litany of foul language. When the wrangler who tended her horses and drove them to events grabbed the reins of the spooked horse, Brittney paused her tantrum and pointed at them. "Get him out of my sight. Take him back to the ranch."

Lacey grinned at Brittney's groupies, but she was disappointed when she looked down to share her smile with the mystery woman. She had disappeared. Lacey turned Denver toward their own trailer just as she was being announced as winner of the competition. She didn't need Brittney's drama spoiling her victory, even if Denver was the only one around to share it. She scanned the rodeo grounds. She didn't normally seek out strangers, or anyone really, but she wanted to talk to the only person who believed the win was hers. How had she known Brittney would screw up? Lacey had seen the woman at the few events held before the year-long pandemic lockdown. She wasn't someone you could easily forget. Naturally gorgeous with no makeup, she turned heads even in faded, worn jeans and a plain white Western shirt. But this was the first time Lacey had seen her this year, and she'd vanished today like beer at a cowboy cookout.

No matter. Lacey had a horse to unsaddle, then a trip to the rodeo office to give them her direct-deposit information. She'd head off to a campground about fifty miles away that she'd discovered five years ago. Time to kick back and rest for a bit. She didn't need to be at the next event for ten days. Maybe she'd hit a grocery store on the way and pick up a big steak to celebrate her win. Yeah. After dinner, she'd light a campfire, put in her earphones, and start listening to the audiobook she'd downloaded yesterday.

❖

Wiloree Rivers didn't stick around to share confirmation of a victory with the intriguing Lacey Bishop. Wil was at the rodeo to prime the money pump for Double R Ranch, which she and her father owned. She walked around to the opposite end of the arena to slide into the bleacher seating next to a group of wealthy horsemen and nodded as they politely touched their hats in greeting. "How's the season treating you fellows?" she asked.

"Been better," Mac Abbott, Brittney's father, said. "My best cutter strained a tendon and is out for the season. And I'm betting Brittney will want another new ride after losing to the Bishop girl. It's not the first time. That girl and her little mare have beaten her three of the last five times they've run against each other."

"Brittney has a great horse." Wil wasn't afraid to speak her mind. "She's just not handling him right. But I'll be happy to sell you another. I have two barrel racers in training. One is pretty much finished. The other's close—maybe another month to fine-tune."

"How's your dad?" Mr. Abbott truly appeared concerned. "Heard he had a hard time with that COVID crap."

"It's slowed him down a bit, but he's on the mend. You know I can't keep him out of the barn. Don's been out for a while, taking care of his wife. She's been really ill with the virus. So, Dad's been working all the horses. He's had plenty of time to bring them along, though, since everything was on hiatus for a year."

"What's your dad have that can cut?"

"He has three ready to go. Two are high dollar. One's from the Cat line, and the other has close Lena bloodlines. The third also has Lena bloodlines, but not as close. All three are looking really good, but the third is also a good reining prospect."

Tom Blackstone interrupted their conversation. "I'm looking for a good reining horse."

"I'll call your dad," Mac said, seeming to ignore Tom. "Might be interested in a new cutter since my best is injured. Tell him not to sell anything to Tom until I get a look at all three."

"Hey, I thought we were friends." Tom gave Mac a good-natured slap on the arm.

"We are, buddy. But horses are business. You understand."

Wil wasn't going to get in the middle of this friendly argument. She rose and turned to the men. "I'll tell Dad you plan to call, Mr. Abbott. Mr. Blackstone, you're welcome to come out, too. He's also got a good crop still in training that you might want to buy an option on for when they're finished."

"I'll do that, young lady," Tom said. "I'm sure I'll see you sooner than later."

"Looking forward to it," she said before climbing down from the bleachers and heading for the parking lot.

❖

Wil was about to open the door to her Double R truck when her name rang out from across the parking lot. "Another minute and I'd have made a clean getaway," she mumbled. She sighed and turned to face Brittney, who was kicking up a cloud in the dusty lot as she trotted toward her.

"Hey, sexy." Brittney didn't stop until she was up in Wil's personal space and practically purring as she displayed her trademark pout that usually got her anything she wanted. "I know you wouldn't leave without saying hello."

Wil had ended her very short fling with Brittney at the beginning of the rodeo season. Brittney had pursued her until, a little drunk and desperate for company during the pandemic lockdown, Wil had given in and bedded her. Brittney was pretty good in bed, but incredibly entitled and fucked anyone in jeans—male or female. She professed to prefer women but slept with men "to keep up her image and in her father's good graces" so she could continue to have unlimited access to his wallet.

Whenever Brittney was at loose ends and Wil was around, she

ignored Wil's gentle but repeated "let's just be friends" speech. And although Wil wanted to tell her that horses would fly before she slept with her again, the Double R needed Mac Abbott's money, so Wil literally couldn't afford to offend her.

"Hey, Brittney. Tough loss today."

Brittney shrugged and tossed her hair. "That hillbilly bitch and her mutt of a horse got lucky. Dash was off his game."

"You need to quit muscling him through the turns. Give him his head. He knows what to do. You should spend more time with him. Bond with him. He's a great horse, but you two aren't working together."

"It's just like you to blame me, rather than the horse."

It was Wil's turn to shrug. "That's free advice. People usually have to pay for my consultations."

Brittney stepped closer and brushed the back of her hand over Wil's breast under the pretense of reaching up to finger the pendant on Wil's necklace. Her expression transformed from pouty to sultry. "Then let me buy you dinner as payment."

"Sorry. I've got horses to feed and bed down."

"Come on, stud. I'm sure somebody at the ranch can do that for you. How about room service in my hotel suite?"

"I thought you were dating Bart Roberts."

Brittney's pouty face was back. "You know that's just for show to keep Daddy happy. Bart and I've been friends since we were kids."

"That doesn't change the fact that I need to head back to the ranch. We're short-handed, with people still getting sick." Wil was vaccinated and would have worn a mask, but the men she was trying to sell horses to were part of the anti-mask group, and the ranch needed their money. She didn't worry about herself and was glad a recent test showed her father still had strong antibodies in his system from his previous infection.

"Killjoy."

"I'm sure your groupies will be happy to party with you tonight."

"I don't feel like a big party, just some private time with you."

"Sorry."

"Maybe I'll let Bart take me out to dinner."

"Y'all have a good time." If Brittney thought the threat would make Wil jealous, she figured wrong. She stepped back and climbed into the truck before Brittney could make a move to kiss her. "Nice to see you, but I have to run. Ranch work is never done. Take care."

CHAPTER TWO

A lthough the audiobook Lacey was listening to was a page-turner, the hypnotic dance of the campfire flames transported her back to the sky-blue eyes staring up as she sat astride Denver watching Brittney's poor run the day before. While eyes that color were fairly common among the professional barrel racers, since almost all were Caucasian, the dark-haired mystery woman's were a mesmerizing, deep-cornflower shade.

Who was she? Although Lacey had glimpsed her at several rodeos in the past, she'd never seen her enter any of the events. Maybe she was married or dating one of the cowboys competing in other events. But this woman's manner and body language were too commanding and self-assured to be trailing after someone else. She'd seen Brittney, who was as subtle as a hound dog drooling over a ham bone, flirting with Blue Eyes—the nickname Lacey had assigned her in her thoughts. But she'd also seen Blue Eyes talking with the men around the stock pens and, once, in the bleachers with an older man, watching the team roping.

"How's our favorite cowgirl doing?"

Lacey put her thoughts aside and tapped her earbud to stop the audiobook she'd have to rewind yet again. She smiled as the wiry, balding man with a crown of Einstein-wild hair stepped out of the shadows and into the light of the campfire. "Hey, Joel. I'm good. Thanks for saving my favorite spot for me."

"Maggie and I are always happy to see you and Denver. I keep an eye out for any rodeos within a hundred miles, because I know you'll likely show up for a night or a week." He held out a foil-wrapped plate. "Maggie's watching that stupid bachelor show or she would have walked down with me, but she sent you a couple pieces of the apple pie she baked earlier today."

Lacey's mouth watered as she accepted the plate. "Oh, man. I love Maggie's apple pie."

"She put a plastic fork in there, too, so you don't even have to get up to fetch one. Said if you come up to the house tomorrow, she'll warm up another piece and put some ice cream on it for you."

"You don't have to ask me twice." Lacey unwrapped the plate and dug in. She loved the older couple, who treated her like family. Their small campground curled around a three-acre pond and included a five-acre fenced pasture where they kept a few goats and a friendly donkey. Her favorite campsite was large enough that she could set up the six eight-foot aluminum fence sections she carried atop the horse trailer to fashion a roomy outdoor stall to bed down Denver, who joined the donkey and goats during the day. If she needed a place to call home, this was it. They refused to let her pay for her campsite, so she usually helped Joel with maintenance work or minded the campground so they could visit Maggie's sister for a few days. "Grab that extra chair over there and sit with me a while."

Joel grinned. "I reckon I can do that. She'll be watching that trash for the next hour. Who in the hell is stupid enough to believe some producer can round up ten women and one of them will be the love of some man's life?"

"I'm not sure there's such a thing as true love anymore," Lacey said between bites of pie. "People are just too self-centered these days."

Joel shook his head. "I don't disagree with you on most being too selfish, but some hearts still belong together. Look at Maggie and me. I've never had a closer friend or better partner, and I've loved her since the moment I set eyes on her."

"You guys are an exception."

"Don't give up, kiddo. That special person is out there for you, too."

Lacey's thoughts instantly flashed back to Blue Eyes, but she shrugged off Joel's encouragement. Blue Eyes might be the only woman who'd made her ovaries sit up and take notice in a long while, but she looked way out of Lacey's league. Oh, Lacey wasn't blind, and she knew the mirror didn't lie. She was fairly easy on the eyes herself. But while Blue wasn't flashy like the other wealthy players on the circuit, she smelled of understated money. Her crisp white shirt seemed immune to the arena dust, and a thick silver chain holding a teardrop pendant carved from high-grade turquoise peeked out from her open collar. The wear on her boots indicated they were expensive distressed leather rather than scuffed from work. But the biggest tell was her confident, easy stride, the straight set of her shoulders, the lift of her chin, and her sculpted cheekbones that screamed good breeding. When she walked past a group of men, they politely touched the brim of their hats in greeting rather than leered.

Blue Eyes wasn't a one-night stand after too many beers, and Lacey didn't intend to get tangled up in anything more.

"Well, I reckon I better head back. You're drifting off on me." Joel put his hands on his knees, preparing to heft himself up out of the camp chair.

"What? No. Wait." She shook away her musings. "I just zoned out for a minute. It's the fire. I tend to get caught up in flames dancing back and forth. Did I tell you I took first place Saturday?"

"Hot dang." Joel's smile was wide. "You're doing real good this year. I've been following the rankings. If you keep it up, you'll qualify for—"

"Don't say it. You'll jinx me. We still have enough events left for me to get edged out of qualifying for the big one or for something to go wrong." She crossed herself, even though she wasn't Catholic or even religious at all.

"The big one?" He laughed at her superstition. "You won't even name it." He leaned forward in his chair. "National…"

She threw her hands up. "Stop!"

"…rabbit-herding finals." He widened his eyes and exclaimed as he pointed in five or six different directions. "There they go. No, over there. Catch that one. Cottontail headed that way."

She laughed at his silliness. "Don't make me tell Maggie that you were smoking weed with the old hippies over in campsite six rather than visiting with me."

"You wouldn't."

She winked at him but shook her head. "No. I wouldn't. Maggie can always tell when I'm spinning tales."

Joel sat back in his chair. "You and me both. Can't fool that wise old bird." They shared a good chuckle, then a comfortable silence while they stared into the fire. The crackle and pop of the flames, the hoots of a nearby owl, and an occasional soft snort from Denver's makeshift stall provided a comforting serenade.

After a while, Joel stirred and grabbed the arms of the camp chair to lever himself up. "Reckon I better head back to the house, or Maggie will be sending Pig to get me."

Pig, a squat, red-nose pit bull, had wandered into the camp-ground one day, half-starved, with a torn ear, multiple bites about her head, and the remnants of a rope around her neck so tight it had cut into her skin. Despite her circumstances and the months needed to heal her infected wounds, Pig was as gentle as a kitten. She'd earned her name from being a shameless moocher of leftovers and treats from any camper who'd give in to her begging. She loved children, all other animals, and especially Maggie. If Pig showed up and tugged on Joel's pant leg, it was as good as a text message that Maggie wanted him home.

"Give Maggie a hug for me, and tell her I'll be up for that second piece of pie tomorrow."

"She said to tell you that breakfast is at seven sharp."

Lacey nodded, because arguing that she could cook her own was useless. Maggie's invitations were more of a command to appear. "I'll be here for most of the week, so we can talk about anything you need help with then."

Joel slapped his hand against his thigh. "Good enough. Night now."

"Good night."

❖

Lacey squirmed a little when Maggie wrapped her substantial arms around her to crush her against her ample breasts.

"I know you don't like hugs, but wiggle out of mine, and I'll feed that pecan waffle you love to Pig," Maggie said. Pig barked her endorsement of the penalty.

"Not a chance, dog," Lacey said to Pig. She happily gave in and returned the hug. "Nobody steals my special waffles."

"Sit, sit, sit," Maggie said, pointing to the table set with three empty plates. She poured two mugs of dark, rich coffee from a commercial coffeemaker on the sideboard and set them on the table before taking Lacey's plate and walking to the stove to fill it with scrambled eggs, grits, sausage links, and a big, buttery biscuit. "Protein first. Then I'll pour you a waffle in the griddle for dessert."

"You're going to make me so fat, Denver won't be able to carry me around the barrels." The menu, breakfast routine, and Lacey's joking complaint were always the same. That's how they liked it. "Where's Joel?"

"Some new campers rolled in about thirty minutes ago. Two brothers. Joel's showing them to their campsite and making sure they know the rules. They said they were bronc riders and were coming from the same rodeo you were at, but they smelled of whiskey, and one of them looked a bit beat-up. I reckon they showed up here so early because they got in a brawl and closed down some bar before heading this way."

"They could be trouble. Which campsite? Maybe Pig and I should go check on Joel."

"Eat your breakfast. I can see the cart coming this way."

Lacey turned in her chair to look through the window behind her. The electric golf cart Joel and Maggie used to zip around the campground was pulling to a stop outside the couple's small house. Seconds later, Joel let the screen door slam behind him.

"There better be some breakfast left for me," he said, his smile making clear the threat was a tease.

"Not if you slam the door again." Maggie went to the stove and began loading a plate for Joel. "I'd swear you were raised in a cave with no door."

"Sorry, love, but if I didn't slam the door once in a while, what would you have to fuss about?"

Lacey loved the easy banter between her two favorite friends. Really, her only friends. "Those two guys check in okay?" she asked. Some of the young cowboys on the rodeo circuit could be a pain in the ass—arrogant and destructive.

"Brothers," Joel said as he buttered his biscuit. "One was still drunk and climbed in his bunk the minute they were parked. That left the other brother with all the set-up chores. I offered to help, but he said he was used to handling it while his brother slept off a binge. He seemed nice enough, but I don't know about the other when he wakes up. Their last name is McCallen. You know them?"

"Can't say it rings any bells, but I don't stick around much to watch the other competitions. I might recognize them if I run into them, just from seeing them on the circuit."

"I didn't tell them you were here. Didn't want them bothering you."

"Appreciate that, but I handle guys like them all the time. The older ones aren't usually trouble. But the young guys think every woman should fall at their feet just because they're fool enough to climb on the back of a bucking horse or a bull."

"Let me know if they go bothering you," Maggie said, her brows drawn together and jaw clenched. "Pig and I will pay them a visit. And if that doesn't reel them in, Joel will throw them out of the campground."

"Don't worry about trouble that isn't here yet," Lacey said. "They're probably just tired and banged up from getting pitched on their heads by broncs. They'll be looking to chill, just like me, I'm sure."

"You too tired to lend me a hand with a few things?" Joel asked between bites.

"Never too tired for that. It keeps me from getting bored and lets me feel less guilty about you guys not letting me pay for my campsite. I've never been a freeloader."

"You don't have to lift a finger if you aren't up to it. You're like a daughter to us. We look forward to any time you can squeeze in a visit here."

"Well, then treat me like a daughter and let me help."

Joel nodded. "I need to mow the pasture, but I can't get that old tractor running. I wish you'd take a look at it before I go and spend money to get Ross out here to fix it. Also, I've been busy putting a new coat of paint on the bathhouses, so I haven't had time to check the walking trails since that big storm three weeks ago. Probably got some limbs down here and there."

"I'll check the tractor first," she said, cleaning the last of the grits from her plate with her biscuit. She pushed her chair back and started to rise. "That was really good, but I've still got room for you to pour me one of your famous pecan waffles."

Maggie sprang from her chair, nothing short of a feat for a woman her size. "Coming right up."

"I can get it, Maggie."

"You sit right there. This old waffle iron has been acting up a bit. You have to handle it just so, or it won't stay on."

They both knew this was an excuse, but Lacey wouldn't dare contradict her. Maggie loved to feed people, just as Lacey loved helping Joel around the campground.

"I'll have one of those, too, if you have enough batter made," he said.

"I don't know how you two put away so much food and stay so skinny," Maggie complained. "I eat half as much and can't lose a pound."

"I don't think I'd like it if you were skinny," Joel said, scowling. "I didn't marry a skinny woman because I didn't want one. I love every one of your voluptuous pounds."

"Do I need to give you two some alone time?"

"Not right now, dear," Maggie said as she slid a golden waffle studded with pecans onto Lacey's plate and set a bottle of warmed maple syrup next to it. "We took care of that last night."

Lacey covered her ears. "Didn't need to know that. It's like thinking about your parents having sex."

Joel winked at her. "Might be snow on the rooftop, but there's still fire in the furnace."

Maggie poured more batter into the waffle iron. "How about using some of that fire to finally finish the paint job on the bath-houses, old man."

Lacey washed down the last big bite in her mouth with the rest of her coffee. "I'm going to go turn Denver out with the goats, then head to the equipment shed to check out the tractor. If I can get it running, I'll mow for you, then take a look at the trails."

"No need to do it all in one day," Joel said, stabbing his fork in the air at her. "You came here to relax, and you'll be here the rest of the week. The trails have waited this long. They can wait until tomorrow or whenever you feel like it."

"I promise to pace myself." She stood and kissed Maggie on the cheek. "Breakfast was the best I've had in a long time."

"Same time tomorrow," Maggie said.

"Maybe she wants to sleep in," Joel said, frowning at Maggie.

"Has she ever slept past sunrise?" Maggie asked.

Joel shrugged.

"I would never sleep through one of Maggie's breakfasts. It's the most important meal of the day. I can always grab an afternoon nap."

"Huh. That'd be something to see. If I ever caught you snoozing, it'd be with a fishing pole next to you down by the lake. Otherwise, Maggie would have me hauling you off to see a doctor."

Lacey laughed. "I'll remember that. If I need a nap, I'll head to the lake to take one."

❖

Several wires on the tractor had been gnawed by mice, and others were just brittle from age, so Lacey decided to replace the entire wiring harness since the old John Deere still had a lot of life left in it. She spent most of the morning, however, tracking down the right part in stock at a store thirty miles away, then driving to retrieve it. She installed it and changed the oil after lunch.

By mid-afternoon, she had the old machine running like the Deere it was and headed out to mow the five-acre pasture. Joel didn't cut it often, because their goats would eat anything from grass to brambles. But horses, unless they are starving, generally graze only on the more tender shoots, and grass blades grow tougher as they grow longer. That's why Joel always hooked up the bushhog mower to the tractor and tidied up the pasture when he anticipated a visit from Lacey and Denver. "Don't want to upset the stomach of that high-performance horse," he'd always say.

The sun was dropping lower by the time she finished, but she relished the calm pace of finding the problem, putting the tractor right, and peacefully mowing up and down the pasture. Her days were usually full of tension—dealing with bad drivers who would tailgate Denver's trailer and pass her in bad spots as she drove from rodeo to rodeo, or worrying that one careless act could injure the legs of her only horse, or one split-second wrong move that tipped a barrel could drop her from the competition leaders.

Still, the cool shade of the equipment barn was a welcome break from the Texas heat at the end of her day. She pulled off her ball cap, wiped the sweat from her forehead, and gathered her hair again to thread it through the back of the cap as she replaced it on her head.

"I thought that was you but wasn't sure with that cap pulled so low over your eyes."

Lacey turned toward the masculine voice to see one of the bronc-riding brothers silhouetted in the wide door of the equipment barn. She squinted at him. "Do I know you?"

"Maybe. I've noticed you around the rodeo circuit. You do barrels on that buckskin mare."

Lacey nodded. "I do."

He apparently took her acknowledgement as an invitation to come inside, strolling over to prop his shoulder against the tractor too close for comfort. He pulled his hat off and gave her a cocky grin. "Brent McCallen. I reckon you've seen me and my big brother, John, around. We ride the broncs and bulls."

"Can't say I have. I don't care for the crowds those events attract so don't usually hang around the arena after the barrel racing. I have a horse to take care of and tack to clean after my event."

"Now, that just hurts my feelings." He reached around her to touch her hair dangling from her ball cap, bringing him solidly into her personal space. "I sure wouldn't mind a pretty little blond thing like you on my playlist."

She glared at him, swatted his hand away, and stepped backward, only to stop because the tractor's huge rear wheel was at her back.

He cocked his head. "Then again, maybe the rumors that you're a dyke are true." His smile turned into a leer. "I bet I could change that. I can guarantee one good ride with me would show you what you're missing."

"There you are." The late-afternoon sun outlined Maggie's bulk in the doorway. "Pig and I were hunting you. The pasture looks great. I thought it was about time you'd be putting Denver up for the night, and I'd walk with you to get in the daily exercise my doctor's always pestering me about."

Brent stepped back when the pit bull sauntered over to nuzzle Lacey's hand but put his hand out for Pig to sniff for an introduction. Pig, however, uncharacteristically growled low in her chest, and her wagging tail stilled. He scowled at Pig. "I'm surprised you keep a dangerous dog around since families with kids camp here."

"Oh, Pig's not dangerous. She loves the children, and they love her," Maggie said. "But she's especially fond of Lacey and seems to feel like you might be bothering her, Mr. McCallen." Maggie walked into the barn, hands on her full hips.

"I was just saying hello." He gestured to indicate Lacey. "We ride on the same rodeo circuit."

"Well, this barn is off-limits to campers. Insurance rules, you know. Can't have anyone getting hurt on all this equipment," Maggie said.

Brent put his hands up. "You don't have to worry about me. I grew up on a farm. Drove a tractor every hay harvest since I was six years old."

"We have to uphold the same rules for everybody."

"Doesn't look like they apply to her." He pointed at Lacey again.

"Lacey's family, not a guest of the campground." Pig leaned against Lacey's leg as if to emphasize the family label. Or maybe it was just to give Lacey a better angle on Pig's ear she was scratching.

Brent placed his hat on his head again and moved away from Lacey and Pig. "I reckon I'll be on my way, then," he said to Maggie before turning back to Lacey. "John and I are at campsite eight. You should come around and have a beer or two with us tonight. John can pull out his banjo, and I'll grab my guitar. We're pretty good at bluegrass and play some country, too."

"My husband would love that. Maybe we'll all drop by," Maggie said, ignoring that the invitation was issued only to Lacey.

Brent shrugged. "Right. All of you." He walked out past Maggie, and they watched as he tossed a wave over his shoulder.

Maggie narrowed her eyes. "Was that boy bothering you?"

"You and Pig showed up when I was just about to handle him."

"I went by their camper earlier. The other brother seemed respectable, but I can't say the same about that one."

"It's all bravado, strutting around like a bantam rooster. It's best to just ignore guys like him. Don't react to them. I see a lot of them around the rodeo. If they think they're getting under your skin, they'll never leave you alone."

"I'm sure you're right, but I'd feel better if you let Pig stay at your campsite at night while they're around. Joel and I'll go over to their camper tonight to hear them play and generally make a nuisance of ourselves, so maybe they'll pack up and leave soon."

Lacey laughed. "I'd show up to witness that if I wasn't worried my presence might be interpreted as encouragement."

Maggie's smile was smug. "The campsite closest to them is empty this week, so I think I'll let Joel sing with them."

Lacey laughed so hard she clutched her sides to catch her breath. Joel was sadly tone deaf but loved to sing after downing three or four beers. "Pig's the only one who can tolerate his noise, and that's only because she likes to howl along with him." She brushed away the tears threatening to leak from her laughter. "That'll run them off for sure."

Maggie's smile widened into an all-out grin. "Works every time."

CHAPTER THREE

Wil rubbed her eyes and sighed as she pressed into the soft leather of the high-backed office chair and raised her arms over her head in an attempt to straighten and stretch her aching shoulders. No matter how she worked the numbers, the Double R ranch would exhaust the last of its cash reserves and available credit in six months.

The business of raising and training top horses for Western events like rodeos, cutting-horse futurities, and barrel racing had always ebbed and flowed with the economy, and Wil's father, Ray Rivers, had been careful to save and invest in anticipation of periodic downturns. But nobody could have predicted a worldwide pandemic would shut down the competitions that generated a hundred percent of their sales and demand for their training services. Meanwhile, mortgage payments had to be made, employees paid, and horses fed and vetted on the thousand-acre ranch.

A few tentative events last year had unleased a stampede of rodeos and futurities reopening for the coming year, but Wil feared it could be too late for the Double R to recover. They'd trimmed the ranch's staff to a minimum, forgone breeding to reduce veterinary bills, and sold the lumber from twenty acres of old forest her father had vowed never to cut. But when he fell sick with the coronavirus, Wil's workload doubled, and medical bills piled up. After long hours working the ranch, she stayed up late to apply for any pandemic financial aid available. The ranch's healthy assets, however, counted against them, even though nobody buys performance horses when they don't have any opportunities for them to compete.

Wil rose stiffly. Sulking in the ranch office wouldn't erase the red ink in their budget. Finding buyers for the stock she'd been training would.

❖

Wil's father, Ray, stood in the training barn's corridor, looking around without seeming to recognize anything. He'd had fewer moments of confusion, a lingering effect of his illness, since he'd been taking a new medicine, but his pallor worried her. He hadn't touched a cigarette in almost ten years, but his former two-pack-a-day habit had weakened his heart and scarred his lungs before he contracted the deadly virus. Wil worried that his week on a ventilator in ICU had accelerated the inevitable decline in his overall health.

"Dad?"

His eyes locked onto her before he closed them and slowly shook his head. "Damned brain fog. I was looking for Don, but I can't remember why."

"We laid Don off last month, Dad."

He frowned, his face red. "Why the hell did you do that? He's the best damn trainer on the farm. You'd probably fire me too if I didn't own this place." She knew frustration fueled his burst of anger.

"Don asked to be laid off so he could draw federal unemployment and take care of his wife. She's still struggling with the virus." The two of them working this arrangement out with Don was the first memory Ray seemed to lose when the befuddlement hit, and she would patiently explain the situation as many times as necessary. "We'll hire him back when his unemployment runs out." This might prove to be an empty promise if Wil couldn't revive their revenue stream in the next six months, but she'd think about that later.

He looked down at his feet. "We've talked about this before, haven't we?"

"Hey. Don't sweat it." Wil worried more about his depression, caused by lingering fatigue and periodic confusion. "I'll keep reminding you until Don's back, leaving his cups of tobacco spit everywhere." She smiled at him. "I guess I can't hope you've also forgotten about the Easter egg debacle last night."

He huffed. "Hell, no. The house is going to stink for months, and you're going to be cleaning exploded eggs off the ceiling, walls, and floors this time next year. Pow, pow, pow." He waved his arms around as he mimicked two dozen eggs exploding after a phone call had distracted her and all the water boiled out of the pot. "The damn cat is still hiding under the bed."

Wil laughed, relieved he'd followed her move to lighten the mood. "Yeah, yeah. You can boil the next bunch since you volunteered us for the egg-painting booth at Saturday's festival."

"Been doing it for nearly twenty years. After that damned virus shut everything down last year, folks need to do something that feels normal again."

"A bunch of calves are waiting in the indoor ring for you to work Lena Smarty Pants and Blue Cat. How's that for normal?"

"What are you going to do?"

"I need to work Pepper and Flash outside on the barrels." She led Pepper from her stall and clipped her into the crossties to saddle her.

"Barrel horses are a waste of your time. We make a lot more money on cutting horses."

"Cutting horses also go for more than roping horses, but that doesn't stop you from training them."

He grunted at her. "Rodeos were started so cowboys could show off their work skills, and roping is what separates cowboys from herders." He clipped Blue Cat to crossties facing Pepper.

Wil loved her father, but they'd debated this topic many times. "And cowboys need horses with barrel-racing skills to flush a herd out of the woods, control a galloping herd, and round up stragglers." They both trained horses for every rodeo category, but her dad also prepared riders for the roping events. He'd never admit to Wil that he longed for the old days when the only women at a rodeo were in the audience, not racing around barrels. But she was okay with that. His opinion came from the rodeo accident that injured and ultimately killed her mother, not chauvinism. "Doesn't matter anyway," she said. "We need to sell any horses we can to get the bank off our backs and pay down the feed bill." She began running a soft curry brush over Pepper's already gleaming hide. "I need to show up at more events to remind people we have well-trained horses available for purchase."

"Did you call that Abbott girl back? She's left about twenty messages for you."

"I saw her last weekend at that rodeo over in Appleton. Saw Mac Abbott, too. He said he was interested in looking at the cutting horses you have ready. His best is on the injured list. Tom Blackstone is interested in a reining horse."

"That's right. Mac called last night. He said his daughter might be interested in a new barrel horse, too."

"She only thinks she needs a new horse. She's got a great one now. She just needs to learn how to ride him." Wil stopped brushing and gave her father a pointed stare. "Or maybe it's just that her father's money is burning a hole in her pocket."

"So, when's she coming out?"

"She's not."

"And why not?"

"Because she's not really interested in finding a horse."

His eyebrows shot up. "What's she interested in?"

"You know what."

He ignored her narrow-eyed glare. "You didn't seem to mind her attentions last rodeo season. And you must have done something right if she's still interested."

Wil's face heated. She refused to discuss her sex life with her father. "Yeah, well, I'm not interested in what's she's offering." Wil pushed aside the vision of the blond-haired winning rider who had invaded her thoughts all week.

He feigned surprise again. "You decided you don't like the ladies after all?"

She huffed at his teasing remark as she bent to lift Pepper's hoof and clean it. "I will always love women, but Brittney only wants a good time and possibly a playmate on the side when she marries a guy and has babies to satisfy her dad." She straightened, then leaned against Pepper's silky shoulder. "Maybe it's because I'm over thirty now, or the whole pandemic thing made me think seriously about what's truly important in life. I want more than a good time. I want a meaningful relationship. I want a partner in life and to start my own family."

Ray straightened from cleaning Blue Cat's hooves, a new light in his blue eyes. "You want to have kids?"

Wil smiled at his hopeful expression, then wrinkled her nose at the prospect of pregnancy. "I never want to experience pregnancy, but I would love to have a partner carry a baby for us or to adopt."

"Grandchildren." Ray stretched the word out as though savoring the idea. "That would be a breath of fresh air around here." His eyes teared. "Your mother would've been a fantastic grandmother."

Wil ignored his last remark, refusing to let him slip into the past. "Hold on. The puzzle still has a few pieces missing…like falling in love with someone who wants the same things I do. And we need to have a ranch that's making money instead of sliding deeper into debt."

"Then we better get busy making some money so you can go hunt down that special woman I know is somewhere waiting for you." He tossed his curry brush into the bucket of grooming tools and unclipped Blue Cat from the crossties. "Let's look at rodeo and futurity schedules after dinner tonight. You can hit some barrel-racing events with whoever you've got ready, while I enter the Cat and Smarty in a few cutting events to show what they can do."

"I'm also going to see if I can interest a stock contractor in buying Tombstone for bronc riding. He's the best bucker I've seen in a long time," she said.

"Sounds like a plan." Ray turned Blue Cat to lead him out the front entrance of the barn. Wil unclipped Pepper from her crossties and followed to where he waited for her outside. He apparently had more to say before they split up and went to their separate training destinations. She waited while he rubbed his chin in a familiar gesture that usually meant he was deciding how to speak. "I hope you know I would never suggest that you compromise yourself for our financial gain, but you need to be careful about how you handle this situation with the Abbott girl. The professional horseman world can be really small if you step on the toes of the big spenders. Her father has a lot of influence among the high-dollar people, so I'm just asking you to do your best to get out of whatever you two had going on without making too big of a stir. You get me?"

"Yes, sir."

He stared at her. "I'm just asking you to handle her with kid gloves, but don't sell yourself out or do anything you feel is wrong. If we end up homeless, so be it. I won't have you prostituting yourself out to some rich brat just to keep this ranch. You understand?"

"Yes, sir. I do."

"Good. That's good." He gave a curt nod, then led Blue Cat to the indoor ring.

Chapter Four

Ray Rivers lowered the stabilizers, then unfurled the large canopy from the side of the Double R five-horse, gooseneck trailer while Wil lowered the windows at the head and tail of each horse to allow a cross breeze that would help the trailer's ventilation system keep the horses cool and the flies to a minimum. Father and daughter worked together in an efficient order honed from many weekends at rodeo events. This trailer was their largest and best, purchased with cash at the end of their most profitable year and right before the pandemic locked everything down the following spring. Wil wished they could sell it—even if they had to take two of their smaller trailers to events—but there was no market at the moment for horse trailers that cost as much as a modest-sized house.

The trailer's living quarters did save them hotel and some meal costs, and driving two trucks with smaller trailers would double their fuel costs. They needed that savings since they paid entry fees totaling around a thousand dollars for barrel racing and team penning.

They were currently in San Antonio, where ropers and riders were gearing up to compete in one of the rodeos sanctioned by the Professional Rodeo Cowboys Association, with prizes counting toward qualification for the Wrangler National Finals Rodeo at the end of the year. With more than 43,000 fans, the large rodeos consisted of a lot more than dust, cows, and contestants. The perks at this arena complex included free electrical hookups for contestants' trailers, locker rooms with showers, free stalling for horses, food and drinks in the hospitality suite for the contestants and their families, and shopping at a variety of vendors.

Wil was entered to ride Pepper in the barrel race, and three of Ray's roping/reining horses—No Cause Rebel, Sip of Whiskey, and Blackfoot—would be in roping contests. Reining and cutting competitions were usually held separately from rodeos. Wil had also brought Tombstone because one of the event's major stock contractors was interested in seeing him buck. If he was impressed, money would change hands, and Tombstone would go home with the contractor.

She and Ray would ride Rebel and Whiskey in the team-roping event. They also paid entry fees for the twin sons of a friend in the area to ride Rebel and Blackfoot in the tie-down roping, since Ray was no longer physically able to wrestle a calf to the ground and tie its legs in the timed competition, and Wil had no interest in competing against the cowboys. The twins, recently turned eighteen, were thrilled to ride for the well-respected Double R because they were trying to earn their first thousand on the circuit to fill the permit requirements to become a member of Professional Rodeo Cowboys Association.

Wil had decided to ride Whiskey in the breakaway roping, which primarily drew female contestants. In that contest, the roper's lariat end was tied to the saddle with a thin string. When the calf was roped, the string would break as the horse and rider slid to a stop and the lariat was stretched tight by the running calf. Time was called the moment the string broke. Cowboys weren't interested in the event because it didn't involve any macho steer-wrestling. The event, however, would give the audience another look at Whiskey's perfect sliding stop.

That's what they were here to do. Not to win prizes but to show prospective buyers the horses they'd trained and were looking to sell.

Wil and Ray were setting out the stall bedding and filling hay bags to hang in the stalls when a silver-haired man and a teenage boy pulled up in one of the rodeo utility carts. The older man grabbed a clipboard next to him on the seat and noted the Double R insignia that decorated the side of the trailer.

"You folks ready to haul your bedding up to the stalls?" He scanned the five horses hanging their heads out of the trailer

windows, then frowned at his clipboard. "Looks like they have you
assigned four stalls, but I see you have five horses. Do I need to call
the office to see if somebody made a mistake?"

"No," Ray said. "The bay on the end is a bucker. Dave Johnson
is interested in buying him and will be coming around in the next
hour to stall him with his other stock."

"Gotcha. Dave's a good one. Treats his animals right." He
gestured to the boy, who exited the cart and began helping Wil load
plastic-wrapped bales of wood-chip bedding onto the back of the
cart and the four-by-six wagon it was towing. Filling four stalls took
a lot of chips. "We've got you in stalls eighty through eighty-three.
I'll move slow so you can follow me if you want to go ahead and
lead two of your horses up there."

"Sounds good," Ray said, taking Rebel's lead rope from Wil
as she walked him out of the trailer. She unloaded Whiskey and
followed their parade to the indoor stalls.

❖

Lacey stared at the arena worker. "Are you kidding me? Nine
dollars a bale for wood chips? I can buy better chips than these for
six."

"Then maybe you should do that. But you'll have a hard time
finding any within fifty miles of here. The event coordinators have
bought up everything. There's a shortage, what with the shipping
problems caused by the pandemic."

He wasn't lying. Lacey had stopped at several farm-supply
and feed stores on the way to the event, but all were sold out and
waiting for more. She knew the arena price would be high because
it included their cost of shipping and labor to unload and stack
an average of ten bales each for more than a hundred ten-by-ten
stalls. But nine dollars? And the bales the guy had pulled out for her
weren't good quality. Probably because she had only one horse and
obviously wasn't from one of the wealthy ranch operations.

"At least let me pick out my own bales. Those look like they've
been in storage for years." The chips were a bit too large and rough,

and most of the bales were graying on one side—a sign that they'd sat exposed to the sun for a long while.

The man casually slid the toothpick he was chewing from one side of his mouth to the other. "No can do. It'd be chaos if we let every cowboy here crawl all over the storage room, deciding on a bale here and there. It's these or none. If you don't take them, the next guy will."

Lacey's anger rose and her face heated. "What about those over there?" She pointed to twenty plastic-encased bales of wood chips stacked on a flat cart like those used by garden-center customers while hers were stacked on the floor for her to carry or make multiple trips with a wheelbarrow. The chips on the cart were small and a fresh yellow-white color.

"Those are for Sonny Stevens." He pointed to an approaching cowboy, who was wearing a shirt bearing several sponsor logos and embroidery over the right pocket that identified him as representing a well-known, large Oklahoma ranch. "Here he comes now to pick 'em up."

Sonny offered a wide smile and gave her a suggestive once-over. "Hey, Bob. Those our bales? We brought a good bit but want to make sure to grab extra before you give away all the good bales to pretty ladies like this one." He touched the brim of his hat to acknowledge Lacey.

She opened her mouth to rip both Bob and Sonny new assholes, but a low, smooth voice behind her made her stop.

"Can you pull ten bales for the Double R, Bob?"

Lacey whirled to tell this newcomer to wait her turn, but her mouth didn't seem to work when she fell into the deep-blue gaze of the woman who'd been enriching her masturbation fantasies the past few weeks.

Bob, who had propped his butt against the chips intended for Lacey, stood quickly. "Yes, ma'am, Ms. Rivers." He hesitated. "I thought you guys brought your own bedding."

"We just want to make sure we have enough before you run out. We have several buyers looking at our horses, so it wouldn't do for them to get stiff from standing on this concrete flooring."

Sonny offered his hand to the woman. "I'm Sonny Stevens,

Ms. Rivers. My boss at Mountain Meadows mentioned the other day that he wanted to look at any cutters your father has ready."

"Please, call me Wil." She smiled and shook his hand. "We, of course, didn't bring cutters here today, but Jake Meadows is welcome to come out to the ranch and take a look. Dad has several ready for the arena, and several more not far off from being finished. But I wouldn't wait too long. We have buyers lining up for the ones ready to go, and we're selling options on a handful of others nearly finished." She turned back to Bob. "Ten bales, Bob?"

Lacey was jarred from her stunned silence. These damned people were acting like she was invisible. She paid her entry fees just like they did, and she was one of the five top money-winning barrel racers so far this year. She cleared her throat and scowled. "I'm sure he'll get your chips as soon as I get mine."

Bob pointed to the chips he'd already designated for her. "Like I said, those are yours."

Lacey narrowed her eyes. "If you think I'm paying nine dollars each for that crap, you son of a fuckin' bitch, think again." Fists clenched at each side, she took a step toward him. "I'm not taking your shit just because—" Wil's warm hand on Lacey's shoulder stopped her.

"How about telling the guy bringing out my bales to pull ten new bales for Ms. Bishop at the same time?"

Sonny stepped closer. "Hey. Why don't you ladies just take the twenty they set out for me. I can wait for them to pull twenty more."

Wil rewarded Sonny with a blazing white smile. "Thank you, Sonny. That's nice of you."

The young cowboy flushed red and touched the brim of his hat again. "My daddy taught me that ladies are always first."

"Well, you can tell your daddy that we appreciate him raising you to be such a gentleman." She winked at Sonny, and his blush deepened.

Bob huffed at Sonny's offer but lifted his radio to tell the workers to bring out twenty more bales. Good bales, he told them, and Lacey gave Bob a sarcastic, sugary-sweet smile before she and Wil took possession of the cart holding their newly acquired stall bedding.

"I'll tell Dad that Mr. Meadows is interested in his cutting horses and to wait before selling off his best," she said as she pulled and Lacey pushed the cart down the aisle toward their stalls.

"Thank you. I appreciate that." Sonny grinned. "It'll earn me some points with the boss."

❖

"You're in the last stall, number eighty-four, right?" Wil steered the cart to the stall's door and stopped.

"Yeah." Lacey's expression was wary. "How'd you know?"

"We're assigned the four next to you." Wil offered a smile she hoped would reassure Lacey and indicated the stalls they'd just walked past. "And your name is on the paper taped to that stall's door."

"Oh. Right." Lacey froze mid-reach in her move to pull a bale of chips from the cart. "You know who I am?"

"Of course," Wil said. "You're on the leaderboard of barrel racers and in a good position to qualify for the National Finals Rodeo." She extended her hand. "I'm Wil Rivers."

Lacey wiped her hand on her jeans before clasping Wil's. "Lacey Bishop." She dropped her chin and shook her head before looking up at Wil again. "But you obviously know that."

"Yeah." Could this woman be any more adorable? Wil wanted to stare into those velvet brown eyes and hold Lacey's smaller, slender hand a bit longer. She was still stunned that her stars had apparently aligned for her to be walking back to their trailer at the very moment Lacey was arguing with the jerk in charge of bedding distribution. They'd had only that one brief exchange the day Wil had congratulated Lacey for beating Brittney, but the attractive blonde had occupied Wil's thoughts a thousand times since then. She was intrigued by Lacey's fearless rides and her refusal to cow to the "princess" racers who had every advantage their wealthy families could buy.

Lacey cocked her head as Wil released her hand. "When I overheard your name a few minutes ago, I realized who you are, Ms. Rivers."

"Please, like I told Sonny, it's Wil." She pitched a bale of wood chips into the stall. "But do tell. What do you know about me?"

"You and your father raise and train some of the top performing horses on the rodeo, reining, and cutting futurity circuits. The Double R is a premium training facility, and your horses sell for ridiculously high prices." Lacey drew a three-inch Buck knife from her pocket and flicked it open to slice through the plastic covering and dump the chips onto the stall floor.

"Don't be too impressed. The ranch operates with a hefty overhead, and we haven't sold a single horse since the pandemic was declared." She closed her eyes and shook her head. If that information got around, Mac Abbott and his buddies would knock thousands off their offers for Double R horses. "I don't know why I told you that. It could be bad for our business if word leaked out." She pitched another bale into the stall.

"There's nobody for me to tell." Lacey sliced the bale open and scattered the chips. "I'm not surprised, though. The pandemic shut down everything. Every business suffered."

They worked in silence for a few minutes, Wil handing over bales for Lacey to split and spread. They stopped after six bales completed a lush, absorbent bedding for Denver. Lacey would store the remaining four bales in Denver's trailer and provide replacement chips each time the stall was mucked.

When they were done, Lacey peered over the solid portion of the wall separating her stall from the last of Wil's. A dark bay mare, standing on a thick layer of fresh wood chips, looked back at her. "Need help with your stalls?"

"Nah. All of ours are done." She gestured to the cart. "We can take your extra bales to your trailer. Then Dad will help me store ours at ours." He'd help her after she explained why she bought ten more bales of overpriced wood chips when they'd already brought more than enough. She grabbed the cart's handlebar to guide it out of the facility and slid over when Lacey bumped her shoulder to join her in pushing it along.

"I'm no pillow princess. You helped me out. I'll help you store your bales. I don't like owing favors."

Wil's traitorous libido flashed an image of naked Lacey, her body bowed taut and head thrown back in ecstasy against a pillow, and a bolt of pleasure twisted in Wil's belly before she firmly reined it to a hard, sliding halt. Damn. How could this woman send her into a spin with two words? Had Lacey intentionally used the pillow-princess sexual reference? Wil normally found people, especially men, easy to read. But this woman was a tornado, touching down all around her in a wildly unpredictable pattern and sure to plow through her at some point. She willed herself to appear calm and turned her head to make sure Lacey saw the truth in her face.

"I appreciate and will accept your offer to help, but I don't expect repayment when I assist a friend."

Lacey was quiet for a long moment while they pushed the cart out of the facility and toward the parked trailers. "I didn't know we were friends. We just met."

"I noticed you long before now, and I'd like to be your friend." Wil held her breath and prayed her insecurities didn't show through her casual and confident façade.

Lacey glanced at Wil, then faced away to shake her head before looking back and pinning Wil with a hard stare as they stopped the heavy cart next to Lacey's dusty trailer. "Why?"

"Why?" The directness of Lacey's question took Wil aback.

"Yes. Why would you want to associate with me? We don't run in the same social or economic circles. We have nothing in common, except maybe horses and a need for wood chips."

"Where do you want to stack these?"

The deflection earned her a sidelong glance, but Lacey lowered the rear ramp of her trailer. "In here, so I can lock them up."

"You've had some stolen before?" This was the professional rodeo circuit, held at top arena facilities. Most of the participants came from wealthy ranches or were sponsored by brand-name companies or rich patrons. She could understand the precaution if they were at one of the unsanctioned rodeos where local ranch hands tested their skills for bragging rights and small money prizes.

"A couple of drunk bull riders once took a couple of bales of my hay and said they'd give it back only if I'd party with them. When I refused, they cut the twine and scattered my expensive orchard grass from here to yonder." Lacey didn't look up but began stacking the bales Wil moved from the cart to the trailer's ramp. "Another time, some of Brittney's friends swiped six bales of wood chips as a prank and stacked them on the other side of the rodeo grounds so I'd have to find them, then haul them back to my trailer. And that place didn't have rolling carts like they do here. They thought it was really funny to watch me haul them one at a time in my wheelbarrow."

"How'd you know they were your chips?"

Lacey took a felt marker out of her pocket and scribbled her initials on the plastic covering of each of her four bales. "Because I always mark my bales to guard against thieves and pranksters."

Wil wanted to grind her teeth at Brittney's bitches pulling pranks like they were high-school mean girls. The bigger crime was that several of them were riding premium racers—horses trained and sold by Wil—but wouldn't dare challenge Brittney, their queen, for the top money. Of course, others outside their group, like Lacey, filled out the top rankings. But, damn. Just because they had the trust funds to buy her horses didn't mean they deserved them. One day, the Double R would be in the financial position to turn down buyers she thought would not fulfill the potential of her elite equine athletes. That was her goal. The pandemic was only a temporary setback.

"Wil?"

She looked up and smiled sheepishly at Lacey's raised eyebrow and amused expression. "Sorry. I zoned out."

"I asked you where you're parked, so we can unload the rest of these and return the cart."

"Oh, right." She looked at the ten bales still on the cart, and an idea began to form. "Actually, our trailer is way down on the end. Any chance I can talk you into letting me stack these in your trailer? It would be a much shorter distance for me to haul them back when I muck the stalls."

Both of Lacey's eyebrows shot up, and her mouth dropped open. "You muck the stalls? You brought four horses and no stable help?"

Wil laughed. "I've been mucking stalls since I was six years old, and I still do almost every day. My dad does not allow laziness or prima donnas."

Lacey went quiet but gestured for Wil to start handing her the Double R wood-chip bales to stack next to hers. After they finished,

Lacey stood propped in the doorway of the trailer. "You never answered my question."

Wil hadn't forgotten the query she'd deflected earlier, but she was afraid if she said too much too soon, Lacey would spook and run like a horse from a barn fire. She stalled again to weigh her answer. "What question?"

"Why would you want to be my friend?"

"Because you're wrong to say we have nothing in common." Wil slowly removed her work gloves and gave in to her impulse to touch Lacey. She cautiously grasped Lacey's forearm—the skin bare and warm between her T-shirt sleeve and glove—and gently squeezed before releasing. "The Double R was only twenty acres with an ancient cow barn when I was born…I'm guessing eight or so years before you were. My dad was working as a farrier and my mother as a teacher to pay the bills while my dad built his reputation by retraining cutting horses and reining horses that weren't living up to their bloodlines because their first trainer did a poor job. I wore my cousin's hand-me-downs and always got one present, a chocolate bar and an orange, for Christmas. My family never ate out in restaurants or went on vacations."

She sat in the trailer and extended her long legs down the ramp, then silently cheered when Lacey sat next to her. "My parents scrimped and saved so Dad could buy his first colt to train, then sell for profit, rather than spend his life training other people's horses for a salary. He reinvested the money he made in more horses to make more profit. I was in college before he bought the ranch that's now the Double R. So, no. I didn't grow up wealthy. In fact, I'm not comfortable around people who flaunt their privilege with expensive cars and designer clothes."

Lacey pointed to the turquoise pendant Wil never took off. "That's some pretty nice jewelry you're wearing to spread bedding in stalls."

Wil touched the pendant in question. "The wife of a Cherokee chief gave it to my great-grandmother because she was a nurse and would help them when a doctor wouldn't come. She acted as their midwife when births were difficult, stitched cuts, vaccinated children, and even performed an emergency appendectomy once. She passed the necklace down to her oldest daughter—my grandmother. When Grandma died, it went to my mother, then to me. I never take it off."

A sudden sadness in Lacey's gaze told Wil that she'd understood but would allow her mother's death to remain unspoken.

"Do I have a pair of expensive boots? Yes. Did we bring our horses here in a new luxury trailer? Yes. It's all part of marketing our product. Appearances matter when you want rich guys to pay close to a million dollars for a horse purchased just to win belt buckles and bragging rights. I don't like those people much, but I do have to associate with them because they're the ones who can afford to pay what my horses are worth."

Lacey covered Wil's hand with hers and squeezed—like Wil had earlier—then retreated.

Chemistry crackled in the air between them, but their nascent bond was too tentative to push further.

"I'd ask you to have dinner with me, but duty calls. Dad and I are dining with Mac Abbott to talk about a couple of our horses he's looking to buy." Her subconscious was jumping up and down, waving a hand like a first-grader to get her attention. *Oh, right.* She smiled at Lacey as a plan began to form in her mind. "What time will you be heading up to freshen your horse's stall in the morning?"

They both stood, and Lacey glanced over her shoulder at the wood-chip bales. "Around five thirty."

"Sounds good. I'll see you then, so I can get some of our chips to clean our stalls at the same time."

Lacey shrugged one shoulder. "Okay." She kicked at the dirt. "It's been a long day. I'm going to have a quick dinner, go check on Denver, and climb in my bunk with the book I've been reading."

Wil was loath to take her eyes off Lacey, so she began to walk backward toward their trailer. "Good night." She started to turn toward the Double R trailer but paused when Lacey called to her. "Yeah?"

A slow smile stretched across Lacey's beautiful face. "I've, um…noticed you, too…before."

They grinned stupidly at each other until Wil turned and tossed a wave over her shoulder as she strode away.

CHAPTER FIVE

Lacey stepped out of the camper end of her thirty-foot, fifth-wheel trailer to find Wil sitting in the lawn chair Lacey had placed under the trailer's roll-out awning the night before. She glanced at her watch. Five thirty on the nose. She cleared her throat. "Been waiting long?" Finding the star of her all-night sex dreams on her doorstep the next morning was disconcerting.

Wil held up a tall travel mug. "Just enjoying my coffee and the quiet before the campground wakes up."

Deciding to let the deflection stand, she saluted the idea with her own travel mug. She locked the door behind her and scanned the semi-dark parking/camping area. A few cowboys were moving quietly around trailers, preparing hay and feed buckets to deliver to their horses in the arena stabling area or enjoying their last cup of coffee under the awnings of their trailers. The rest of the camp would be stirring soon, and the campground would be teeming with people and horses by the time the sun was fully up in about an hour. "We better start moving before things get too busy," she said, walking over to unlock the trailer's ramp so she could prepare Denver's breakfast and start hauling wood chips up to clean Denver's stall.

"I'm sure your horse will appreciate that. She was indignant that her breakfast wasn't served when I fed mine a half hour ago."

Lacey laughed, relieving some of the awkward tension between them this morning. "She can be a demanding diva. I'm sure she'll let me know about her displeasure."

"The good news is that the stable area was nearly deserted, and I was able to snag the cart we used yesterday, so we won't have to make multiple trips from here."

Lacey wasn't used to working with someone else. She hesitated, then rewarded Wil with a wide smile. "You might be worth keeping around." She put a freshly filled hay bag and a bucket containing Denver's measure of sweet feed and supplements on the cart, and Wil gave her an affectionate shoulder bump before pushing the lightweight cart toward the stables.

❖

Lacey and Wil scanned the order of competitors for the first round of the barrel races.

"Wait." Lacey turned to Wil. "You're riding in the barrel races?"

"Well, yeah. How else can I show people what my horse can do?"

Lacey frowned. *Damn. How good is her horse? Better than Denver? And how good is Wil? She trains other people and their horses, in addition to her own horses.* The San Antonio rodeo was one of the larger events sanctioned to award points toward an invite to the National Finals Rodeo in Vegas, and she needed first-place points to put some distance between her and Brittney in the rankings. Wil seemed to read her thoughts.

"Hey, hey. Don't worry. You and Denver have this." Wil's brow drew together, her expression worried. "My horse is green and has never run in an arena with loud, distracting crowd noise. You're smaller, maybe forty pounds lighter, and riding an experienced barrel racer. I promise I'm not going to steal the points you're going after."

She wasn't totally convinced, but Wil seemed so intent on easing her doubts, Lacey decided to play a little. "What about stealing points from Brittney?"

Wil placed an overly dramatic hand over her chest. "Would I sabotage a client who is probably going to buy my best barrel racer?"

"Hmm. I doubt it." She leaned in close to Wil. "But would you cut the legs out from under an ex-girlfriend who's a real snot?"

Wil's eyebrows shot up before she straightened, threw her head back, and laughed loud and long. Lacey loved the surprised and happy abandon of her laughter.

"Oh my God!" Wil wiped tears from her eyes when she regained her composure. "I can't believe you asked that, but the answer is yes. I would. I will. If you're in first place and Brittney second, I'll absolutely try to knock her out of the second-place slot. And if she's in first place, I will do my damnedest to best her."

"You might lose a horse sale if you piss her off."

"On the contrary. If I beat out Brittney, she'll be obsessed with buying the horse I rode that beat hers."

Lacey shook her head at Wil's smug grin. "I'm beginning to see how you could afford to buy that fancy trailer you're hauling."

"Common sense more than trade secrets, but the Double R would go down in a wash of red ink if there was even a hint that I was conspiring with you against Brittney."

Lacey shook her head. "My lips are sealed as long as you don't try to manipulate me."

"I would never," Wil said, raising her hand with three fingers extended. "Scout's honor."

"Yeah, yeah." Lacey's cheeks were going to be sore if she didn't stop smiling so much, but she was enjoying the easy banter between them.

"Can I buy you breakfast?" Wil asked.

Lacey hesitated. After mucking Denver's stall, she'd helped Wil clean the Double R's four stalls. That was payback for Wil's help with idiot Bob yesterday.

"We'll probably beat the crowd if we go over to the hospitality dining room now," Wil said. She didn't indicate that she'd noticed Lacey's hesitation. "I hear this rodeo puts out a pretty good spread."

Lacey relaxed. Wil's offer to "buy" breakfast was a euphemism because the hospitality buffet was free to competitors and their families. "Absolutely. I'm starving." She rubbed her hands together in anticipation. "Their buffet is the main reason I always enter this rodeo."

❖

Although the bacon was a bit undercooked, the buffet was pretty amazing. Lacey ate a plate full of grits, scrambled eggs, link sausage, a bagel with cream cheese, and a bowl of fruit. Then she went back for a made-to-order, full-size waffle. She'd been really happy when the lady making the waffles asked if she wanted anything added to her waffle batter or sprinkled on top. Lacey had scanned the available fruit, then nearly did a happy dance when she spotted the bowl of chopped pecans. Yum.

"I have no idea where you're putting all that food, and why you aren't as round as you are tall," Wil said, shaking her head while Lacey poured a generous amount of maple syrup over the large waffle.

Lacey chewed, then swallowed the huge bite she'd stuffed into her mouth. "High metabolism." She pushed her sleeve up, then lifted and curled her arm to show off her well-developed bicep. "I'm all muscle, and muscle burns more calories."

Wil laughed. "Indeed it does. But I'm four, maybe five, inches taller, and although my body fat is very low, my frame is at least three sizes larger. I think, in your case, genetics must keep you slim even though you eat enough for three teenage boys." She stood and picked up her empty coffee cup. "I'm going for a refill. Want me to refill yours, too?"

Lacey downed the last swallow in her cup and handed it to Wil. "Please."

"Flavored creamer or plain?"

"Plain. Three sugars and three of the little half-and-half things."

"Noted. I'll be right back." Wil started to leave but turned to her again. "Should I put in an order for a second waffle?"

"Thanks, but no." Lacey patted her stomach. "I have to save room for lunch."

Wil feigned an exaggerated expression of disbelief. "That's hours away. How will you survive until then?"

Lacey pretended to consider this question, then offered Wil a bright smile. "I'll swipe a bagel and a cream cheese packet for a snack. Maybe an apple, too."

Wil shook her head and headed toward the coffee station on the other side of the large room. Lacey dug into her waffle again, mentally reviewing the things she would need to do before the first round of barrel racing scheduled to begin at noon. She was halfway through her list when Brittney Abbott sat down on the other side of the picnic-style table, next to the remnants of Wil's breakfast. She eyed Lacey with disdain.

"I don't believe you have the money to hire Wil Rivers as a coach, much less buy one of her horses. So, I figure you must be paying the same way your mother got what she wanted."

Lacey wanted to snarl. "You don't know anything about my mother, much less about me."

"Oh, honey. Everybody knows who and what your mother was. The stories have been recirculating since you and your mutt of a horse pushed your way into the top-ten rankings." Brittney made a tsk-tsk noise with her tongue. "And she showed such promise as a barrel racer...until she got preggers and the penniless cowboy who sired you left without even saying good-bye."

"You'd better shut up before you're wearing the rest of my breakfast."

"Impulsive. Just like the whore who spawned you."

Lacey glanced toward the coffee station after Brittney looked that way and stood to leave. Wil was on her way back, her eyes narrowing when she spotted Brittney. "Oh, good." Lacey intentionally laced her words with bored sarcasm. "Wil's bringing me some hot coffee you can wear before you slither back to your minions."

Brittney ignored the threat. "Here's a piece of advice. You're nothing but Wil's attempt to make me jealous, because she knows that when I'm ready to settle down, it will be with a man my daddy approves. And she doesn't want to share me." Brittney lowered her voice as Wil drew closer. "But she'll come around, so you better work quick to get what you want from her."

"Good morning, Brittney." Wil's demeanor was relaxed and casual, but her eyes were cold as shards of blue ice. "You and your entourage are up and out early today. I'd offer for you to join us, but Lacey and I were just leaving." She had exchanged their ceramic coffee mugs for two large to-go cups full of steaming coffee.

"I was mad at you for ducking out after dinner last night, but I forgive you. I know you were just jealous because I went over to Bart's table to talk to him for a few minutes." Brittney's exaggerated pout morphed into a sugary sweet smile. "So, I'm glad I ran into you this morning to let you know I forgive you."

"I was not jealous. I left because I needed to bed down our horses and call the ranch to make sure everything is going well there."

"About those horses. I see you're riding a new one in the barrels today. I might be interested if it runs well."

Lacey reached for her coffee, but Wil shook her head, refusing to hand it over.

"Could you grab my plate and drop it with yours in the trash on our way out?" Wil asked. "I'll carry the coffees."

"Sure." Lacey frowned but stacked Wil's paper plate on top of hers while Wil turned back to Brittney.

"Pepper isn't my best horse. The fastest racer I've ever trained is back at the ranch because I'm still working to get him consistent on the turns. I'm sure you'd be more interested in him when he's ready."

Brittney smiled and stepped closer to finger Wil's collar. "Let me check my calendar. I can probably spare a weekend soon to check out the horse and maybe enjoy a few rides, if you're up for it."

Wil stepped back and held up the coffees clutched in both hands. "Careful. That blouse looks expensive, and I'd hate to spill hot coffee on it."

Lacey snorted in disgust. Could Brittney be more obvious? Her sultry expression made it clear she wasn't talking about horseback rides. Lacey was tempted to divert Brittney with a little trash-talk about today's competition. She and Denver had beaten Brittney and Dash the last time they competed at the same rodeo. But Lacey didn't want to jinx herself, and Wil wasn't hers to rescue. "I've got things to do," she said, heading for the trash can next to the exit.

"Right behind you," Wil said. "Bye, Brittney."

Lacey dumped their breakfast trash and turned to take the coffee Wil held out for her. When she glanced past Wil, Brittney glared at her. If Wil was trying to make Brittney jealous, it was working. Lacey smiled and gave Brittney a little wave as they exited.

CHAPTER SIX

L acey whirled Denver in a tight circle again. The mare was super-charged after their ten-day rest and would be a challenge to slow enough for the precision turns needed to post a top time. She worked the bit to keep Denver's attention on her rather than the open arena at the other end of the starting chute.

"Next up, Lacey Bishop, riding Dust Storm Denver. Ms. Bishop is currently ranked seventh in the national standings." The announcer's deep voice still reverberated over the arena speakers when she and Denver exploded into the arena with the first barrel in their sights.

Half Arabian and half Quarter horse, Denver was an oddball among the mostly registered American Quarter horse racers on the professional circuit. The mare, however, had inherited the best tools of both breeds for barrel racing. She had the Arabian short back for exceptional agility but the muscled rump of her Quarter horse sire for powerful sprints. Her longer-legged opponents had an advantage in that final sprint to leave the arena, but Denver made up time with tighter, faster turns.

Their first was a bit wide as Lacey struggled to slow Denver's wild charge, but both horse and rider settled into their task with a flawless maneuver around the second barrel and a determined dash for the third one. Their approach was precision perfect, but as Denver dug into the turn, her inside hind hoof slipped in the soft dirt, and they lost three-hundredths of a second while she scrambled to regain her footing and sprint for home.

Lacey was off Denver the minute they left the arena, watching carefully for any sign of lameness as she walked her out to the warm-up ring. Wil and Pepper were still in the outdoor ring, preparing to go inside since the lineup after Lacey included Brittney, then Wil, and then the top three nationally ranked racers. The only other rider in the ring was Ray Rivers, showing off one of his reining horse's moves to three men leaning against the railing.

Wil immediately rode over to Lacey. "What's wrong? Is she injured?"

Lacey didn't look up. "She slipped going around the third barrel." She wasn't surprised that Wil immediately knew something was off when Lacey led Denver into the ring rather than riding her in to cool down. "I hate drawing the last position before they drag the arena. They're, of course, dragging it now before Brittney's run."

"Not like we get a choice. Once they post the order of the competitors, it takes an act of Congress for them to change it," Wil said, riding behind them and eyeing Denver's legs. "At least it applies to everyone. Not even a princess like Brittney with all her daddy's money can get them to revise it."

"I know. But, damn, they should plan to drag the arena to even out the dirt before any of the top ten riders perform. Not just after every eighth or tenth competitor." Lacey understood the reasoning behind peppering some of the best riders throughout the schedule but saving those at the very top until last. It ensured the crowd would mostly stay in their seats rather than come late or leave early. And if they didn't have an audience, sponsors wouldn't be shelling out dollars to advertise at the arena and on the clothing of the best athletes. But damn it all. "Those of us who've climbed to the top have too much invested to lose it all because of a slip that can put a horse out of competition."

"You're right, but if they dragged the arena for the top players rather than just at regular intervals, that would hardly be fair to the riders at the bottom, trying to work their way up." Wil cocked her head, listening as the announcer introduced Brittney. "Denver looks sound from the back, but I'd keep walking her for another twenty minutes, then do some leg stretches."

"You'd better get in there, or you'll miss your run."

"Yeah. I'm going. Dad and I have team roping tonight, but I'll check with you before then to see how she's doing." Wil urged Pepper into a fast trot and disappeared into the arena entrance.

❖

Lacey walked Denver around the grassy field behind the arena complex. It seemed every area except the arena floor was paved, and she was sure she'd find concrete there, too, under the tons of dirt hauled in for the event. This arena was also used for events ranging from concerts to basketball to knife and gun shows. The warm-up ring, of course, consisted of dirt, but it was filled with cowboys readying their horses for the roping and steer-wrestling events. So, even though the field was littered with trash, and a few of the city's homeless had camped at the other end, it was the best footing for a horse trying to stay loose and not go lame by morning.

She could hear the crowd cheering and the low tones of the announcer's voice over the speakers, but it was just faint white noise while she let her thoughts drift as she watched the ground for any sharp objects that could harm hooves.

Wil was a mesmerizing conundrum. While Lacey had been drawn to the dark-haired beauty since the first time she'd noticed her several years ago, she'd presumed Wil was one of those women privileged by wealth from birth. She'd also concluded Wil was part of the rich-girl social group because Brittney's body language around Wil clearly indicated they were more than friends. She couldn't blame Brittney. Wil was smoking hot. But associating with Brittney was a poor reflection on Wil's character…at least in Lacey's eyes.

As it turned out, she'd been wrong. So wrong. Wil had no respect for Brittney's clique, and little for Brittney. Whether Brittney had lured Wil into her bed was none of Lacey's concern, but Wil was adamant that the only relationship currently between them was horse business.

Lacey had been initially conflicted over Wil's friendly overtures. But, damn, she was hard to resist and not at all the person Lacey had imagined. She was smart, considerate, fun, and indifferent to what other people thought. Wil's dark looks, tall athletic frame, and startling blue eyes screamed sexy.

She put her hand to her own face to confirm a sudden realization. Yes. Wil also made her smile, as evidenced by the unbidden grin currently stretching her cheeks. As she and Denver completed their circuit of the field and neared the arena complex, the announcer's voice boomed, clear and distinct.

"That concludes the first round of steer wrestling, folks. Todd Gentry is in first place, with Bret Saunders in a close second, and Donnie Rodriguez trailing in third place. But that could all change during the next two rounds this weekend, so make sure you come back to see how it shakes out. Until then, keep your seats, because team roping is next, and then the crowd favorite…bull riding."

Team roping. Isn't that what Wil said she and her dad are entered in tonight? Lacey turned toward the stable area. Denver showed no signs of lameness from her slip, so she should be fine while Lacey watched the rodeo competition for a few hours. Denver nickered when they passed the Riverses' stall next to hers. A bay gelding answered, then thrust his nose against the steel bars that separated the top half of the wall between them. Lacey chuckled to herself. It appeared Denver had made a new friend and wouldn't miss her at all. She smiled. So, she was free to go see how good *her* new friend was at roping calves.

❖

Wil wiped the sweat from her forehead with her sleeve and readied her lariat, the stiff rope easily forming a large loop in her right hand, while the rest of the rope was coiled in her left. Then she glanced at her dad on the other side of the steer chute as she backed Sip of Whiskey up for a running start when the calf was released. Since he was a master roper, he would be the heeler—the one who would lasso the calf's back legs after Wil's rope settled over the fake horns strapped to its head.

Cowboys had developed team roping to restrain a calf. Although it was still useful for catching and holding a wounded calf in the pasture, most modern ranches now herded the animals into safe, narrow chutes to brand and vaccinate them. Rodeos added the fake horns strapped to the calves' heads to eliminate possible injury to the animal when roped around the neck.

Ray backed Rebel into place, nodded his readiness, and added a wink that helped Wil relax. She wasn't normally nervous, but they hadn't ridden together in competition since six months before the pandemic lockdown, and she might be rusty. She took a deep breath and nodded to the stockman. He opened the chute, and the young steer bolted for the other end of the arena.

Whiskey needed nothing more than a slight squeeze with Wil's legs to set him after the calf. He knew his job so well, the reins gathered in her hand that held the extra loops of rope were extraneous. The gelding paced the calf while Wil swung the large loop of her lariat overhead. Her aim was true, and she yanked the rope tight when it settled over the calf's hat of fake horns. Whiskey slid to a stop and backed up a few steps, a move that swung the calf around to face them and place his hindquarters in perfect position for Ray to lasso both hind feet as the calf kicked out. He pulled the rope tight to show both feet were ensnared, but released it with a flick of his hand so the calf never fell down or was actually stretched tight between the two horses.

Wil flicked her lariat loose, and the calf ran for the open gate where other ones stood waiting after their run. She grinned at her father. That had to be among the top three times, and their horses had performed perfectly. They weren't interested in accruing points, but she was changing her mind about trying to win the competition. The Double R sure could use the prize money.

"That show of precision roping puts the father-daughter team from the Double R in second place and advances them to tomorrow's round."

An ear-splitting whistle drew Wil's attention to the upper seats, where Lacey was on her feet and cheering wildly. She gave a fist pump when Wil smiled and waved.

"That's a pretty cute cheerleader you've got there," Ray said, tipping his hat back for a better look. "You know her?"

"That's Lacey Bishop, one of the barrel racers."

He nudged Rebel to walk alongside Whiskey. "Ah, the one you tried to woo with wood chips. I thought I taught you better. You give a girl flowers or candy, not wood chips."

Wil affectionately pushed his shoulder. "You don't know Lacey. She's not the flowers type. She appreciates practical things for her horse's stall more."

"Women still like to feel pretty and cherished. Trust me." Ray squeezed Wil's shoulder. "You can give her wood chips for her horse, but also give her something nice for herself."

"What do you know about wooing, old man?"

"I won your mother over, didn't I?"

"She took pity on you."

He laughed. "That's probably true, but I still got the girl."

Wil loved their teasing, and she was considering his advice. Although she doubted Lacey would appreciate flowers, maybe she'd like something else. But what? Ray was a great father, but she wished for the millionth time that her mother was still alive to help her navigate certain important aspects of her life. She'd have to think on this for a while, because Lacey wasn't just any girl.

❖

Wil lingered in Pepper's stall, grooming her an unnecessary second time that day. With the first round of team roping over, they remained in second place. But there were two more rounds, and unlike the barrel racing, the team-roping prizes and points were awarded for the top three cumulative scores after the final round.

She smiled when she heard the door on Denver's stall roll back, then turned to see Lacey also smiling at her.

"That was some awesome roping for a fancy cowpoke," Lacey said.

Wil tried her best to look indignant. "Who are you calling fancy?"

Lacey pushed her hat back on her head. "The woman who wears a white shirt all the time and dares the rodeo dust to touch it."

Wil laughed. "You think I can intimidate rodeo dust?"

"That and three-quarters of the men around here." Lacey's eyes shone with challenge as she propped against Denver's side while the mare contentedly munched on a mouthful of hay.

Wil didn't stop to think about what she was doing. She just went with her heart...or maybe it was her libido. But, damn, she was so easily sucked in by this woman's flirting. She stepped into Denver's stall and rested her hand on Denver's rump, the angle almost trapping Lacey against her horse. "And what about the women? Do I intimidate them?"

Lacey hesitated, then lifted her chin. "Not this woman."

Wil stared into her eyes, the brown of her irises so deep, inviting yet wary. Wil had her own doubts, but Lacey's lips were a vortex, spinning her emotions and sucking her down to touch, to taste them with her own. Yet when she bent to drown herself in the softness of those lips, her father called her from outside the stalls.

"Wil, where are you?"

Lacey jerked back, making Denver snort.

Wil closed her eyes and sighed. Her father always did have bad timing, and she was beginning to believe it was on purpose. They normally would joke and laugh about his intrusion later, but it wasn't funny this time. She'd never felt so drawn to someone. She didn't understand why, but no woman had ever felt this important to her. "I'm here." She stepped out of the stall and glared at him. "What's wrong?"

"Nothing's wrong. Just wondering where you were." He smiled brightly.

Wil could tell he'd had a few beers. He wasn't a big drinker, so it didn't take but two or three to light him up, and she didn't begrudge him an occasional buzz.

"I think I'm gonna turn in." He yawned. "You coming? It's getting late, and you've got breakaway roping first thing tomorrow."

"I'll be along in a few minutes, after I take a quick shower in the locker room to knock the dust off before I crawl into my bunk."

His eyebrows shot up. "You hate public bathrooms."

"I don't want to use all the water in the trailer's tank." She looked away, knowing he'd see the small lie in her eyes. "We're basically camping in a dirt parking lot since we got here too late for the few spaces that have electricity and water hookups."

Lacey stepped out of Denver's stall. "Uh, I got here early and do have water and electricity. You could use my shower." Her face flushed pink. "Sorry to eavesdrop, but it's hard not to hear a conversation just outside the stall." She shifted her feet and shoved her hands into the pockets of her jeans while silence hung in the air for a few seconds. "Hi, Mr. Rivers. I'm Lacey Bishop."

Denver nickered and pressed her nose against the metal bars of her stall.

Lacey chuckled. "And this is my horse, Denver."

Her dad glanced at Wil, and she saw he'd finally caught a clue. "I'm so sorry my daughter has forgotten her manners and failed to introduce us." He held out his large, callused hand. "I'm Ray Rivers...Ray to you, Ms. Bishop. And I know who you are. Yes, siree. You guys are the blonde and the buckskin shoving your way into the barrel racers' top ten."

She shook his hand, a broad smile lighting her face. "That's us. Hoping to push our way high enough for an invite to Vegas."

"I have no doubt you'll get there. That's a fine horse. I wouldn't mind chatting about her bloodlines when I'm not half asleep."

Wil slapped him on the shoulder. "Off to bed, old man. I'll be along soon."

Ray harrumphed. "Not so long ago, I was sending you off to bed, brat."

"Yeah, yeah." Wil gave her father an affectionate one-armed hug and whispered in his ear before kissing him on his cheek. "Don't forget your breathing treatment."

He nodded to confirm he'd heard her but turned back to Lacey. "Ms. Bishop, would you join us for breakfast tomorrow at our camper? We eat early—six thirty—but I guarantee nothing in the hospitality buffet can touch my made-to-order omelets and melt-in-your-mouth biscuits."

Wil smiled. "I can confirm that fact, if you're interested."

"Thank you, Ray," Lacey said. "I never turn down a free meal, especially one that has me drooling already. But you have to stop being so formal and call me Lacey."

"Can do. I'll see you in the morning, Lacey." He grinned, flashing teeth as white as his daughter's. *These people must have a great dentist.*

"Good night, Dad," Wil said.

"I'm going." He strode out of the stable building, waving over his shoulder.

"He's sweet," Lacey said as they watched him leave.

Wil chewed the inside of her cheek, staring after her dad. "It's been just me and him since my mom died when I was in high school. I've been worried because he got really sick with the coronavirus. He was in ICU on a ventilator for a week. He obviously pulled through, but the aftereffects are very real—depression, fatigue, brain fog. I'm scared to death he'll come down with one of the variants and not make it through a second time."

Lacey rubbed soothing circles between Wil's shoulders. "Shouldn't he be wearing a mask with all these people around?"

"I did insist he get vaccinated because they don't know how long antibodies last in your system after you've had the virus, but he's damned hard-headed about wearing a mask. He says Mom is looking after him from Heaven."

Lacey seemed to suddenly realize she was stroking Wil's back and quickly pulled her hand away. Wil decided it was best to ignore the withdrawal. She picked up the backpack that held her clean clothes and shower essentials. "I'll take you up on that offer for a shower. I really do hate locker rooms."

"It's small and might be a tight fit, but you're welcome to it."

"Thanks. I'm used to being too tall for showers, but at least I know yours hasn't had hundreds of people using it and doing God knows what in it." Wil exaggerated a shudder.

Lacey laughed. "Come on, then."

They walked companionably through the temporary village of horse trailers. Lights shone through the windows of some that included living quarters. People in dusty jeans and T-shirts lounged by an occasional trailer—most smoking or sharing a drink and quiet conversation. The younger, rowdy crowd were likely sowing oats at several of the Western bars in town. Lacey's three-horse, slant-load trailer was ten years old but gleamed inside and out as though barely used. The little bathroom and shower were smaller than the Double R trailer's but larger than Wil had imagined, given the efficiently compact living quarters.

"This is great," she said to Lacey. "Somebody has taken very good care of this rig. It looks almost new."

Lacey smiled, apparently pleased that Wil approved. "It belonged to my great-aunt, but she used it only a couple of times before my uncle died and she quit showing horses. It had been sitting in their barn for eight years when heart disease claimed her. The farm was double mortgaged and sold to pay her bills, but she signed the trailer over to me before she died."

"That was lucky." Wil set her backpack on the closed toilet. "I won't be long."

"I don't doubt that," Lacey said, chuckling. "The water heater holds only six gallons."

Wil wasn't concerned. Unable to stop thinking about the almost-kiss, she definitely needed the shower to be cold.

❖

Lacey stepped outside to pace under the trailer's canopy. Wil Rivers was in her shower right now—tall, beautiful, and naked. Lacey had seen and slept with plenty of naked women, but never in her trailer because this was her home. But, oh my God. Wil was the most stunning, interesting, intelligent, caring woman she'd ever met.

If she'd been invited, she'd have found a way to squeeze herself into that tiny shower with Wil. *Wait.* No, she wouldn't. While part of her wanted to strip and fling herself at Wil, a bigger part wanted to take what was developing between them slowly. She wanted to savor each minute before they parted. And Wil would lose interest at some point.

People always left. Her father disappeared when he found out her mother was pregnant. Her mother ran off with her latest sleazy boyfriend when Lacey was fifteen. And her first girlfriend ditched her when she chose to follow her barrel-racing dream instead of taking the college scholarship she was offered.

So, she wasn't looking for anything permanent. But, damn, she sure was willing to take a ride with Wil, even if it lasted only a few months or until the National Finals Rodeo.

Lacey heard the shower stop and hurried inside. She couldn't let Wil catch her pacing and mumbling to herself. She stood in the middle of her tiny living quarters. What to do? She could grab the book from her bed in the gooseneck portion of the trailer and lounge on the short couch like she'd been casually reading while Wil showered. Should she turn on the television across from the couch instead? Still rooted to the same spot by her indecision, she felt the air being sucked out of her lungs when the bathroom door opened and Wil stepped out in an oversized T-shirt and very, very skimpy running shorts. Holy Mother, she had legs for days. Lacey would have swooned with an attack of the vapors—her great-aunt's words—if she hadn't been so preoccupied with the fantasy of running her hands up those smooth, muscular thighs and under those cute shorts.

"Lacey?"

She mentally shook herself. Wil was saying something to her.

"Sorry, sorry. It's just…damn. You've got great legs."

"Uh, thanks." Wil smiled but stared at the floor, flushing red.

Lacey's confidence bloomed with Wil's unexpected bashful response. "Do you run?"

"I did track in high school and college. Now I jog a couple of times a week to burn off stress." Wil rested her back against the closed bathroom door, showing no sign of leaving. "Do you?"

Lacey stepped into Wil's personal space. "Not from smart, gorgeous women." She brushed her fingertips over Wil's lips to signal her intent, then caressed her cheek before sliding her hand behind Wil's neck to tug her closer. "I want to kiss you."

"Yes." Wil's whispered answer was warm and toothpaste minty before Lacey closed the distance between them.

She brushed her lips gently against Wil's, then again more firmly to taste them. Wil's arms closed around her, melding them together, and Lacey gave in to her persistent urge to glide her hand over Wil's smooth, muscled thigh. When Wil brushed her tongue against Lacey's lips, she opened to her, and they explored each other with a building urgency. So hot. So sweet. She hadn't even realized she'd slid her hand under Wil's shorts and underwear to grip her smooth, warm buttock until Wil grasped her hand over her shorts.

"We have to stop." Wil gasped.

"Why? I don't want to." Contrary to her response, Lacey withdrew her hand. "Sorry. I don't normally grope women." She looked up into Wil's dilated pupils. "I just…I seem to lose my mind around you." She stepped back and combed her fingers through her own hair, trying to regain her control.

"You make me kind of crazy, too." Wil's chuckle was tight. "But I don't want to jump into bed with you."

"You don't?" Lacey was confused. She couldn't have misjudged the kiss. Wil absolutely was into it.

Wil shook her head. "I mean I do…want to make love with you. But that's just it. I want a relationship, not just sex. I want time to get to know you. I want to take you to dinner, then sit under the stars to share secrets and life goals. I want to know your favorite color, your favorite food, and where you spend your time when you're not at a rodeo." Wil sucked in a deep breath, then ducked her head and looked away from Lacey. "If that scares you, or if you were only looking for a quick fuck, then we're not on the same page and should stop before one of us gets hurt."

Lacey stared at Wil for a long moment. Wil wanted a real relationship with her. Why would somebody like Wil be interested in a homeless rodeo vagabond? Was this a cruel trick Brittney had talked Wil into? She couldn't believe Wil would do such a thing. She liked Wil. More than liked her. But could she risk her heart? "You want something other than incredibly hot sex?"

Wil looked up at her again. "I want it all…especially the incredibly hot sex. I just want to explore whether this could be something more than a summer fling." Wil held out her hand.

"I…I don't know." Lacey was wary. No. She was scared. Should she trust Wil? While her misgivings and deep attraction waged a mental war, Lacey somehow took Wil's offered hand. "I've never been in a real relationship, so I'm not sure I know how to do this."

Wil smiled, her gaze soft and affectionate. "It scares the hell out of me, too," she said, lifting Lacey's hand to her lips. "But I want to try. Will you try with me?"

She might regret this decision, but she smiled back. "As long as incredibly hot sex isn't too far down the agenda."

Wil threw her head back, her laugh light and joyful. "Agreed."

"And can I get another kiss? You can hold on to my hands to make sure they don't wander."

"I need to get some sleep. How about a good-night kiss outside? Then we won't have to worry about getting carried away."

"Good idea." Lacey tugged Wil toward the door.

Outside, the night was cooling, but moist humidity still blanketed the area. Wil looped her backpack over one shoulder and reached for Lacey's face with both hands. Despite the heat, Lacey shivered as Wil's callused palms cupped her cheeks, then satin lips touched and tasted her own. She opened willingly to take in Wil's hot, wet tongue and suck it before pushing her tongue into Wil's mouth. She reluctantly withdrew, her hands on Wil's hips as she held her an arm's length away.

"Wow." She shook her head. "Are you sure—"

Wil gathered Lacey's hands in hers and held them to her chest. Lacey could feel Wil's heart pounding in sync with her own.

"You make it really hard, but yes. This thing between us is special. I can feel it, and I think you do, too. I want to do this right."

"Hottest woman I've ever kissed, and she has to be old-fashioned." Lacey smiled to let Wil know she wasn't unhappy about waiting. Well, not too unhappy.

"I want to court you first."

Lacey laughed in delight. "Court me?"

Wil straightened her shoulders and nodded. "Yes. I'm not counting breakfast because Dad will be there." She adjusted the backpack on her shoulder. "But I'd like to take you to dinner tomorrow night."

"You don't have team roping again?"

"No. They've scheduled broncs and bulls for the Saturday-night contests. We'll compete earlier now that the number of contestants has been narrowed down. So, dinner? Nothing dressy."

"Good. Because I don't do dressy."

"Is that a yes?"

Lacey stepped forward and pulled Wil into another brief kiss. "Yes," she whispered.

Wil brushed her lips against Lacey's one more time, then began to back away. "See you in the morning." Then she turned and jogged toward her own trailer.

"Special. Yes, you are." Lacey mumbled the observation aloud to herself. If she didn't give voice to the feeling, her fear might try to talk her out of it.

CHAPTER SEVEN

Wil took Lacey's hand and led her to a path nearly invisible in the dense tree line.

"You're not taking me into the woods to murder me, are you?" Lacey's tone was teasing. "I've seen you admiring my horse, but that's not the way to get your hands on her."

Wil laughed, light with anticipation rather than weighed down by expectation. "Oh, I'm after way more than your horse."

Ten minutes after Lacey had arrived at their trailer for breakfast that morning, she and Ray were chatting like best friends. Wil was amazed and Ray delighted at the amount of food Lacey, barely five feet, five inches tall with a slim build, managed to consume. Ray refused help cooking, but Lacey and Wil filled coffee cups and passed out plates and silverware, and then all pitched in to clean up afterward. The conversation was easy, centering around horses, rodeos, and how the pandemic had changed life in general. In a moment of strong déjà vu, Wil realized the last time she'd felt this comfortable and…complete…had been when she shared a Saturday morning breakfast with both her parents present. Before, it'd been Mom and Dad, and her. Today, it'd been her and Lacey, and Dad. The dynamic was different but just as comfortable. Her father seemed happier than he'd been in years, as though he felt the rightness of it, too.

But she was getting ahead of herself. She still had a woman to woo.

She'd called on the twins, who were riding Rivers horses in the tie-down roping, to help her provide a special dinner on the banks of a river within walking distance of the arena complex. They reached the clearing, and Wil said a silent thank you to the boys. She'd asked for a picnic format, but a small table covered in a white linen tablecloth was set for two, complete with wineglasses and the bottle of wine she'd bought icing in a silver bucket. Sundown wouldn't take place for another hour or more, but the flames of four tiki torches filled their outdoor dining site with the faint scent of citronella.

Lacey stopped at the edge of their destination, eyes wide. "Wow. When did you do all this? You rode in three events today."

"I enlisted a couple of elves to help."

Lacey turned in a half circle to fully take in the view of the river and the city lights beyond as dusk began to settle around them. "This is perfect."

"And you are beautiful," Wil said, drinking in Lacey's profile softened by the diminishing light.

Lacey turned to her but glanced away. "Nobody has ever said that to me," she said quietly.

Wil touched Lacey's cheek, then gently curved her fingers under her chin in a silent request for Lacey to meet her gaze. So many unspoken questions passed between them as they searched each other's eyes, and then Wil drew her close. Their kiss was slow and soft, reassuring rather than enticing. When they drew apart, Wil pulled out a chair for Lacey, who raised an eyebrow at her chivalry but let Wil seat her.

She poured bottled water into their glasses, then took the chilled Shiraz from the ice bucket and dried the bottle before presenting it to Lacey. "Would you like wine with your meal?"

Lacey made a show of unfolding her linen napkin and settling it in her lap. "Of course." She chuckled as Wil folded a white towel over her forearm and laid the bottle against it like a waiter presenting the wine so the diner could read the label.

"This is the flavorful Estate Shiraz of Elderton Wines in Australia," Wil said. "A steal at twenty-five dollars," she added when Lacey frowned. Admitting this wasn't a two-hundred-dollar wine reignited Lacey's smile, so Wil uncorked it and poured. Lacey examined it like a professional before swishing it around her mouth and swallowing.

"Excellent. I approve," she said.

Wil poured the wine, then lifted the cover from the chafing pan to reveal beef stroganoff poured over thick egg noodles. It would have all been very elegant if the plate of four soft dinner rolls and the two spinach salads in creamy balsamic vinaigrette hadn't been covered with a colorful assortment of mixing bowls to protect them from insects or leaves falling from the surrounding trees. Nonetheless, she removed the covers and spooned up a healthy serving of the stroganoff onto each of their plates.

"Dinner is served, Miss Bishop."

Appearing amused, Lacey eyed the table. "No vegetable?"

Wil scowled and pointed to the salads. "Spinach is a vegetable."

Lacey shrugged. "Okay." She tasted the salad and gave it the same nod as the wine. But she closed her eyes and moaned as she closed her mouth around a forkful of the stroganoff. "I have to know where you bought this. I want a quart of it for my freezer before I leave town."

"I made it."

"Shut up. There's no way you had time to cook this today."

"I didn't say I did it today. It's my mom's recipe. Last time I cooked it, I made double what Dad and I could eat, then froze half of it to bring with us. I did boil the noodles today." She dug into her own dinner.

"This is amazing." Lacey shoveled another forkful into her mouth.

Wil studied her. "I'm really glad you like it. I didn't think an expensive restaurant would impress you. And, as much as I want to do that, I'm not in the position right now to blow two hundred dollars."

"I would be pissed if you did," Lacey said. "But this…this took planning and couldn't have been easy to execute with your busy schedule today."

"Dad helped arrange things, too."

Lacey ducked her head. "Oh my God. Your dad?"

Wil smiled at Lacey's sudden flush. "He likes you."

"He doesn't really know me."

"He knows you're a hard worker, and he respects that you're

a self-made woman. He really enjoyed breakfast with you this morning, and most importantly, he knows his daughter is besotted with you."

Lacey's blush deepened, but she looked up from her dinner to hold Wil's gaze. "Besotted?"

Wil felt her own blush heat her cheeks. "Yeah. An old-fashioned word, but it's a good one to describe how I feel." She held her breath, waiting for Lacey's reaction.

"It's possible that I might also be a little besotted with you, too?" The upward inflection in Lacey's reply revealed her uncertainty.

Still, Wil was elated. "Okay, then. We're on the same page." She grinned and scooped up a forkful of stroganoff. Lacey smiled and did the same.

After dessert, they walked hand-in-hand along the river's bank. Lacey pointed out a falling star, and then Wil sprinted around in a field they came upon and caught two fireflies. She regaled Lacey with tales of catching fireflies with a girl on a neighboring ranch when she was eleven years old. The girl was her first crush, and they'd catch the fireflies and smash the part of the insect that held the illumination and rub it on their earlobes to pretend they had glow-in-the-dark ear piercings.

"You put bug guts on your ears?" Lacey's grimace was teasing.

"Worse. I was crushing on her so bad—at that age, I didn't know why I wanted to be with her every minute—that I caught some more and put their guts on my forehead like a Hindu woman, then on my eyelids like eye shadow."

"Yuck. That's just nasty."

Wil shrugged. "She said it made me look enchanted."

"Enchanting?"

"No. Enchanted…as in ethereal or fae."

Lacey laid her hand against Wil's cheek, and Wil leaned into the touch. "Please don't put bug guts on your beautiful face for me," Lacey said.

Wil released the fireflies in her cupped hands, then bent to kiss her slow and deep with all the feelings overflowing her heart. They both smiled when she pulled back and took Lacey's hand again to continue their walk in a comfortable silence.

Finally, Wil spoke. "Actually, they're beetles, not flies or bugs."

"Beetles aren't insects?"

"Technically, bugs are insects whose mouthparts pierce and suck, like bedbugs or mosquitoes. People just use 'bugs' as a generalization."

Lacey peered at her in the semi-darkness. "Are you a botanist or something?"

Wil laughed. "No, but I was in the pre-vet sequence in college and took a lot of biology classes and some botany ones. I just never went to veterinary school. Biology lab where we had to dissect baby pigs convinced me pretty quick that I'd rather train horses than doctor them. I switched to a business degree to learn how to better manage the ranch finances because no college professor could teach me more about horses than Dad already had."

"It's cool that you're so close to your dad. My father took off before I was born. I don't even have a name to look him up. Mama said she didn't know who got her pregnant because she was drunk at a party. My great-aunt, who took me in when Mama ran off, said Mama did know, but she wouldn't give me his name either. She said he was a worthless drunk and probably dead or in jail somewhere."

Wil dropped Lacey's hand to pull her close with an arm around her shoulder. They fit together perfectly. She wanted to know Lacey better, but it was time to lighten the mood. "God, don't tell Dad that you're an orphan, because he'll want to adopt you. That would make you my sister, and then I couldn't do this." Again, she drew Lacey into a lingering kiss before whispering to her. "And I really like kissing you."

Lacey didn't answer but put her arm around Wil's waist to draw Wil's arm around her shoulder again as they resumed walking. When they returned to where they'd dined, everything had been cleared away.

"Wood elves?" Lacey teased, dropping her arm and taking Wil's hand instead.

"Yep. Little thieves, they are. Good thing we finished off the wine and ate dessert before taking our stroll." The night had grown cloudy, and the wind began to sway the trees around them. Wil could smell the impending rain. She flicked on the flashlight of her phone and tugged Lacey toward the path back to the roadway. "May I walk you back to your camper?"

"No, but you can run with me." Lacey didn't release Wil's hand but began to jog.

They stopped at the stabling area, only to find Denver and the Riverses' horses had been fed, their stalls cleaned, and fresh bedding added for a cozy night's sleep.

"Those are some great elves," Lacey said after they checked each stall.

"Well-intentioned, but a bit pushy. I can see Dad's hand in this." Wil scowled to exaggerate her frown. "If I can't woo you, he's likely to throw me off the ranch and adopt you."

Lacey bumped Wil's shoulder affectionately as they headed down to the trailers. The drenching rain had ended as quickly as it started, which was not unusual for summer cloudbursts in the area. "That would never happen. He adores you."

Wil caught Lacey's hand and entwined their fingers—a bold move even though the lighting was poor in the parking area. They'd shared at least a dozen lusty kisses, but they smiled shyly now because their linked hands represented more than physical chemistry. Although Wil had only dreamed of having the connection that was developing between them, she was confident her feelings were real. And she planned to persist until Lacey was sure, too.

"Well, well, well. Looks like Ms. Rivers is slumming tonight." Caroline Early, the leader of Brittney's fan club, stepped out from between the trailers across from Lacey's. Two of her cohorts trailed her.

Wil slipped her hand from Lacey's and crossed her arms over her chest as she turned to face them. "What are you three doing here, Carrie?" She knew Caroline hated having her name shortened.

She put her hand on her hip and smirked at Wil. "Brittney was looking for you earlier. She said y'all were supposed to talk about a horse she might buy."

"I told her I had a previous engagement tonight and would talk with her and her father tomorrow if she's serious about a purchase."

Caroline shrugged. "She says your ranch is one missed payment away from foreclosure, so you should be grateful she wants to buy one of your horses and meet with her at her convenience."

Wil narrowed her eyes. "First of all, only my horses are for sale. If Brittney thinks I'm part of the purchase package, she's sadly mistaken. Secondly, Brittney has no knowledge of the Double R's finances, and anyone spreading false rumors that we're desperate to sell horses is affecting our business. I won't hesitate to sue them for slander."

Caroline tilted her head, her smile mocking. "It's your funeral. Or should I say foreclosure?"

Wil struggled to maintain her composure as her anger rose. "Careful, little girl. You're wrong if you think Brittney will have your back when you're sued, too."

Caroline made a dismissive noise, but fear showed in her eyes. She whirled around with a flip of her hair and stalked away, her two minions following.

Wil watched them for a few seconds to make sure they were leaving, then turned back to find Lacey gone. Shit. This couldn't be good. She scanned the area, hoping Lacey had just stepped between two of the trailers to remove herself from the confrontation. No Lacey. Wil knocked on the door to her trailer but had no response. She knocked again, louder this time. "Lacey, I know you're in there. Don't let those little bitches get between us. That's exactly what they want."

When the door still didn't open, Wil started to stalk off toward her own trailer but stopped mid-stride and turned back toward the arena. The horses. Of course. Lacey would check to make sure the trio of mean girls didn't double back and try to sabotage their chances in the finals tomorrow.

Lacey spoke to Denver in a low, soft voice. No matter what upset her, she always found solace in the presence of horses. Denver stretched out her neck and raised her upper lip in obvious pleasure when Lacey brushed a particularly itchy spot, so she returned to it several times. She tried to lose herself in the rhythm of her strokes as she reviewed the tweaks she hoped would shave a few hundredths of a second off her run tomorrow, but all she could feel, the only image in her head, was Wil releasing her hand and turning away when Brittney's minions showed up.

She shouldn't be surprised that Wil didn't want to be seen with her. Hadn't they always been alone when Wil flirted? Hadn't their only "dates" been out of public view? Nobody wanted to be seen with the one-horse girl living out of a decade-old trailer—certainly not the stunning, sexy Wil Rivers. So, why was Wil courting her? Was she trying to make Brittney jealous, or get back at Brittney for ditching her every time Bart Roberts came around? Maybe she planned to sabotage Lacey's quest to qualify for the national finals.

"Lacey."

She closed her eyes, stilled her hand that held the soft grooming brush, and cursed her traitorous libido that warmed her cheeks and raised goose bumps down her arms at Wil's low, sexy timbre. She resumed brushing, brisk and rough, then lightened and slowed her strokes when Denver flinched away. "What are you doing here?" Her tone was intentionally sarcastic. "Didn't Brittney send her sidekicks to summon you to her hotel?"

"I think that's what they were sent to do, but Brittney Abbott has no claim on me."

Lacey rested her forehead on Denver's silky flank, soothed by the unique smell of horses and fresh hay. "And you can't afford to burn your bridges with a wealthy client."

"I'll tell you the same thing I told Caroline—my horses and my training sessions are for sale, but I'm not. My heart is mine to give only to the right person, and that's definitely not Brittney Abbott."

Lacey turned to Wil, searching her eyes for traces of a lie or uncertainty. She saw none. She sighed and allowed Wil to pull her into an embrace. She rested her head on Wil's shoulder. "That's a very romantic notion," she said. "But what you dream about having and what real life deals you are rarely the same."

"You don't believe in a love that lasts?"

She pulled out of Wil's embrace and turned away so Wil wouldn't see the tears welling in her eyes. "Why should I? My parents didn't love me enough to stick around. Then my aunt left me with nothing but a horse trailer and five hundred bucks. So why should I trust something as stupid as love? It's just a big lie."

"Lacey, don't."

"Don't? You dropped my hand like it was burning yours when those girls showed up, then stepped in front of me so they couldn't see who you were with." Damn it. She was not going to cry. She was tougher than this.

"That's what you think? That I was ashamed to be seen with you? Is that why you left?"

Lacey kept her back to Wil and stared at the ground.

"I let go of your hand so I could get between you and those little bitches. I don't trust them and wasn't about to let them hurt you. I know it's sort of Neanderthal of me, but I was trying to protect you." Wil's arms came around her from behind. "Don't write us off because of some pathetic girls who act like they're still in high school. We are adults, and you and I have something pretty good growing between us. Please trust me. Give me a chance. I promise I'm worth it."

Lacey let her shoulders slump. She was so tired of fighting the world. Maybe Wil was right. If she was truthful with herself, she already was a little in love with Wil. She turned in Wil's arms to face her, startled by the worry clouding Wil's blue eyes. She reached up to cup Wil's face, then pulled her down for a soft kiss. "I guess you're as good a bet as I've seen in a long time. Just…just don't hurt me…please."

"I would never intentionally do anything to hurt you." Wil's smile was soft as she drew Lacey into a longer, deeper kiss that left them both breathless. "This seems like déjà vu, but can I walk you to your trailer?" She held out her hand.

Lacey hesitated, then placed her hand in Wil's.

Chapter Eight

They walked in easy silence until they reached Lacey's trailer, then turned to each other without speaking. Lacey looked up, and Wil didn't hesitate to meet her in a long, deep kiss. When they were both breathless, Wil withdrew but pressed her forehead against Lacey's. She wanted to say so much, but Lacey wasn't ready to hear what was in Wil's heart. That kiss, however, said Lacey was ready for more.

"Come inside, Wil. Please." Lacey's whisper was hot in Wil's ear.

"Are you sure?" Wil couldn't resist kissing along Lacey's neck. She'd never been so hungry for someone.

"Positive. But only if you're sure, too," Lacey said, drawing Wil into a kiss that would have weakened her defenses if she was unsure…which she wasn't.

Wil tried to resist one last time. "I promised to date you properly before we jumped each other."

"Shut up. We just had a date." Lacey unlocked the door, and Wil followed her inside. Lacey seemed as hungry as Wil, drawing her into a hot, urgent kiss and working her hands under Wil's shirt.

Wil moaned when Lacey's thumbs raked across her nipples over her sports bra. "Bed now," she growled. Lacey turned and began to climb the built-in ladder to the queen-sized bed that filled the loft over the fifth-wheel hitch. Wil followed close behind, but far enough back that she could admire Lacey's trim hips and tight buttocks. Something low in her belly clenched at the fleeting vision of what those hips must look like sans jeans, and she took a deep breath. God, she hoped she didn't orgasm in the first two minutes like some virgin boy.

Wil was barely on the bed when Lacey grabbed her shirt. "Clothes off," she said, before yanking Wil's shirt open. Good thing Western shirts had snaps instead of buttons.

The next minute was more like a wrestling match until they were naked and both moaned as skin met skin, breasts skimmed over breasts, and tongues began to explore. Wil flipped Lacey onto her back and hovered over her, but Lacey countered, rolling them so that Wil was pinned beneath her. She kissed her way down Wil's neck and shoulders to her breasts, where she flicked her tongue against each nipple in turn.

"Lacey, wait, wait." Wil trembled with the effort to hold back the orgasm threatening to explode in her belly. "Give me a minute." Lacey moved up again, and all Wil could feel was Lacey's mouth, hot and wet, sucking and nipping and shooting bolts of pleasure that made her hips buck. Her words were a whispered pant. "You're going to make me come too soon."

Lacey used her teeth to tug at Wil's earlobe. "Are you saying you're a one-and-done?" Her voice was a few sexy octaves lower than usual. Holy Mother. Lacey was a cloudburst, flooding Wil's senses and sweeping her headlong toward the dam that was holding back her orgasm.

"Just let it go, baby. Take the edge off. Then we can go slower." Lacey slid her hand between Wil's legs, making her gasp as two of Lacey's fingers pushed inside to massage that sweet spot and jerk as her thumb stroked Wil's rock-hard clit. She was lost.

Wil's body bowed upward, and her lungs refused to draw breath as she clenched her teeth to hold back a scream. She clamped her legs together to still Lacey's hand as aftershocks rolled through her. Her arms and legs felt paralyzed by the force of her orgasm, and she could easily close her eyes and drift into an exhausted slumber.

But Wil was no pillow princess either. With a growl, she forced her limbs to move, rolling to hover over Lacey. God, she was beautiful. Her ponytail had come loose from its tie to splay silky blond strands across the pillows, and desire had softened her doe-brown eyes. Wil wanted to devour her. She wanted to savor her. She kissed along her neck, relishing the way Lacey lifted her chin and shivered at the touch of Wil's lips. She nipped at Lacey's earlobe, then captured her mouth again for a deep, lingering kiss before sliding downward to nuzzle and kiss along Lacey's breasts, then her belly. She paused at Lacey's groin to inhale her enticing scent. Lacey spread wide as Wil shouldered between her legs to taste her. She tickled Lacey's hard clit with her tongue, then licked her with a broad stroke when Lacey moaned and tightened her fingers in Wil's hair.

"Don't tease. Please, Wil. Not this time."

Hoping she'd have other opportunities, Wil sucked hard on Lacey's clit and plunged two fingers inside, finding the stroke that made Lacey go still, then quake as her orgasm exploded. She paused when Lacey went limp but kept her fingers inside while she moved up to lick and suck her hardened nipples.

"I don't know if I can…oh."

Wil resumed her strokes, deeper and more forceful. "You are so beautiful. Come for me again so I can see your pleasure in your eyes." She kissed along Lacey's neck and sucked at her pulse as she increased the pace of her firm thrusts.

"Oh, crap. Don't stop."

Wil moved to ride Lacey's thigh with every thrust. God, it felt good as Lacey pressed hard against Wil's wet sex and dug blunt fingernails in her ass to urge her on. Her thrusts grew erratic with the pressure building in her, and she added her thumb to stroke Lacey's clit. She struggled to hold back, then let loose her climax when she felt Lacey stiffen once again in her arms. Pleasure exploded inside her, her cry matching Lacey's. She continued to stroke as her orgasm defused in waves that rolled through her limbs, then fell limply to lie beside Lacey.

"Damn." Occasional aftershocks cooled her sweat-slickened skin and confirmed that she could still feel her arms and legs… and fingers still encased in Lacey's warmth. She pulled out slowly, triggering Lacey to jerk and moan.

"Wow." Lacey shivered and rolled to lay her head on Wil's shoulder and fling a leg across her thighs. "I think you fried my circuits."

Wil chuckled and lazily stroked Lacey's bare back. "I'm sure you burned out a few of mine."

They fell into a comfortable silence, and when Wil felt Lacey's breathing even out, she closed her eyes and let sleep claim her, too.

Chapter Nine

A great time for Brittney Abbott. Fourteen-point-three-oh moves her into first place, with only two competitors remaining in this final run." The announcer's voice boomed over the noise of a sold-out audience. "Next up is Wiloree Rivers, riding Red Pepper."

Lacey tried to block the urge to leave the warm-up area early so she could watch Wil's run. She needed to focus only on her and Denver's performance coming up next. She loped Denver around the edge of the oval-shaped area after closely examining her feet and legs, then added a few sprints and tight turns. Denver felt great under her, responding instantly to her cues and prancing with eagerness the entire way from the warm-up area to the arena.

Wil and Pepper thundered past the timer and skidded to a stop in the exit chute just as Lacey and Denver arrived.

"Woo-hoo!" Ray Rivers waved his hat in the air to celebrate his daughter's successful run. "Bet that put you on top."

As if confirming his declaration, the announcer's voice boomed over the speakers. "That's a blazing fourteen-point-two-five seconds for Wil Rivers and Red Pepper, moving them into first place with only one competitor left to run, but that rider is Lacey Bishop, who's been burning up the barrel-racing circuit on her horse, Denver, since January."

Wil guided Pepper to where Lacey was holding back an eager, prancing Denver. She leaned close and spoke in a low voice.

"You can beat that, Lacey. Do it, and we'll bump Brittney back to third place." Wil backed Pepper away to give Denver more space.

Lacey nodded and shot Wil a small smile as she let Denver twirl in a circle several times to wind her up, then curled forward over the horse's neck and, with a squeeze of her legs, spoke a soft "go."

Denver rocketed into the arena. Their first turn was textbook, and they shaved the second turn so close the barrel vibrated but stayed upright. Denver was focused and flowing smoothly around the barrels at a such a blazing pace, Lacey simply shifted her weight into the turns and let her run. They curled around the last barrel, and then Lacey crouched in her stirrups like a jockey and leaned over Denver's withers with hands extended so they were nearly touching the mare's ears. Fast. So fast, she felt like Denver was on the verge of sprouting wings to fly past the timer.

Lacey blinked as the summer sun glared into her eyes. They had cleared the timer and the arena in what seemed like a split second. She sat back in the saddle and gave little tugs on the reins to slow Denver. When they turned back to the stadium tunnel, Wil trotted Pepper toward them.

"Hot damn, woman. You rode like your horse's tail was on fire." She reined Pepper to walk beside Denver, who was prancing from adrenaline. "You might have broken fourteen seconds, but I'm not sure of the exact time. It's first place for sure."

"Really?" Lacey knew they'd been fast, but breaking through to under fourteen would put her time among those of the top four barrel racers in the country.

They both froze when the announcer began. "The official time for Ms. Bishop is thirteen-point-nine-five—a scorching final run that lands her securely in first place. Wil Rivers comes in second at fourteen-point-two-five, and Brittney Abbott places third in this final competition with fourteen-point-three-oh. Congratulations to all three ladies for giving us a great show this weekend. Next up is saddle broncs, starting after a twenty-minute break."

"YES!" Wil twirled Pepper in several tight spins. "Amazing."

Lacey covered her open mouth with her hand. They had beaten their former best time by nearly a half second. "I can't believe it." She bent down to wrap her arms around Denver's neck and give her a tight hug. "We did it. This gets you two apples tonight, girl." Her head was swimming with the win. It unexpectedly, shockingly changed everything. Lacey had been head-down trudging toward her dream of reaching the National Finals Rodeo. She realized now that she had never believed deep down that she could actually do it. Today proved she could, but that epiphany settled on her shoulders like a heavy weight, and her fears blossomed. She'd been going from rodeo to rodeo in an old truck, pulling a beat-up trailer on a shoestring budget. She'd eaten more bowls of ramen noodles than she could count because buying Denver's feed and supplements came first before groceries.

"Damn. You didn't just do it. You aced it." Wil's eyes, magnetic blue beacons, lured Lacey from her whirlpool of emotions. She seemed to read Lacey's thoughts, her fears. "You and Denver are as good as any barrel-racing team I've ever seen."

But she was basically homeless with no sponsors supplementing her dash to the finals. Her trailer tires were nearly bare of tread. Her truck was beginning to drink oil. Yet those facts seemed less scary while she basked in the confidence radiating from Wil. Yes. She could do this.

"Well, well. Looks like you got lucky today with that little horse of yours." Brittney, still riding Dash, returned to the arena to hear Lacey's official time. "You wouldn't be in first place if I wasn't riding this burned-out nag. He's ready for pasture, so I'll see you next weekend, Wil."

Wil frowned. "Next weekend?"

"Daddy's driving to your ranch to pick out a new cutting horse, and a barrel horse for me." She made a show of running her gaze over Pepper. "I'm interested in the one you're riding. If she had a smaller, lighter rider like me, she'd be walking off with the top prize money today. I also want to see what else you have in your stable. Your horses *are* for sale, aren't they?"

Wil shifted in her saddle, her jaw working. "You know they are. That's what we do…train and sell horses."

"You aren't racing next weekend?" Lacey's mind was jumping ahead to the next rodeo on her calendar. It was a three-day event, smaller than the one she'd just won, but offered decent prize money. Without Brittney there, she had a solid chance at the top prize. She needed money to put those new retreads on her trailer, and her truck too, which would scratch a big item off her worry list.

Brittney shot her a condescending smile. "It's all yours. I don't need the pocket change they're offering for prize money, and it won't add any points toward qualifying for the finals." She started to turn her horse away to leave but stopped. "Have fun wearing your horse out by running her every weekend." She wiggled her fingers in a silly wave. "Ta-ta."

"Bitch," Lacey growled under her breath. "Denver is half-Arab. She's got more stamina that any pampered Quarter horse."

"Whoa. I trained and sold her the one she's riding now," Wil said. "He's not burned out. She rides him wrong."

As they turned their horses toward the warm-up area to cool them down, Lacey mentally reviewed the last time she'd watched Brittney race. She nodded. "You mean the way she muscles her mount through the course?"

"Exactly. She's ruined the mouth on every one I've trained for her, so much that I hate selling her any of them. But I can't afford to handpick my buyers, especially since we're standing right on the line between profit and bankruptcy."

They walked the horses in silence, each contemplating the cruel reality that even when you worked hard every day, a pandemic or catastrophic illness or economic recession could snatch everything away.

Finally, Wil broke the silence. "So, you pulling out tonight?"

"Yeah." Lacey's good mood deflated.

"Where you headed next?"

"I'm planning to hit some smaller rodeos for the prize money on my way to Abilene, then on to Big Spring." Small rodeos shot up all over Texas almost every weekend during the summer months.

"Which ones between here and Abilene?"

"Santa Anna next weekend, then San Angelo."

They hadn't talked about when or if they might see each other again, and Lacey skirted the uncomfortable subject now, changing the subject to ask about other horses at the Double R as they walked their horses to the barn area, washed them down, and wrapped their legs for travel.

Ray grinned at them through the bars of the stalls. "Figured this was where I'd find you ladies."

"You look happy." Wil smiled back at her father.

"Sold two of the three roping horses we brought, plus that bucking one."

"That's fantastic, Dad. That might catch us up on our mortgage payments and pay off the vet's bill."

He comically wiggled his eyebrows. "That's not all. Mac Abbott wants to drive out next weekend to look at the cutting horses I've been training. The others are pocket change compared to what he'll pay for a cutter. And his daughter has her eye on Pepper, but she's coming with him to see what else you have that can run barrels."

So, Brittney wasn't just goading them when she said she'd see Wil next weekend. Lacey was happy to see Wil grimace at the news.

"Are you ready to load the horses to leave?" Wil asked, unnecessarily lifting Pepper's front hoof she'd already cleaned and scraping briskly at the bottom with a hoof pick.

"Nope. I found out they're not breaking down these stalls until tomorrow, so I'm having dinner with an old friend. We can leave around midnight."

Lacey's heart jumped a little. A few more hours with Wil? She'd take it. "That sounds like a great idea." She smiled at Ray. "I think I'll wait a bit to leave, too."

"Why not until morning?" Wil asked.

Ray shook his head. "We'll miss the worst of the traffic between here and Bowie if we take off tonight, and I want to get back to the ranch and work a couple of cutters I think Abbott will want to see."

"Okay."

"Grab a few hours of sleep," he said to Wil, waving over his shoulder as he walked away. "You'll be driving first."

They watched him go, then turned to each other. Wil, eyes smoky and smile seductive, stepped toward Lacey. "Want to take a nap with me?"

Lacey cocked her head and narrowed her eyes as if considering the offer. "Maybe I'm not sleepy."

Wil traced her fingertip along Lacey's neck and down the *V* of her Western shirt. "I bet I can help you with that."

Their flirtation was fun, but Lacey couldn't stop weighing the consequences. Wil's life was waiting for her at the Double R. Lacey lived on the road, driving from rodeo to rodeo to earn enough to keep Denver and her financially afloat. She was already becoming too infatuated with Wil. She pushed her reservations to the back of her mind. She deserved a little fun, and Wil definitely was nearly six feet of delicious entertainment.

"My trailer or yours?"

"Yours. I don't know how long Dad will be at dinner."

"Good point." Lacey tilted her head and raised an eyebrow, hoping it was a sexy, not stupid, look. "You done here?"

Wil's eyes flashed. "Waiting on you."

Lacey took Wil's hand and led her out of the stable area and toward her trailer.

CHAPTER TEN

Wil touched the smooth skin of Lacey's naked back. They'd made love over and over until Lacey finally fell into an exhausted slumber an hour ago. Wil, however, felt energized rather than sleepy. She loved the way Lacey tucked her hand under her chin while she slept, her eyelashes so long they nearly touched her cheeks. She trailed her fingertips along the curve of Lacey's back to where the sheet bunched low on her hips, then pressed her lips to Lacey's shoulder blade. Lacey stirred under her touch.

"What...what time is it?" Lacey blinked sleepily.

"Eleven o'clock." Wil wished she could stop time to spend just a few more hours in their warm cocoon that smelled of their lovemaking and Lacey's warm skin. But reality beckoned. "Dad will be looking for me to help load our horses." She tugged Lacey into her arms, reveling in their skin-on-skin connection. "I don't want to leave—"

"But you have to," Lacey said. "I'm going to sleep a bit longer and take off just before sunrise. I don't have as far to drive and can't check into the campground outside Santa Anna where I have a reservation until morning."

Wil groaned. Knowing Lacey would stay snuggled in their nest made it even harder for her to leave. "I wish Dad and I had driven here separately." She pressed her naked body tighter against Lacey's. "I'd stay until you had to go."

They both jumped at the loud banging on the door of Lacey's trailer. "Wil Rivers. You in there?" Ray shouted. "Let go of that girl and come help your old man load the horses. We need to get on the road."

Wil groaned again, her cheeks heating with embarrassment. "Coming," she yelled back. She covered her eyes. "Lord. I hope nobody heard him."

Lacey laughed. "That's what you get for lying abed and not taking care of business."

Wil tickled Lacey's sides, making her laugh harder and squirm away. She stopped and yanked her close again to kiss her long and deep. Lacey's eyes were dreamy, her breaths coming in short exhalations when Wil pulled back. "That's so you don't forget me before I can see you again."

Lacey's expression turned serious. "I'm booked at some rodeo almost every weekend until the finals in December."

"Abilene is in three weeks, right? Our ranch is outside Bowie, only a couple of hours from Abilene. I could drive down." Suddenly uncertain, she swung her legs over the side of the bed and reached for her clothes piled on the floor. "I mean, unless I'd be in the way."

Lacey grabbed her hand and entwined their fingers. "I do want to see you. I'm just not sure how, since you need to be at the ranch to train horses, and I'm on the road most of the year." She stared down at their joined hands. "Maybe we should keep it light…friends with benefits whenever we cross paths like this weekend."

Wil was taken aback for a few seconds but realized Lacey's fingers tightening, clinging to hers belied her offer to limit their budding relationship to no-strings sex. She shook her head, then slid off the bed and turned to Lacey so their eyes met. "I want more than a sex arrangement, sweetheart." She touched Lacey's cheek in a brief caress. "I think we might have something special growing between us, and I want to explore it. If you don't feel the same way, please be honest with me now."

Lacey looked away, chewing her lip for a few seconds. "I'm not used to thinking about anyone but myself and Denver."

"The ranch consumes a lot of my attention."

"I can be a grumpy hard-ass."

"I turn into the devil incarnate after spending all day working on the monthly paperwork to keep the ranch solvent, not to mention the demon I become when I have to calculate and pay quarterly taxes."

Lacey looked up, a tentative glimmer of hope lighting her eyes and a hesitant smile surfacing as she studied Wil. She shrugged. "Okay."

"Okay?"

Lacey's smile grew. "No promises. You'll probably realize the error of your decision soon enough, but we can see how it goes."

The hard knot in Wil's belly loosened and faded away. She cupped Lacey's face and brushed her lips against Lacey's. "Can I call you tomorrow?"

"Yeah. But you better go now, or your father will be banging on my trailer again."

Wil knew that was true but was reluctant to leave and kissed her one more time, deeply and thoroughly. "Get some more sleep before you hit the road, too." She brushed her lips across Lacey's once more, then stood. "Sweet dreams."

Lacey fanned her face with her hand. "My dreams are going to be anything but sweet after that kiss."

Wil laughed. "At least you can dream in the privacy of your trailer. Be glad you don't have to spend the rest of the night trying to think of something, anything else because you're cooped up in a truck with Dad for the next five or six hours."

Lacey's laughter followed Wil as she left the trailer.

Lacey punched her pillow into submission and squinched her eyes closed, trying to quiet her mind…and body. She had about four hours before she needed to shower, load Denver, and get out of town to beat the morning commuter traffic, but Wil had left her wet and wanting. Geez. She'd already orgasmed twice in the short time they'd had, but she felt primed and ready again. How could that be?

The sudden memory of Wil's dark head between her legs and the feel of Wil's tongue flat and warm against her sensitive clit made her belly clench and legs tighten.

"Damn you, Wil. I'm never going to get to sleep," she muttered to the walls.

She threw back the sheet as heat suffused her naked body until she was covered with a fine sheen of sweat. She slid her hand down her belly until her fingers touched the wiry curls covering her sex. Could she…one more time? She closed her eyes and reached lower to finger her turgid clit. She was amazingly close just thinking about Wil—eyes impossibly blue in the sunlight and dark, silky hair gleaming in the wind. Wil naked and hovering over her. One stroke, two, and she nearly doubled over as exquisite pleasure exploded in her like a frothy wave crashing, then lapping against rocks as it dissipated. She panted, and her heart pounded in the aftermath. Then as heart and breath slowed, she closed her eyes and drifted into a sound, dreamless sleep.

❖

They'd wound their way out of the city to Interstate 35 before Ray broke the silence without lifting the brim of his hat that he'd tipped forward to cover his eyes for a nap. "So, you've taken a liking to that little blond filly."

Wil smiled and shook her head in resignation. "I wondered how long it'd take you to bring that up."

"That's not an answer." He sat up from his slumped position and pushed his hat back.

"Yeah. I like her." Wil could feel him studying her, waiting for her to elaborate. Still, she kept her eyes on the road.

"This one's different, though." His remark held no question.

Wil sighed. He could be like a dog worrying a fresh soup bone when he latched onto a subject.

"She's honest and says exactly what she's thinking, unlike Brittney's little crowd of back-stabbing, rumor-mongering friends."

"And she's really cute," Ray said, grinning.

Wil was instantly in the trailer again, watching Lacey throw her head back in orgasm and a flush spread from her breasts to her cheeks as she thrust into her. She licked her lips and hoped the faint light in the truck's cab would hide the wave of heat traveling from her own chest to her ears. "She's beautiful." Her words were a reverent whisper.

Ray nodded, his teasing expression turning wistful. "The first time I saw your mother, I was infatuated. After I finally worked up the nerve to talk to her, I was enchanted."

Wil could have laughed at the rough old cowboy using such a

romantic word, but it was true. She knew how much he missed his wife of forty years and had feared his desire to join her in an afterlife was stronger than his will to live when he was hospitalized with the coronavirus. But he'd pulled through, and she'd held his hand as she wept in relief. He'd squeezed hers and mumbled, "I'm not going anywhere just yet. Your mama said you still need someone to look after you."

"Lacey's had a hard life. She's had to make her way all on her own. I don't think she trusts anybody but her horse." Wil had loved her mother but always felt a closer kinship to her father because of their mutual love and understanding of horses. He was the parent in whom she'd confided her deepest secrets. His patient presence allowed her to finally put words to her fear. "She might break my heart, Dad."

He didn't respond for a long moment, then nodded. "Maybe. Maybe not. But I didn't raise you to be a coward, Wiloree Rivers. If you feel this Lacey might be the woman for you, like your mama was meant for me, then you go after her. Don't give up until you convince her the grass is sweeter on your side of the fence."

She laughed, relieved by his support. "I plan to do my best."

CHAPTER ELEVEN

Lacey pulled into the campground where she and Denver would stay until the three-day rodeo was held the following weekend. She'd decided to wait until Friday morning to move to the noisy fairgrounds where the event was to be held. These smaller towns had few of the large rodeos' perks, but the entry fees were sometimes as low as thirty dollars and the prize money easy pickings. She would likely be the only ranked professional rider entered since it wasn't sanctioned by the Professional Rodeo Cowboys Association to award points, and the five-hundred-dollar first prize for barrel racing would buy gas, groceries, and horse feed for a couple of weeks.

The shady campground was well-kept, the lots spacious. She'd begun staying there each year after Joel and Maggie told her to check it out and called the owners to vouch that Denver would be no trouble around the other campers. A network of small private campgrounds dotted the state, but most still depended on local vacationers or word-of-mouth to attract travelers, even if they'd established a website for booking the lots. This campground included hiking trails and two pools fed from natural springs—one for families and the other for adults only. Lacey preferred the family pool because she liked to watch the kids play, and most of the adults were married. The adult pool tended to attract single people, and she hated being hit on by prowling dudes.

She was exhausted after only four hours of sleep and setting up camp and Denver's temporary corral, but she smiled and welcomed the group of five children, who had seen her walking Denver to get the kinks out of her legs after traveling.

"Hi. Y'all come on in. Did you want to see my horse?"

"Are you a cowgirl?" The boy appeared to be one of the oldest, probably around nine.

"I'm a professional rodeo rider." Lacey tried to steer him away from boy-girl labels.

"You ride bulls?" a younger boy, eyes wide, asked. "I seen that on television one time."

"You saw that on television." An older girl corrected him. She apparently was the chaperone of the group. Lacey guessed her to be about twelve.

"Travis says 'seen.'" The kid looked at the boy who had spoken first.

"Girls can't ride bulls," the first boy said, scowling and ignoring the younger boy.

Lacey smiled at the girl, causing her to blush, but spoke to the boy. "Yes. Women can and do ride bulls, but I don't. I race horses around barrels."

"Wow," the younger boy said.

"Can we pet your horse, miss?" one of the twin girls, about six years old, asked.

"My name is Lacey, and my horse is called Denver." She smiled at them. "She loves to be petted."

"I'm Samantha, but everybody calls me Sam. That's Travis," she said, pointing to the older boy. "That's Bodie, and the twins are April and Mae." She pointed to each child as she named them.

"It's nice to meet you guys." Lacey held up a large red apple. "I was about to give her this treat. Do you want to feed her?"

The three youngest children jumped up and down, clapping their hands. "Yes! Yes!"

Lacey sliced the apple into six pieces with her pocketknife, feeding one slice to Denver to demonstrate how they should place their apple slice on their palm, fingers held straight so the horse wouldn't mistake them for part of the apple.

The twins stepped up first and giggled when the mare's lips brushed their hands.

"His lips tickle," one twin said.

"Denver is a she, and all horses—boys and girls—have whiskers."

"My dad has whiskers, but he shaves them off every day," Bodie said.

"Well, I trim Denver's whiskers, too, but not every day. They tickle because it's time to give her another trim."

The kids spent another twenty minutes petting Denver, until Lacey told them it was time for Denver's nap.

"Could we come back tomorrow?" Sam asked.

"I'll be here until Saturday morning, and I'm sure Denver would love for you to visit." She held up a finger in warning. "But only if I'm here and Sam or an adult comes with you." She considered setting visiting hours so the kids wouldn't end up hanging around all day, then decided to hold off in case it wasn't necessary. They would probably be spending most of their time at the pool.

They smiled and nodded. "We promise," the twins chorused.

Lacey waved to send them on their way. "See you tomorrow, then."

She sighed as she watched them run away. Her childhood had been such crap, she loved to see happy, inquisitive children, still unscarred by life. She opened the door to the camper portion of the trailer. "Nap time, Denver."

Flash danced through the barrel pattern once again, constantly mouthing his bit to get it into his teeth so he could take off running as though he was back on the racetrack. Wil wheeled him in a tight circle, trying to distract him from his compulsion to grab the bit and sprint to the other end of the large oval ring.

Ray watched from the sideline, his foot propped on the second rung of the metal bars fencing the practice ring. "Did you lunge that horse before you got on him?"

Wil brought Flash to a standstill and glared at her father. "Have I ever trained a horse without lunging him first?"

Ray shrugged off the question and moved the toothpick he was chewing to the other side of his mouth. "I think you should give up and cut your losses on that one. Those racehorses only retrain if you get them when they weed out the two-year-olds before they get a good taste of the track. That boy raced for three years. His legs are likely used up because they start them too young, and his brain is too firmly wired to all-out run."

"His legs are fine, and his bloodline has produced some outstanding barrel horses. He's learning. It's just taking a bit longer." Wil took him past the electronic timer, wheeled him around, and headed for the first barrel. His turn was wide because he didn't slow when Wil sat back in saddle, but he did whip around the barrel and sprinted toward the second. He took the second barrel wide again, but at a pace so fast that he nearly unseated Wil. Then he sprinted right past the third barrel, even though Wil pulled his head around so far, his nose was nearly touching his shoulder. Only the fence at the other end of the ring slowed him enough for Wil to regain control and trot him back to the barrels.

Ray took the toothpick from his mouth and put it in his pocket. A toothpick stuck in the soft frog of a hoof could lame a horse. "Like I said. You need to sell that horse and invest in a better prospect."

Wil, grumpy from too little sleep after driving most of the night, didn't reply as she turned him toward the barn.

❖

Lacey stared into her campfire, but she wasn't seeing flames. Her mind conjured Wil smiling up at her after Lacey's fantastic thirteen-point-nine-five run, Wil's great ass as she walked away, and Wil leaning toward her as sunset turned the sky into hues of pink and orange. She closed her eyes and could almost feel Wil's breath on her face and the soft brush of her lips. The thoughts made her vibrate with pleasure. Wait. She really was vibrating. Lacey pulled her phone from her back pocket and smiled at the caller ID as she accepted the call. "Hey, you."

"Hey, yourself." Wil's sonorous voice warmed Lacey's heart and other parts. "Everything go well with your drive?"

"No problems. Well, if I don't count nearly oversleeping because somebody wore me out."

"Same here. I could barely keep my eyes open while Dad napped for a few hours."

"Tell me he didn't realize why you were still so sleepy."

Wil laughed. "Of course he did. He knows I'm a grown woman. But he didn't razz me too bad about it."

Lacey covered her face even though no one was there to see it heat with embarrassment. "I'm never going to be able to face him again."

"He'll forget all about it before you ever see him...unless you switch from barrel racing to cutting and start entering those futurities. He's got several cutting horses ready for sale and wants to show them off at a few competitions." Wil was quiet for a few long seconds.

"Hey, is everything okay?"

Wil's sigh was heavy over the phone. "Yeah. It's just...his memory isn't all that good since he was sick."

"Oh, no. Was it bad?"

"Yeah. He refused at first when they wanted to put him on a ventilator, but he finally got so bad I had to make the decision. I was sure I was going to lose him. I don't know what I'd have done if I had."

"God. I'm so sorry." Lacey thought about the jovial, handsome man she'd met at last weekend's rodeo. "He seems fine now."

"He is...mostly. He gets that brain fog they talk about that lingers, and he tires easily."

"He seemed strong and healthy at the rodeo, but I understand you still worrying about him." Lacey wished she could reach out and wrap her arms around Wil. She was beginning to realize that inside the competent, confident woman most people saw, Wil was still a motherless girl who'd had to grow up fast.

"Is he going by himself?"

"No. I'm sending our foreman, Jimmy, with him. It'll mean more work for me here at the ranch, but I'll feel better with Jimmy watching over him."

"Good. That's good."

"How was your day?" Wil asked. "Do you like the campground there?"

Lacey decided to go along with the change in subject and talked happily about the campground's facilities, then recounted the visit from the children. "I'd be surprised if they don't show up tomorrow with a handful of carrots."

Wil chuckled. "They sound cute. Have you ever thought about having offspring of your own?"

"I can barely support myself and Denver, and children need to have a home, especially when they reach school age. In case you didn't notice, I live the nomad life of a rodeo vagabond."

"What if things were different? I mean, if you were settled in one place, would you want some?"

Lacey thought about the ones she'd met earlier. "I like them, but I didn't exactly have a good role model. I'd probably be a terrible mom."

"You're a good horse mom."

Lacey snorted. "Kids aren't horses, Wil. You can't put them in the corral or close them in a stall when you've got something else you want to do."

"I know that."

"Do you want some? Did you ask that because your biological clock is ticking?" She wasn't accusing, just curious.

"I like them, and Dad would love a couple of grandkids. But I can't picture myself pregnant and giving birth. Nuh-uh. Not going there."

"You could adopt," Lacey said. "A ranch is a great place for a kid to grow up."

"You could cut down on the small rodeos and settle down somewhere. You're winning enough now at the big rodeos to do that."

Lacey had considered that possibility. She had even dreamed about buying a small place—twenty acres or so—and giving riding lessons, training horses, or figuring out some other way to make extra money. "My nest egg would have to be a lot bigger than it is now," she said.

"Yeah. Mine, too," Wil said. After a long pause while they both seemed to be thinking over their feelings on the matter, she spoke again. "What were you doing when I called?"

Ah. Lacey smiled as she formed her answer. "I was mostly staring into the flames of my campfire after reading the same two lines in my book over and over."

"Really? What do you see in those flames?" Wil's voice was low and sexy.

Lacey spoke slowly as she laid out the scene in her mind's eye. "You naked, under me. Your hair is like black silk fanned across the pillow, and your head is thrown back, mouth open as you orgasm."

Wil's groan was loud over the phone. "Are you trying to kill me, woman? I'm on the porch and need to go to my bedroom if we're going to have phone sex."

Lacey wished they were on a video call so she could see her face. Even better, she wished Wil was in her bed rather than in her thoughts. "Sorry. No phone sex. I'm sitting outdoors where anyone could walk up, and I'd have to make sure the fire was out good before I could go inside. I'm afraid the mood would be lost."

"Dream about me when you do go to bed?" Wil nearly purred the words. "I know I'm going to dream about you."

"I don't think I can avoid it," Lacey said, smiling. Damn. She'd been smiling way too much lately. Her cheeks were going to be sore because her face wasn't used to it. She sucked in a deep breath and exhaled to calm her raging hormones. "It's late, and while I might be able to sleep in tomorrow, I know life on a ranch starts early."

"Yeah. The farrier will be here at seven in the morning, and I have to feed and get the horses lined up before he arrives."

"Wil?"

"Yeah?"

"I'm glad you called."

"Me, too. I wasn't sure…I was afraid I might be bothering you," Wil said. "I've been grouchy all day. I thought it was because of getting very little sleep, but now I think it was because I'd rather be hanging out with you."

"I like hanging out with you, too." Geez. They sounded like a couple of teenagers who didn't want to be the first to hang up. "Hey, maybe we can video-call next time." Damn it. Could she sound more infatuated? "I'd like, you know, to hear about the horses you're training."

"Okay." Another pause. "Uh, is tomorrow night too soon? Because, you know, I like hearing about your day."

"Really? I don't do much that's interesting. I read a lot when I'm between rodeos."

"We can talk about what you're reading. I read a lot, too. Honestly, I'm the only woman on the ranch, and while Dad and the guys are great, sometimes I feel kind of isolated."

Lacey knew that kind of loneliness—feeling alone even when you're in a crowd of people. She wished she could teleport herself to the ranch and give Wil a tight hug. She softened her voice. "Then tomorrow night will be perfect."

CHAPTER TWELVE

Wil sat back in the saddle and concentrated on anticipating the quick moves of her dad's best cutter, Lena Smarty Pants, as the horse denied the black calf's attempts to rejoin the small herd of other calves at the opposite end of the ring. This mare was so talented, all she had to do was stay centered in the saddle as Ray and Mac Abbott watched from outside the ring.

"She definitely got a good piece of her Lena bloodlines," Ray said to Mac. "I don't think I've ever trained a horse with so much instinct. See how she latches on, staring that calf down? She's moving to cut him off even before his legs get the which-way-to-turn message from his brain."

Mac nodded, stepped back from the fence, and waved Wil over. Mac had business in the area so hadn't waited until the weekend to check out Ray's cutters. They'd already watched Blue Cat work a couple of calves, but he seemed satisfied after watching Smarty work just one. Wil disengaged and let the calf slip past them before riding over to the two men. Mac ducked between the bars of the metal fencing and walked around them when Wil brought the mare to a stop. He eyed Smarty's relaxed demeanor and her body structure.

"How much you asking?"

"This is definitely my high-dollar horse. She's the best I've ever trained. I'm looking to get $500,000."

Mac whistled and shook his head. "That's pretty steep, Ray. I'd have to spend the money I set aside for when Brittney gets married. I know she and her mother are going to want to put on a big extravaganza." Mac made a show of shifting the wad of tobacco in his right cheek to the other side of his mouth, then spitting. "I'll give you $400,000."

Ray shook his head. "She'll earn that much during her career, then give you foals that can sell for just as much as her price because of the strength of the Lena bloodline."

Wil listened but didn't speak. She loved watching her dad work through this ritual. They both knew Mac's oil wells were pumping out that much profit every week. And Mac was aware they knew this, but the men loved the ritual of posturing and dickering over price.

"If she got injured the first time she competes, I'd be out a half million dollars. Her foals wouldn't bring in near her price if she can't compete to show off her worth. How much for Blue Cat?"

"Smarty's health and legs are solid. I have a recent vet statement confirming that fact, but you're welcome to pay for your own vet to check her out. I'm looking to get $250,000 for Blue Cat. He can also compete as a reining horse, but he's gelded. He won't make you any money after you retire him. That's why his price is so much lower."

Mac spit again, then kicked some dirt over it before bending to run his hands up and down Smarty's legs. He sighed when he straightened and looked at Ray. "I reckon Brittney's gonna have to elope. I'll send my foreman over with a certified check for the mare as soon as you shoot me a copy of her X-rays and health report for my vet to approve." He held out his hand, and Ray shook to seal the deal.

"I'll call my vet today," Ray said.

Yes! Wil wanted to jump up and down. Mac's check would put the ranch back in the black, but Ray also would want to invest some of it in new stock. They had five or six promising yearlings, but their bones needed several more years to fully develop before those young horses could begin serious training. They needed some horses old enough now to turn around in a year to sell, and Ray was good at finding ones that weren't reaching their potential at the cutting futurities and fine-tuning them so they began to place in the money. She also suspected her father had his eye on buying an older mare from the Lena bloodline for breeding. To keep their stock current and rehire Don to help Ray train, they'd need to find buyers for the other horses.

Wil waved over their grizzled foreman, who'd been propped against the fencing on the other side of the ring. "I'll get Jimmy to make sure she gets an extra rubdown tonight." She led Smarty to the middle of the ring and handed the mare off to him. "I don't care if you have to sleep with her. Treat this mare like she's the love of your life until Mac Abbott's foreman comes to get her in a few days. Dad just sold Smarty for a crap-load of money."

Jimmy's shaggy, handlebar mustache twitched with what she suspected was a grin if she could see his mouth. "Hot damn. You going to get Don back? Ray's not up to snuff yet, and I worry he's pushing himself too hard."

Wil saw the concern in the old man's faded brown eyes. Jimmy had been a fixture on the ranch most of her life after he broke his back bull riding and Ray gave him a job and a bunkhouse to live in. "If his wife is well enough, I'll have Don back here before the week's gone."

Jimmy nodded but shifted his gaze to over Wil's shoulder. "Well now, here comes trouble."

Wil turned to see Brittney park her BMW next to the ring and get out to saunter over to Ray and Mac. She shook her head. "She's pushing her dad to buy her another barrel horse because Lacey Bishop and I beat her pretty good last weekend."

"Didn't you sell Dash to her a few years ago? She can't do much better than him."

"Yeah, and there's nothing wrong with her horse. She's not riding him right, but you can't tell her that. I better get over there."

"I'll tag along in case she tries to jump you."

Jimmy was aware of the brief fling between Brittney and Wil, and he reveled in teasing her about it.

Brittney gave Wil a sultry smile when they approached. "Wil, tell Daddy how much you want for the horse you beat Dash with last weekend."

Mac was shaking his head. "If you want another barrel horse, you need to quit toying with those penniless cowboys and marry Bart Roberts. Then you can spend his money instead of mine."

She laughed and playfully slapped her father's arm. "Oh, Daddy. I know you don't mean that, but Ray and Wil are going to think you're serious." She slipped her arm around Wil's waist and raised up on her toes to plant a kiss on Wil's cheek. "Maybe I'll marry Wil." She gave her father a challenging stare. "It's legal now, you know."

Wil laughed nervously and edged back from Brittney. She had to tread a thin line between insulting and encouraging her in front of Mac. "No money here. All the sales we make go right back into keeping the ranch solvent and taxes paid."

"You ain't marrying no woman because it'd kill your mother." Mac looked at Wil and Ray. "No offense intended."

Wil didn't hesitate. "None taken."

"And I'm not going to buy you another horse." Mac's red face and lapse into bunkhouse grammar told Wil that Brittney had pushed him too far.

"Actually, Dash would have beaten Pepper's time if you'd tweak how you ride him a bit," Wil said. She needed to steer the conversation back to congenial levels.

Brittney's expression flashed from sultry to indignant. "I've been riding horses since I was six years old. I don't need lessons."

Mac crossed his arms over his chest, his smile smug. "That's a great idea. Wil trained Dash, so she can coach you to ride him for optimum performance. How much would you charge to do that, Wil?"

Wil sputtered. The last thing she wanted was to spend more time with Brittney. "I…I'm pretty busy, with Don taking off to care for his wife."

"How about two thousand for ten lessons, and a five-thousand-dollar bonus if she places in the money at the National Finals Rodeo in Vegas?"

Wil was stunned by Mac's offer and looked to Ray for help.

"Five thousand for ten lessons, plus the bonus, and a guarantee that Wil will not marry your daughter under any circumstances," Ray said.

"Dad!" Wil was incredulous—over the offer and her father injecting himself into her business.

"Done," Mac said. "But I want that guarantee in writing. It'd be just like Brittney to talk Wil into something just to piss off her mother."

"We can do that," Ray said, holding out his hand to shake on their second deal of the day.

❖

The kids came back the next day with carrots, as expected, but on their third day Sam's mother was with them. She was an attractive brunette with long, curly hair held back by a large barrette at her nape and a light brown complexion hinting of either Latino or mixed-race heritage. She also had the solid build of an athlete and a confident posture that pinged Lacey's gaydar loudly.

"Hi. I'm Sam's mom, Andie…that's with an *ie*." She held out her hand, and Lacey shook it in greeting.

"Lacey…with an *ey*," she said.

Andie smiled at Lacey's mimic. "Don't I know it. If I've heard your name once, I've heard it a million times from Sam."

"Mom." Sam's face reddened, and she elbowed her mother.

Lacey laughed. "It's okay. You've probably heard my horse's name, Denver, a few times, too."

"Almost as much as yours." She smiled at Lacey.

"Mom, come meet Denver." Sam grabbed her mother's hand and dragged her toward Denver's temporary corral.

Andie looked back over her shoulder. "I guess I'm going to meet the real celebrity now."

Lacey laughed and followed them to Denver's side.

Sam held up a carrot for Denver, while she schooled her mother on how to feed the mare. "You can let her bite off the long end, but then you have to put the short end on top of your hand like this," she explained, demonstrating what Lacey had taught the kids. "That's so she doesn't mistake your finger for a carrot."

"That's really smart," Andie said. She looked at Lacey. "It's so nice of you to put up with them coming by every day. I can find something else for them to do, if they're bugging you too much."

"No. It's fine. How are kids going to have new experiences and learn new things if adults don't take time to teach them?"

"Are you a teacher?" Andie asked.

"Mom. Lacey's a rodeo rider. I told you that."

"No. I'm not a teacher, but a lot of riders have full-time jobs like teaching and just rodeo on the weekends. I'm fortunate enough that Denver is a really good horse, so we win enough prize money to pay for our expenses most years."

"Wow. You must be real good," Andie said, her eyes widening. "I'm sorry for not recognizing your name, but I don't follow the rodeo. I have seen it on television from time to time, though."

"No worries. Until this year, I usually supplemented my income by working at ranches hiring temporary help to harvest hay or brand herds. I've pretty much done everything possible on a ranch, and my overhead is low."

"You must be in great shape."

"I don't have to exercise, because you do a lot of heavy lifting when you travel from rodeo to rodeo."

"Well, if you ever give it up, you'd make a great teacher. You're good with the kids."

"Thanks." Lacey scanned Andie's toned body, but not in a sexual way. "You look in pretty good shape yourself, not like someone who spends all day in a classroom."

"Thank you," Andie said, her tanned cheeks glowing pink. "I do teach a few classes at a small college, but mostly I coach the women's softball team. I played for the Texas Longhorns in college and got my degree in sports management."

Lacey quickly changed the subject to avoid the inevitable question of where she went to college. She'd qualified for a need-based scholarship at Baylor, but her great-aunt's death had opened the door for her to pursue what she really wanted—to follow the rodeo circuit. Her grades had been good—not spectacular—in high school, but she saw school as an inconvenience when she needed to work to keep food in the house and the rent paid while her mother drank her life away.

"Hey. Why don't you kids take turns brushing Denver like I showed you yesterday?" She held out the brushes she was using when the group walked up.

The kids instantly began squabbling over who got the brushes first, but Sam stepped in as the group's leader. "We'll take turns until everybody gets a chance to brush her." The boys grumbled but didn't challenge her, and the twins beamed at being assured they would have the same chance as the older kids.

Lacey turned to Andie. "We can sit down over there," she said, indicating two canvas chairs placed near the campfire. She wasn't expecting visitors, but she always set out two chairs to give the impression she wasn't alone in case some nefarious person wandered into her camp.

"So, is Sam's father with you guys?" She'd always found the easiest way to avoid answering a lot of questions was to keep the other person busy answering hers. And she was curious whether her gaydar was right about this woman with a child.

Andie tilted her head as if considering how to answer. "Sam's father was a sperm donor, and her other mother took an offer a few years back to coach softball at Arizona State University and start a new family with their basketball coach."

"Damn. That's harsh."

Apparently emboldened by Lacey's lack of reaction to "other mother," Andie raised an eyebrow. "Is a significant other waiting for you at home?"

Lacey pointed to her camper's door. "This is my home, and no one's napping inside. I'm a modern-day nomad. It's not exactly conducive to setting up housekeeping with someone."

"Look at you with that sexy cowgirl thing going on. I can't believe nobody has tried to corral you. No girlfriend or boyfriend at all?"

Lacey began shaking her head, but her face heated as visions of Wil invaded and filled her thoughts.

"Well, damn. There is someone," Andie said. "I was hoping I might have a shot at a little recreational romp this week." She held up her hands, palm out, to forestall any adverse reaction from Lacey. "Not that I'm assuming you're an easy hookup, but it's been a while." She sighed. "It's hard to meet people when you have a kid that has to be in bed by nine on school nights."

"No offense taken," Lacey said. "I did meet a woman I really like at the last rodeo, and we've been video-calling this week."

"So, you think you'll be seeing her again?"

"Maybe. She says she'll be at the Abilene rodeo in three weeks."

"She's a rodeo rider, too?"

"She and her dad train and sell horses at their ranch, the Double R, in Bowie, but she competes sometimes to show off a horse and drive up her asking price."

Andie instantly began tapping away at her phone. She raised both eyebrows when she found the Double R's website and tapped on the "trainers" page. "Wow. Is this her?" She passed the phone to Lacey, and Wil's blue eyes looked up at her.

"Yeah. That's her."

"She's super-hot," Andie said, taking the phone Lacey handed back to her. She looked again at Wil's image. "Wiloree Rivers."

"She goes by Wil." Lacey looked away, pretending to be watching the kids. "We hit it off, but I don't expect anything to come of it. She's pretty much out of my league."

Andie cocked her head. "Why would you say that?"

Lacey shrugged. "She's nothing like me. I'm pretty much homeless, going from rodeo to rodeo and living off prize money. She owns that ranch with her dad and went to college and grew up with a mother who had dinner on the table every night."

"Those things might not matter as much as you think."

Lacey didn't answer, but that seemed to be okay with Andie. They sat in comfortable silence for a few minutes.

"Hey. I've got some lasagna I was going to toss in the oven for dinner. I know you probably don't want to leave your horse unattended, but you can walk her over to our campsite and tie her there, or we could bring dinner here to your campsite."

Lacey hesitated.

"Just a friendly meal. I love my daughter, but I wouldn't mind having another adult to talk with for a change. You can leave when your friend calls, and we won't be offended."

Lacey's mouth was already watering at the mention of lasagna. She thought of the long, lonely weekend ahead at a rodeo full of locals where she was unlikely to know anyone. She frowned. She'd never felt lonely before, but the offer to have a meal with another human being was sounding good. "Okay. But only if I can provide a salad to go with it."

"Sounds good to me. Any time after six is good. I'll wait until you show up before I put the garlic bread in to warm."

❖

Wil flicked the loose end of the lunge lead to push Flash into a trot, ignoring that her dad had walked up and was leaning against the railing of the round pen. He waited patiently while she stopped the horse, stepped sideways to turn him in the other direction, and flicked the rope to set him into motion again.

Finally, he spoke. "I thought you'd already worked him today."

"I did, and I'm working him a second time. He needs to know he's not going to stand in a stall twenty-two hours a day to hype him up to run flat-out every time a saddle goes on his back. You know that's what they do on the racetrack. I want him to relax so he can concentrate on making the turns around the barrels and not be afraid he'll get out of that box only once a day."

"Your horse, your call."

Flash was small for a racing Quarter horse but had the big butt of a powerful sprinter. She'd bought him with her own money when her dad disagreed with his purchase, and she was determined to prove Ray wrong when he said Flash was fast, but his butt was too big for him to make the turns without tipping the barrels.

"Yep. He is."

Flash shone with sweat and obediently turned to Wil and approached her when she slowed him to a stop. She led him to the rail where a saddle and bridle were laid out, and Ray waited.

"You need something?" Wil didn't look at Ray but proceeded to saddle Flash for another run at the barrels. She could feel her father's eyes on her.

"You mad at me for something?"

"Why would you think that?"

"Because you've been at my heels since you were a toddler, and although I don't profess to have any insight into a woman's moods, I can tell when you've got your britches in a snit."

Wil checked the tightened girth to make sure it wasn't pinching Flash's skin anywhere, then turned to face her father. "Since when do you hire me out like a leased horse without my consent?"

"Since our richest client agreed to pay us a half million dollars for one horse. I don't think it's unreasonable to coach his daughter through a few lessons, especially for the price he's offering."

"It's a quarter of the price he'd pay if we'd given Brittney time to browbeat him into buying Pepper. And that's exactly what she'd do."

"She's already probably ruined Dash. You want to sell Pepper to her?"

Feeling like the scolded twelve-year-old she once was, she paused before bridling Flash, leaned against the railing, and looked down to dig her boot toe into the dirt. "No. I'm thinking to run Pepper at Big Spring to interest some new buyers."

"What if Mac makes an offer for Pepper before then?"

Wil shrugged. "Then I'd have to sell her to Brittney." She finally looked up and gave Ray a slow grin. "I could sell her Flash."

"We want her father to keep buying our horses at extravagant prices, so I don't think we want to kill his daughter by selling her an untrained racehorse."

"Ten lessons, Dad. I've been trying to distance myself from my bad decision to date her, and you chain me to her for ten fricking lessons. She doesn't want coaching from me. She wants to get into my pants again."

"Well, then you'll need to lock your bedroom door at night."

"Wh-what?" Wil stared at him. "Are you whoring me out now?"

"Watch your mouth, young lady. I'm still your father, and I'd do no such thing. She asked if she could stay in our guest room while she's training here. What was I going to say? Mac was standing right there. And it makes sense. They live more than an hour away."

Wil didn't like it. Not one bit. But her father was right. She pointed at him. "I'm going to ride this horse, and while I do, you're going to put an extra lock on my bedroom door."

"Okay." Her father laughed. "I'll put an extra one on the bathroom door, too, in case she gets a mind to share your shower."

Wil pointed a threatening finger at him, then strode toward the big ring with Flash in tow.

Her father's last teasing words followed her. "I can't believe you're so afraid of that debutante bombshell," he shouted.

CHAPTER THIRTEEN

Lacey had decided to wait until tomorrow to call Wil because it was late when she returned to her campsite after a pleasant evening of dinner and chatting with Andie and her daughter Sam, then bedding Denver down for the night. When did she become so social? But when she checked her phone, she had a missed call and a text from Wil.

Call me when you get this, no matter how late.

Had something happened? There was always a risk in working with powerful animals like horses, even for experienced equestrians. Not to mention the inherent danger of working around farm machinery—tractors, mowers, baling machinery, and the like.

The tensed muscles in her shoulders relaxed when Wil, apparently already in bed, answered her video call. "Damn. I'm sorry. Did I wake you up? Your text said to call no matter how late." It was only eleven, but that was at least an hour past bedtime for ranchers, who rose before dawn to start their day.

"No. I've been in bed for a while, but just tossing and turning." Wil was adorably dressed in an old college T-shirt worn so thin, Lacey could clearly see her hardened nipples.

She smiled. "Thinking about me, or is your air conditioner turned too low?"

"A little of both." Wil laughed, and the lines of stress visible on her face softened. "But that's not what's keeping me from sleeping." Wil looked away from her phone's camera, her expression turning shy. "When I think about you as I'm falling asleep, you visit me in my dreams. I, uh, well…I had a sex dream about you last night and woke up in the middle of an orgasm."

"Oh my God." Lacey's face heated, and she hid behind her hands for a second. Could Wil see her turning red? "Me, too. Could we have possibly visited each other's dream? Forget I asked. It's impossible, and stupid to think it could happen. Nothing but coincidence."

Wil laughed. "True, but it's kind of cool to think we might have come together in our dreamscapes."

"Dreamscapes." Lacey grinned. "You're a Xena fan."

Wil chuckled. "And you must be, too, if you knew where the reference came from. I'm guessing you've seen all the episodes?"

"I was just a baby when the series was on television, but I have the entire thing on DVD. I thought the fan fiction I found online was better because it didn't just hint at a relationship between the two women."

"Yeah. Me, too," Wil said.

They both paused a long moment, absorbed in each other's gaze. Wil finally glanced away. "I wish you were here or I was there," she said in a near whisper, almost as if she was admitting it to herself.

"One to beam over. Engage," Lacey said in her best Captain Picard voice. "Damn. The transporter is offline again."

Wil smiled as she shook her head. "Nerd."

"Back at you." *Enough joking around.* "I know you're usually early to bed, early to rise, like me. So, tell me what's keeping you awake so late…unless you don't want to talk about it."

"No, no. Maybe it'll help me sleep if I do." Wil sighed and, after a few seconds, said, "Brittney and her dad, Mac Abbott, came out to the ranch today."

"You knew they were intending to, right? You and your dad talked about it before you left the rodeo last weekend."

"I did. Mac wanted to see all the horses Dad has for sale so he could be sure Smarty was Dad's best cutter. I was happy to see Mac show up without Brittney, but she came in her own car after I had ridden Smarty and a few others while he and Dad watched and dickered over Smarty's price. Mac's one of the few fairly local clients who can afford to pay top dollar for horses."

"Did he buy Smarty?"

"Yep. For a half million. That'll pay off our taxes and let us rehire Don, who was doing a lot of the training with the cutters before the pandemic hit. We'd have more horses ready for sale if we hadn't needed to lay him off."

"That sounds good. What else happened today that's keeping you up?"

"Brittney wanted to buy Pepper, but Mac said she already had a good horse."

"How much are you asking for Pepper, if you don't mind saying?"

"Thirty thousand, because of her great bloodlines. Mac, however, wasn't willing to pay that."

"Oh. I'm sorry it didn't work out."

"I'm not. I'd rather sell Pepper to someone who'll care more about their horse than the prize money."

"What's still troubling you, then?"

Wil's shoulders visibly raised and lowered as she heaved a deep sigh. "Brittney's father wants me to coach her to get better results out of Dash. He offered me two thousand dollars for ten lessons and a five-thousand-dollar bonus if she places in the money at the National Finals Rodeo in December."

"That's a lot of cash. Did you agree to do that?" Lacey had all but written off Brittney as a competitive threat, but that could change if Wil coached her.

"I told Mac I was really busy, but Dad jumped in and countered with an offer of five thousand, plus the bonus option and a promise that I wouldn't under any circumstances marry Brittney."

"Wh-what?"

"You had to be there. Brittney had threatened to marry a woman after her father told her to marry Bart Roberts and spend his money rather than Mac's."

"Ten thousand dollars is a lot to turn down."

"I was on board with the part about not marrying her, but no amount of money is enough to have to spend ten days coaching her. She won't listen to a thing I say, so there's no danger of her doing well at the finals. The competition there is very tough. Before I could decline, though, Dad and Mac were shaking hands on the deal."

"Your father hired you out?"

"Worse than that. He agreed to let her stay at the ranch the whole time but didn't tell me until after they left."

"She's going to be living with you for ten days?"

"She's not living with me. She'll be staying at the house. I told Dad he better get busy putting a double lock on my bedroom door and windows…and the bathroom I'll have to share with her."

Lacey's insecurities ignited. "Yeah. Like he'll do that." Ray had been very friendly to her, but keeping Brittney happy would keep his wealthiest client happy. She shouldn't be surprised. She'd known from the start that Wil was out of her league. Brittney would likely worm her way into Wil's bed by the third night.

Wil's face grew larger in the screen. "Look at me, Lace. I'm serious about the locks, and Dad knows it. If he doesn't install them tomorrow morning, I will."

"Don't sweat it. It's not like we're serious or anything. We were just having fun."

"Stop it. This is more than a fling," Wil said, frowning. "At least it is to me. If you don't feel the same, I want to know now before I let you break my heart."

Lacey couldn't meet Wil's eyes. She felt like running. But she also wanted desperately to give the instant bond between them a chance. Was she brave enough? "Why would you want me, Wil? I have nothing to offer. I often live off noodles and sandwiches because I'm one horse away from losing my rodeo career and having to beg for a low-paying wrangler job. If Denver ever gets injured, I'm done." She hadn't meant to spill her guts, but Wil seemed to have that effect on her.

Wil's expression softened. "You are a survivor of life. You're beautiful and smart and accomplished. Despite the obstacles you've had to overcome financially, you're a few points away from qualifying for the National Finals Rodeo."

Lacey shook her head and opened her mouth to respond, but Wil held her hand up, palm out, to stop her.

"Who can say what causes chemistry between two people? All I know is that after the week we spent together, you're all I think about."

Lacey finally returned her smile. "I hope your mind isn't on me while you're handling horses. That could be dangerous."

"Okay. Every moment I'm not training horses."

"Or Brittney."

Wil frowned. "I had to spend some time today considering what locks to put on my bath and bedroom."

Lacey laughed at the fire in Wil's eyes. "How about concentrating on the good parts? Your dad sold a horse for a half million dollars. It's hard to even imagine being able to pay that much for one horse."

"Yeah. Taxes will get a lot of it. But let's change the subject. You get to answer my questions now."

"Your questions?"

"Let's start with what you were doing that kept you busy past your usual bedtime."

"Oh. I made a new friend and got an invitation to eat dinner at their campsite. I usually prefer my own and Denver's company, but I had fun tonight."

"A new friend. That's great. How'd you meet?"

"I told you about the kids. It's the mother of the oldest girl, Sam. Andie teaches at a small college and coaches their softball team. Her partner left her after they had Sam."

"That sucks." Wil tilted her head this way and that, as if loosening the muscles in her neck, then looked down at her lap. "Is she beautiful?"

Lacey laughed. "She is cute, but I told her we were sort of dating—I hope that's okay—and she immediately googled you on her phone." She paused for dramatic effect, then grinned at Wil. "She thinks you're super-hot."

Wil laughed. "She must have seen my website picture. A professional photographer took it. She should see me after a day of training horses or slinging hay bales."

"Crap, woman. Now I won't get to sleep thinking about a sweaty you in a tank top, jeans, and chaps. Mmm-mmm." Lacey lowered her voice. "I could lick that sweat off you."

Wil grabbed the front of her T-shirt and fanned it against her body. "You're making me sweat right now. What else would you do to me?"

Lacey laughed. "It's late, and I'm not having video sex with you."

"Aww."

"I might not have a lot of work to do tomorrow, but you do. You need to get some sleep."

"I think I can now. It did help to talk tonight."

Neither seemed to know how to end their call, until Wil spoke up. "Just for the record, we're not 'sort of dating.' From my point of view, we *are* dating, and I date only one woman at a time."

Lacey's heart skipped a beat. Was Wil insinuating they already were a couple? Her face heated as a wave of shyness washed over her. "For the record, my past has been nothing but a few hookups. One woman at a time sounds like all I can handle since this dating thing is new for me."

"Okay," Wil said with a soft smile.

"Okay," Lacey echoed, then paused. "Talk to you tomorrow?"

"Absolutely."

"Good night, Wil."

"Sexy dreams, Lacey."

CHAPTER FOURTEEN

Brittney arrived late, as expected, so Wil was working Flash in the round pen in preparation for some barrel training when she got there.

"Hey, sexy."

Wil acted as if she hadn't heard her.

"Are you ignoring me?" Brittney assumed her often-used pouty face.

Wil slowed Flash to a stop and turned to Brittney. "I'm sorry. I thought you were speaking to someone else. My name is Wil, not sexy."

Brittney climbed over the round pen's railing and exaggerated her hip-swinging approach. "Now, don't be that way. I'm only a little late. I had to stop by Mandy's place to help her pick out a dress for the party this weekend. We have ten fun days ahead of us, and I don't want to start off with you being all fussy."

Wil gave her a hard stare. "We have ten days of hard work if you want to make the finals. I'm headed to the ring to work Flash on the barrels. You need to go groom, saddle, and warm up Dash to be ready to run the barrels when I'm done."

Brittney waved her hand dismissively. "Gabe can do all that. That's why I had him come along when Cal dropped off Dash and picked up Daddy's new horse. I figured you had space for him in your bunkhouse since I heard you had to lay off some of your wranglers."

"I sent him back with Cal. You don't spend enough time learning Dash's moods and quirks, and letting him get to know you. Horses aren't cars. They're athletes, and you have to learn the best way to coax a top performance out of them." She gathered up the long lunge line as Flash walked toward them. "So while you're here, you'll take care of Dash yourself."

"And what if I don't want to?"

"Then you can go home and tell your father that you aren't willing to put in the effort needed to win." She opened the gate to leave the round pen.

"Then you won't get paid."

"The bonus is the only thing making this worth my time. But if you're not going to try to learn something, you don't have a chance at placing in the finals, and I'll never see that bonus." Wil started for the barn to saddle Flash, and Brittney followed.

They walked in silence while Brittney appeared to be weighing things.

"I know how to ride my horse. Maybe I'll get in my car and just go back home."

Wil could use the money, so she played the last ace she had. "That's fine. I reckon you don't want to win bad enough and don't mind if Lacey Bishop beats you again in Abilene." She held back a smile when Brittney let out a long, frustrated growl.

"I do want to win."

"Then you can start by getting your horse ready for a training session."

"I'm not mucking his stall."

Wil decided a small concession wouldn't hurt. "One of our stable hands will clean his stall while you're training."

"Okay then."

❖

Horses and riders were everywhere in an unorganized chaos, crossing right in front of Lacey and Denver or riding too close behind and beside them. Denver pranced with barely contained anticipation and anxiety through the churning mass of animals and humans as they made their way to the warm-up area.

Lacey grimaced when she reached their destination, where a cluster of about eight riders gathered on their horses in the middle of the medium-sized ring sat chatting. They should go somewhere else if they weren't actually warming up to ride in an event. She loped Denver around their group several times, then executed a few spins close enough to their horses to make them move away after glaring at her.

"Sorry," she called out. "There's just not enough room for those of us who need to get ready to race with you guys sittin' and talking in the warm-up area." Then she smiled at the repeated glares and grumbling.

Same as last year, except for the whispers and comments. She had very good hearing.

"Wow. That's Lacey Bishop. I read she had a really fast time in San Antonio."

"What's a ranked racer doing at our rodeo? It's not fair to the local riders."

"Look, Mom. That's Lacey Bishop. I can't believe she's here and we get to see her run."

"She's probably here 'cause she thinks our grand prize is easy picking. I've got a horse that's going to give her a run for the money."

"I bet you twenty bucks that she'll smoke you."

"I'll take that bet."

"I hear she's a high-and-mighty lesbian bitch."

"I'm guessing you tried to hit on her, and she shot you down."

Lacey smiled at the strong but feminine voice making the last comment.

Although one of the larger local rodeos, the event was organized by the town's local civic clubs, in conjunction with the county fair located adjacent to the rodeo stadium. Most of the civic clubs' members were city folks—merchants, ministers, teachers, and bankers—who didn't understand some basic precautions needed to ensure the safety of the audience and the contestants. And it didn't help that the generous prize money drew every would-be amateur cowboy within a hundred miles. To enjoy as much quiet as possible, Lacey always parked her camper/trailer as far away from the stadium and fair rides as she could in the huge grassy field designated for parking. After all, her behind-the-back commenters were right about one thing—their top prize was easy pickings for her.

This barrel racers' competition was cumulative. The entire field of thirty posted times on Friday, but only those among the twenty fastest were invited back to run on Saturday. Then the top ten of Saturday's racers advanced to race for the biggest prizes on Sunday. She and Denver easily posted the best time—nearly two full seconds ahead of her closest competitor—on Friday.

She exited the warm-up area when she heard the stadium announcer introduce the contestant two ahead of her in the lineup. As she approached the stadium, she saw Andie and Sam waving.

"Hey. I wasn't expecting fans in the crowd."

"We're not stalking you or anything," Andie said. "Sam really wanted to see you compete."

"I'm glad you came. It'll be nice to have someone cheering for me," Lacey said, and she meant it. Denver, hyped from the warm-up and familiar competition sounds coming from the stadium, was focused on the race to come. Lacey had to spin her in a tight circle several times to exchange even a few words with them. "I better get on up there before Denver wears herself out fretting, but come find me at my trailer later if you're not in a hurry to get back." She pointed to the field of horse trailers. "I'm parked in the back corner."

"Yes!" Sam turned begging eyes on her mother. "Please, please, Mom."

Andie smiled. "That would be great. We'll find you after we watch a bit more of the rodeo."

Lacey touched the brim of her hat in acknowledgement, then let her overeager horse trot the rest of the way to the stadium.

❖

"Next up is Lacey Bishop, riding Dust Storm Denver." The announcer's introduction didn't note she was the only rider ranked among the top twenty-five nationally participating in their rodeo. It could have been intended as a local snub, but she wrote it off as ignorance, since he was likely just a civic-club member with a good voice but little background knowledge of the rodeo circuit.

She twirled Denver at the mouth of the entry chute, then rocketed down the tunnel to break the timer beam.

Denver was in the zone, just like during the last rodeo. Lacey simply had to hold on, lean forward, back, and to the inside so she didn't impede the mare's momentum and balance. They shaved each barrel so close, Lacey had to make sure she didn't have the toe of her boot or an elbow sticking out to tip a barrel.

When they rounded the third barrel and hurdled toward the finish line, she knew they'd turned in another great run—not as fast as in San Antonio, but the footing at these smaller rodeos wasn't as good, and the barrels were likely no longer precisely placed since they'd been tipped over several times.

"That time of fourteen-point-one-five, combined with her time yesterday of fourteen-oh-eight, keeps Miss Bishop solidly in the lead heading into Sunday's round."

As much as she wanted to go find Sam and Andie, she had to walk Denver to cool her down, then bathe and check her over before hanging a full hay net in her trailer. She'd walk her again later, because the field for trailers was too crowded for Lacey to set up her small corral.

She put out three camp chairs by the trailer and hung a few mosquito- and bug-killing lanterns nearby, then sat alone for barely ten minutes before she saw Sam and Andie coming her way. When she made eye contact, Sam broke away from her mother's side and sprinted to Lacey.

"Wow! You and Denver are the GOAT," Sam said. "I didn't know she could run that fast. She was lit, spinning around those barrels without touching them, then turning into the Flash after the last barrel."

"I can translate for you if needed." Andie, laughing, arrived at a more sedate pace.

"No, no," Lacey said. "I'm not around preteens much, but I do stream Netflix and buy a WNBA league pass for streaming games every year. I've seen all the superhero movies more than once and know Sue Bird is the GOAT." She gestured for them to sit down in the chairs she'd set out. "And I think I can figure out the rest."

Andie rolled her eyes and nodded. "Sorry. I didn't mean to insinuate you were a hermit, but you go to bed so early, and I didn't know if you had internet since you move around so much. Plus, I've never seen you watching a television or using a laptop. You seem to prefer to sit outside until bedtime."

Lacey stretched her legs out in front of her. "Contrary to belief, it does rain in Texas. I pay for a satellite internet, but that's iffy in bad weather. I try to check Hulu, Netflix, and Amazon Prime when the weather's good to see if they have any movies I want to download to watch later."

"You might be a nomad, but you don't seem to be missing out on much."

"There are concessions. Rodeos like this one don't have shower facilities. I have a fifty-gallon water tank, but I also need that water to flush the toilet, wash a few dishes, cook, and water Denver. There is a place where I can rinse Denver off after a run, and I usually fill a five-gallon bucket from that hose for some of her drinking water."

Andie wrinkled her nose and made a show of moving her chair a few more feet away from Lacey's. "So, you don't shower all weekend?"

Sam leaned closer and sniffed. "You smell okay to me."

Lacey chuckled. "I took a wh…uh, sponge bath last night, but I bathed in my trailer a little while ago. You just have to take a military shower to use as little water as possible."

Sam frowned. "What's a military shower?"

"You turn the water on to get wet, turn it off to soap up, then back on to rinse off. And no standing in the shower and running the water just because it feels good."

"Mom likes to soak in the bathtub. Sometimes she's in there a whole hour."

Andie covered her face with her hands. "It's true. I like to fill it to my shoulders, and when the water starts to cool, I let some out and add more hot water."

"Mom, I looked it up online. That tub holds forty to sixty gallons of water! It's one of our most important natural resources, and you're wasting it," Sam said, giving her mother a scolding glare.

Andie smiled and pointed to her daughter. "I think I'm raising a future environmental terrorist. She'll be joining marches and carrying signs by the time she hits high school." She gave Lacey an imploring look. "Please explain to her that long baths are a mental-health treatment for her poor, stressed mother."

Lacey laughed and shook her head. "Nope. You could take up yoga instead, you water-waster."

❖

Wil banged on the bathroom door. Brittany had ignored her polite knock and request for Brittney to wrap up her bath. "Brittney. You've been in there nearly an hour. You're wasting water, and it's my turn. I want to shower so I can go to bed."

"I just love this big old claw-foot tub. I can't seem to drag myself out of it. The door's unlocked. You can come in and use the shower. I have seen you naked before, you know."

Wil growled under her breath. She'd known Brittney would pull something like this. If she did as Brittney offered, she wouldn't be in the shower alone for long. "Not going to happen."

She marched down the hall and knocked on Ray's bedroom door. "Dad?"

"Come on in," he said. "I'm decent."

He was crawling into bed when she opened the door, but growing up, she'd often seen him in his loose boxers and T-shirt. "I was just about ready to tuck myself in. You should be doing the same soon."

"I would already be in bed if Brittney wasn't still monopolizing my bathroom."

He waved at the door to the master bathroom. "Go ahead and use mine. I'll read a little until you're done."

"I'll be quick," she said as she closed his bedroom door and practically jogged to his shower.

She was done in fifteen minutes, but when she came out, her father was already asleep with a book on his chest and readers slipping down his nose. Since he'd had COVID, he seemed to crash more than tire. She gently removed his glasses and book to put them on his bedside table, then kissed him on his forehead and turned out his light.

Brittney was propped against the wall next to Wil's bedroom door. "There you are. I was waiting to tell you I'm done in your bathroom."

"I showered in Dad's. I'm tired and get up really early every morning. We feed the animals first, then return to the house to have breakfast at six thirty. If you're not up, I'll leave you a plate in the microwave, but you need to set an alarm for yourself. We'll do two sessions tomorrow—one at ten and a second one at four in the afternoon. That means you need to have Dash groomed, lunged, saddled, and waiting at the barrel ring at ten sharp."

"Just coffee for me. I don't eat breakfast. I'm not much of a morning person, so could we make the lesson at eleven?"

"No. Our vet is coming out at noon to ultrasound some mares for me."

"Then we can just do the four o'clock lesson."

"The contract I signed with your father stipulated I would coach you twice a day for ten days, with each session lasting a minimum of one hour. The contract also says that my only obligation is to be present during the designated time, and I'll be paid whether you show or not. So, skip the morning session if you want, but I'll be there to fulfill my obligations." She took a key to unlock her bedroom door from the pocket of her robe she'd wrapped tight around her and securely tied with a knot.

"You lock your bedroom door?" Brittney's tone turned sultry. "What are you hiding in there? Sex toys you don't want your father to find? I wouldn't mind seeing them."

"I didn't lock it until I found out you'd be staying here. My phone and bed are in my room, and I don't want you scrolling through my phone or waiting in my bed."

Brittney glared at her, then softened her expression and ran her fingers along the lapel of Wil's robe as if Wil hadn't just insulted her. "You still sleep naked, don't you? I don't know how I'm going to calm myself enough to sleep with that picture in my head."

Wil grabbed her exploring hand and held it in front of Brittney's face. "Use this to take care of your urges and put yourself to sleep." She opened her door and stepped into the room before turning back to Brittney. "If you get any ideas about picking the door lock, I have a hefty slide-bar lock on the inside." She closed the door on Brittney's frown and engaged the slide bar forcefully so it could be heard in the hallway.

❖

"Y'all feel free to check out the fair food if you want," Lacey said. "I've had enough burgers, corn dogs, and turkey legs from over there to last me a lifetime. A Chinese restaurant on the highway will deliver to me because I give the driver a big tip."

"I've been thinking about a funnel cake all day, but Chinese sounds good right now," Andie said.

"How about you, Sam?" Lacey asked.

"Do they have dumplings?"

"Yep."

"Then let's have Chinese for dinner, and we can split a funnel cake for dessert."

Andie grinned. "Sounds like a plan to me."

"I'm in," Lacey said. "I'll order the Chinese and wait for it while you guys check out the fair and bring back a funnel cake."

"You don't want to go with us?" Sam was clearly disappointed.

Lacey shook her head. "The only way Denver and I could fail to get the grand prize is if we don't run at all tomorrow. I trust people on the professional tour because they know the implications of messing with someone's horse. But I can't be sure some local yahoo at this rodeo wouldn't do something to keep Denver from running so his girlfriend could win the big prize. Not that these folks aren't good people, but there's always one guy around with bad judgment. So, I don't want to leave her alone."

"Understood," Andie said. "Come on, Sam. Let's go search out funnel cake."

❖

Two hours later, they had consumed all the food, and each had a dusting of powdered sugar on her shirt from the two funnel cakes—Lacey and Andie shared one, while Sam consumed the other by herself—when Lacey's iPad buzzed with a video-chat request. She lifted it from the pocket on the arm of her camp chair to check the caller.

"Hey, Wil. Andie and Sam came to see Denver and me run today." She checked the time. "They're still here, so can I call you back if it's not too late?"

Andie stood while Lacey was talking to Wil. "Don't hang up. It'll be dark soon, and we need to get back to the campground. I plan to wake us up early to pack up and head home. Teachers have to go to work Monday to get ready for school reopening in two weeks."

"Is that your girlfriend?" Sam asked. "Can we talk to her?"

Andie's nodding head and bright smile confirmed she would like an introduction, too.

She looked down at the pad. "You up for meeting my new friends?"

Wil looked uncertain for a second, then nodded and checked the tie on her robe to make sure her modesty was intact. "Sure. I've at least showered off the barn dirt, but I'm in my robe, and my hair's still wet. If they don't mind, I'm okay with it."

"We'll come around behind you," Andie said as she directed Sam to lean down behind Lacey's right shoulder while she did the same on her left side.

"Wil, meet Andie and her daughter Sam," Lacey said, pointing to each. "Guys, this is, uh, my, um, my girlfriend, Wil Rivers."

Wil's smile expanded to a grin. "Was that hard to say? Girlfriend?"

Lacey's face heated, but she smiled and shook her head while the others laughed. "I don't think I've ever said 'my girlfriend' about anyone."

Wil gave a little wave. "Hi, guys. I'm Wil, Lacey's girlfriend."

"Hey, Wil. We drove over from the campground since it wasn't very far. Sam was really excited to see Denver and Lacey run the barrels."

"You should have seen how fast Denver ran," Sam said. "Way faster than any of the other horses."

Wil nodded her agreement with Sam's exuberant report. "What was your time today, Lace?"

"Fourteen-point-one-five. Not as good as yesterday, but they aren't adding dirt to the arena each day like the big rodeos do. The footing's getting slow. This is a cumulative competition, though, and I'm about two full seconds faster than the next-fastest rider."

"I'm afraid she's got my twelve-year-old considering a career as a barrel racer instead of last week's career choice—environmental activist," Andie said.

"Where do you work, Wil?" Sam asked, dismissing her mom's comment.

"My dad and I own a ranch where we train horses for cutting, reining, barrel-racing, team-penning, and roping competitions."

Sam's eyes widened and her jaw dropped. "That must be so much fun."

Wil laughed. "I enjoy it, but it's also hot, sweaty work, and some horses just refuse to learn. So, it can be frustrating."

Andie waved again at the screen. "It was great to meet you, Wil, but we really do need to be going."

"Nice to meet both of you, too. I'd love to show you around our ranch if Lacey will bring you by sometime." She waved at them. "I'm going to hang up now, though, so you guys can say good night. Call me back after, babe."

Lacey's face heated again, at the affectionate "babe," as the screen went dark. She stood and laid the tablet in her chair. "It was great to see you guys. Thanks for your support today, and for taking time to meet Wil."

Andie gave her a quick, one-armed hug while Sam was saying good-bye to Denver. "I wanted to make it clear I am not stalking you or hoping to steal you from her. I don't go after anyone who isn't absolutely single, and I don't respect anyone who does."

"Thanks," Lacey said, rubbing the back of her neck. "I don't have much practice at this dating thing. I haven't been a hermit, just hooked up for a night or two. I don't want to screw this up, but I'm feeling around in the dark here."

Andie smiled and patted her on the shoulder. "Feel free to call me if you need advice or just want to talk about it. I think that failure to communicate is the biggest hurdle for our relationships."

"I'll keep that in mind."

"You'll be okay. Wil is gorgeous and seems very sweet." Andie raised her voice. "Time to go, kiddo."

Sam ran over and wrapped her arms around Lacey. "Can we come see you again?"

Lacey returned her hug. "Sure. I'll email my rodeo schedule to your mom."

"And you can come visit us if you're in our neck of the woods. We live in an old neighborhood with large one-acre lots. My house is small, but I have a double drive and a big, fenced backyard Denver could stay in."

"That sounds great. Thanks." Maggie, Joel, and their campground were like family and home. Andie and Sam felt like friends—something she'd never had...or let herself have. And there was Wil. The very thought of her warmed Lacey inside, and not just in her crotch. Her world was expanding fast, and it was a little scary.

Chapter Fifteen

Abilene at last. The three weeks since Wil had shared breath, kisses, cuddles, touches, and bodies with Lacey had seemed like three years.

However painful the separation, Wil believed their long, nightly video chats were helping build a foundation outside their haze of lust. They traded childhood memories—good and bad. They talked about television shows, music, and movies. They shared pet peeves, likes and dislikes from people to food to brands of boots.

But she was more than ready to share some of the lust in person that they couldn't, uh, hadn't in a video chat. They were still too shy with each other to bring up phone or video sex. Geez. They'd spent only a few nights together—mind-blowing, heart-pounding nights. Wil fanned her face with her hand as she parked her truck and two-horse trailer next to Denver's trailer. God. She didn't want Lacey to think she was a total horndog.

Wil stepped down from her truck, suddenly feeling bashful because of her lascivious thoughts and her decision to bring Buckeye, the roper her father wanted her to show off, in their small trailer that had no living quarters. Was it presumptuous to assume she would be sharing Lacey's bed?

All doubts disappeared when the door to Lacey's living compartment swung open before she could knock, and Lacey hauled her inside. There was no preamble, just lips and mouths and tongues and the two of them pressed as tightly as the clothes between them allowed. Both drew back after a moment, chests heaving. Wil locked gazes with the woman she'd been pining after for weeks.

She cupped Lacey's face in her hands and kissed her again—slowly and tenderly. "I missed you," she said. "And, wow, I like the way you say hello."

Lacey cocked her head and smiled. "I saw you hesitate to knock, so I thought maybe I hadn't made it clear how much I want you here. Are you feeling better?"

"Yeah." Wil tugged Lacey into a tight hug, hiding her face so Lacey couldn't see her embarrassment. She hated being sick and didn't want Lacey to think she was hiding some big health problem. "I get migraines only once or twice a year, but when I do, they knock me out for a day or two. I'm fine now." She released Lacey and redirected the conversation. "What smells so good?"

Lacey gestured to the dining booth. "It's nothing fancy, but one of my favorite single-dish recipes."

"I need to unload Buckeye and get him stabled." Her mouth watered at the aroma of the chunks of chicken breast, rice, and mixed vegetables Lacey was ladling into bowls. "But he can wait while we eat." She scooped up a spoonful to taste while Lacey retrieved two bottles of water and hummed as she chewed the tasty dish. "This is so good. How did you make it?"

"It's easy. Just cover the bottom of a casserole dish with uncooked rice and throw in a can or frozen package of mixed vegetables and chunks of chicken breast. Then pour cream-of-mushroom soup over it all and pop it in the oven for thirty or forty-five minutes."

"I've got to make this for Dad. He'll love it."

"My friend Maggie is a great cook, and I get tired of take-out food when I'm on the road, so she taught me a few recipes I can make in my little kitchen without much fuss," Lacey said.

"I'd like to meet her and Joel. They seem important to you."

Lacey's cheeks pinked, but she nodded. "I stay at their campground three or four times a year and help Joel with some of the upkeep he can't manage by himself. They're more like family than just friends—sort of the parents I wish I'd had."

Wil reached across the table and squeezed her hand. Both sadness and hope flared in Wil's heart at Lacey's unspoken longing—sadness for her tortured childhood and hope that Lacey might one day claim her and Ray as family, too.

❖

Lacey echoed Wil's moan as they came together naked, heated skin on skin. She settled on top of Wil, who she knew could easily bear her weight, and used her tongue and teeth to explore her mouth, her neck, her ears, and down to her breasts. Wil smelled of shea butter soap and faintly of horses and the fresh hay they'd put out for their mounts. She pressed her hips to Wil's as Wil's hands moved down her back to grip her butt. God, she wanted to devour this strong yet feminine woman the way she had in her dreams each night since they'd last been together.

Wil's hands on Lacey's buttocks trembled as Lacey held her nipple in her teeth and flicked her tongue back and forth over the hardened peak.

"Oh, God. Yes. Like that. Feels so good."

Wil moaned her encouragement, but Lacey abandoned her breast to slide lower, rimming her sensitive navel, then shouldering between Wil's legs. She sucked the pulse throbbing in the crease where her thigh joined her hip, then licked along Wil's upper thighs and danced her tongue lightly over her exposed sex. She tasted so good, and her swollen clit practically taunted her, dared her to take a long swipe. So she did and held on as Wil's hips bucked with the contact.

"Yessss," Wil hissed. "I'm gonna…I'm going to—"

Lacey felt Wil's belly tighten and her hand clamp onto the back of her head to keep her from moving away. The power she had over Wil's pleasure swelled her own desire. She used teeth and tongue on Wil's clit as she had on her breast and plunged two fingers inside the hot, moist heat of her lover. Lacey pumped in and out, in and out as Wil's insides convulsed around her fingers. Wil slapped a pillow over her face, muffling her cry as her body bowed, and Lacey's blood sang with each thrust.

She sucked as Wil's clit softened, then immediately began to harden again, and Lacey's world spun. Wil was on top now, hunched over her and pushing Lacey's legs up to her chest to rub their clits together. Holy crap. She didn't know this position was even possible, but she was so swollen and hard, so aroused by Wil's steady pumping over her, she instantly felt the sweet tingle of her clit engorging for release. She moaned and dug her short nails into Wil's back. "Oh God, oh God. Don't stop." Every muscle in her body tightened as pleasure exploded through her. Her cry was met with Wil's shout, and then Wil pushed two fingers inside before Lacey's orgasm could dissipate. She'd never come twice so close together, but when she opened her eyes to see Wil's hot blue gaze and felt the fullness of her fingers pressing in and out, in and out, she instantly succumbed to a second wave of pleasure.

"Enough. Enough." Lacey was limp from the intensity of their coupling. Wil collapsed next to her, and they lay panting together for several minutes. Lacey moaned again as Wil slowly withdrew her fingers. "I think you killed me," she said.

"You make me completely lose my mind." Wil was quiet for a few long seconds. "I…I wasn't too rough, was I?" She raised up on one elbow, studying Lacey's expression.

"I appreciate that you think I might be some kind of fragile flower, but this cowgirl likes a rough tumble as much as slow and tender."

Relief showed on Wil's face.

Lacey frowned. "You weren't really worried, were you?"

Wil looked away and half shrugged. "I don't know what came over me. Everything is just, uh, more with you."

Lacey guided Wil to meet her gaze again. "It's okay. We're okay." She wanted to say she felt the same way, but that tiny, insecure voice inside held her back. They'd known each other little more than a month. They might burn hot for a short time, then fizzle. She had nothing to offer their relationship, while Wil had a home and family. She turned on her side away from Wil but tugged at her to encourage Wil to spoon behind her. Thinking about tomorrow wouldn't change anything, so she would just enjoy every moment of today.

❖

Lacey walked Denver away from Wil and back again. "She seems a little off."

Wil shook her head. "I can't see any signs of lameness."

"Her time was off at the last rodeo, but I didn't sweat it because we were well ahead of the rider in second place."

Wil ran her hands up and down each of Denver's legs. "That right front knee does seem a bit warm, but I don't detect any swelling. When was the last time you had her legs x-rayed?"

"I usually have that done each year when she gets her annual vaccinations, but that was eight months ago. Until last weekend, our times have been getting better and better. I thought the dirt on the arena floor was a bit thin, but she didn't seem to have any problem with it. At least nothing I could detect." Lacey scratched the back of her neck. "Maybe I'm obsessing."

"You thinking of pulling from the competition?"

Lacey shook her head, despite feeling that Denver wasn't one hundred percent healthy, Abilene's prize money was too much to give up without any real sign of injury. Plus, she was counting on placing in this and the Big Spring rodeo to finance her expenses for the Wrangler National Finals Rodeo, pay next year's membership dues to the WPCA, and keep her solvent until after the holidays, when the circuit started up again. "I don't guess so. I don't have a lot of wiggle room in my budget. If I don't run here, I'll be eating ramen and scrambled eggs the rest of the year." Lacey paused in her indecision. "But I don't want to ride her if something's wrong."

"I can't see anything that would make me pull her if she was my horse," Wil said. "You can't get a refund on your entry fee this late."

Lacey swung up into the saddle. "I'm going to warm her up some more. If she feels off during our run, I won't push her. Ramen or not, I need her sound for the national finals."

❖

"Woo-hoo!" Lacey stood up from her seat and whistled long and loud. "Way to go, Wil." She took the stairs two at a time in the section reserved for rodeo participants and their families to watch other competitors. The breakaway roping wrapped up with Wil and Buckeye at the top of the leaderboard, and she couldn't wait to congratulate her girlfriend. She almost stumbled at the thought. Girlfriend. She smiled to herself. She was in the lead after the first barrel-racing session, Denver was showing no signs of lameness, and she had a girlfriend. Life was getting better every minute.

She slowed her trot to a walk when she spotted Wil and Buckeye. Wil was talking to a middle-aged man, who appeared to be a prospective buyer because he was giving the horse a good once-over. Wil waved her over anyway.

"Congratulations," Lacey said as she neared them. "Great roping."

Wil grinned. "Buckeye makes it easy. He seems to have an instinct for putting you right where you need to be for a good throw." She indicated the man, who straightened from feeling along Buckeye's legs. "Lacey Bishop, this is Ross Martin. He's in the market for a good roping horse."

Ross held out his hand, and Lacey shook it. "Pleased to meet you, Miss Bishop," he said. "Nice run you had earlier. My daughter is racing in the junior division, and you're one of her favorite professional racers."

"Really? I had no idea I had fans…well, at least one fan." Wow. She had a girlfriend, friends, and fans. She felt her cheeks begin to warm, embarrassed by this sudden wealth of good things in her life. Time to change the subject. "So, what do you think about Buckeye?"

Ross lifted his hat and scratched his crewcut before settling it back on his head. "I like what I just saw in the arena, and he seems sound."

"We've had him fully vetted. We always do that when a horse is ready for sale, to protect us and the buyer," Wil said. "I can have our vet email copies of his X-rays to your vet, or you're welcome to have your vet take another set."

"No, no. Ray Rivers has a stellar reputation. But if I buy him, I would like a copy of his medical records for my vet to put on file."

"No problem. We do that anyway," Wil said.

Ross rubbed his chin and walked around Buckeye for another look. "My boy's birthday is coming up. He's been learning to rope on several of the ranch horses, but I was thinking to surprise him with a competition roper. I'd like to see how this guy does as a heeler in team roping, though."

"Dad trained him for both single and team roping, but I'm not entered in team roping because I'm here by myself this week."

Ross smiled at her. "I happen to know there's an open slot tomorrow where someone didn't show up. I can call in a few favors to get you in as a late entry and, of course, pay your entry fee if you can find someone to team up with."

"I can do it," Lacey said. "I'm probably a little rusty, but Denver's had a good bit of experience roping."

"There you go," Ross said, then looked at Wil. "You up for that?"

"Well, sure."

"Then I'll go take care of the arrangements and check back in with you later." He turned and hurried off to the rodeo office.

"Are you sure about this? You're not still worried Denver might be going lame?"

"No. That was probably just me getting too much inside my head. She didn't run her top time today, but near it. And she's not showing any bad signs."

"Okay, great." Wil's eyes were affectionate, her smile warm. "I appreciate the help."

Their gaze said everything they wouldn't express in the middle of a conservative rodeo crowd. They weren't afraid for their safety, but they were rather private and preferred not to flaunt their sexuality in public.

"How about we bed this guy down and grab a couple of chili dogs back at the trailer, then catch the second session of barrel racing," Lacey said. "I saw Brittney's trailer pull in this morning, and I want to see her run."

Wil's smile vanished "The chili dogs sound good, but I've seen enough of Brittney over the past two weeks to last me a lifetime." She began walking Buckeye toward the stabling area.

Hesitating a second, Lacey caught up and fell into step with Wil, puzzled by her sudden mood change. "I thought maybe you'd want to see if she'd learned anything from the lessons you gave her."

They had almost reached the huge metal building set up with temporary stalls before Wil spoke again. "The contract I signed didn't stipulate that she had to learn, only that I had to teach her. That woman has a head as hard as a rock. I seriously doubt she digested anything I tried to show her."

"Uh, okay."

"You can go watch and tell me if you think she learned anything." Wil led Buckeye into his stall and began unsaddling him. Halfway through the task, she stopped and sighed. She turned to Lacey. "I'm sorry for going grouchy on you. Just the mention of her name irritates me."

"I won't mention her again."

"If her father wasn't Dad's biggest client—"

"I get it. It's okay. I don't have to watch her. I'm sure we'll both advance to the final round, and I can do it then."

"No. It's fine. You go. I should circulate and see if anybody else is horse-shopping. After we paid taxes, the money Dad made from selling Smarty caught up all our bills and let us rehire Don, but we won't stay in the black unless we sell more of the horses we have ready. Dad's medical bills when he had COVID ate up the cash we'd set aside to buy more stock to train."

"Okay. I know this is work for you, not just a booty call."

Wil finally smiled again. "Booty call, huh?" She glanced around, then reached quickly to give Lacey's butt a squeeze. "Forget chili dogs. Let's have booty for lunch."

"No. I'm hungry, woman." Lacey pushed her away, enjoying Wil's playful side. Her one-night stands were simply sex and never involved affection and frisky banter. "Besides, if we start something now, I'll miss checking out my competition."

Wil looked upward as if pleading to the heavens. "Okay, Mom. I get it. This is punishment for all those times I kept knocking at y'all's bedroom door when it was locked."

Lacey laughed. "I'm picturing young Wil standing outside her parents' bedroom door." She knocked on the wall of the stable building three times. "Mom, Dad." Three rapid knocks. "Mom, Dad." Three rapid knocks. "Mom, Dad."

Wil laughed, too, acknowledging the reference to a nerdy television sit-com.

"Well, well. Sounds like you two are having fun." Brittney lounged in the doorway to Buckeye's stall. She locked her gaze on Wil. "Coming to watch me and Dash turn in the top time this afternoon?"

Wil stiffened. "No. I have business to take care of."

Lacey sauntered over and stuck her arm out to prop against

the stall's side so she was between Wil and Brittney. "I'm going to watch, but I've already clocked a better time this morning than your best."

"That might be true at the moment, but in case you didn't know, Wil has been coaching Dash for the past two weeks, and we've been burning up the barrels." Brittney's smile remained smug.

"Hmm. The way I heard it, your daddy paid her to coach you on how to ride, since nothing was wrong with the horse she trained and sold to you."

Brittney cocked her head. "Is that what she told you?" She waved a dismissive hand. "Doesn't matter. You can believe what you want, but when you pick up that second- or third-place check this weekend, remember to thank your friend over there."

Lacey felt Wil's hand on her lower back, nudging her to displace Brittney in the stall doorway.

"Oh, look at the time," Wil said. "You probably should start getting Dash ready. Lacey and I are going to have lunch."

They pushed past Brittney, and Wil closed the stall door and made a show of double-checking the latch was secure and looking up at the security camera that recorded any motion in the aisle between the rows of stalls. Understanding Wil's pointed stare at the camera, Lacey kept her voice casual.

"Don't worry," she said loud enough for Brittney to hear. "I checked with their security people when I first brought Denver in here. The cameras are all working and record every time they detect motion in the aisles."

❖

"I changed my mind," Wil said as they walked from the RV parking toward the arena. "I'll watch with you this afternoon, but let's look in on the horses before we head over there."

"Okay." Lacey was amused that Wil had been glued to her side since they'd seen Brittney. Wil had pulled her into a passionate kiss the moment they were inside Lacey's camper, but they restrained themselves from stripping off their clothes and jumping into bed because they both knew they'd be there all afternoon if they did. "What changed your mind?"

Wil shrugged but didn't look at Lacey. "I thought about what you said, and I am curious to see if she learned anything last week."

"You mean other than how to pick your bedroom lock?"

Wil almost tripped over her own feet.

"Whoa. You okay?" Lacey grabbed Wil's arm to steady her.

"I get clumsy sometimes when I'm tired. I could use a cup of hot coffee about now." Wil rolled her shoulders and stretched her arms across her chest.

"Tell me again about Brittney breaking into your bedroom."

"I'd forgotten I let you know about that." Wil looked relieved. "She figured that if she could pick the doorknob lock while I was in the shower and climb into my bed naked, I'd give up and get in there with her. I wish I'd taken a picture of her face when I turned around and said, 'Fine. Dad has a king-sized bed, so I'll sleep with him.' I knew she wouldn't dare go into his room, even if he hadn't been in there."

Lacey shook her head and laughed along with Wil.

"Anyway," Wil said, "she apparently has taken my advice to groom and saddle Dash herself so they can bond, rather than have Gabe do it. Dash is a good horse. I hate to see her holding him back."

Lacey nodded. She understood the sentiment and appreciated that Wil was all about the horses, because she felt the same way. She hooked her arm in Wil's like any two female friends might. "Well, I reckon I can bump you up to the front of the line."

Wil looked at her. "What line?"

"You know, the line of women waiting to sit next to me in the stands."

Wil pretended to growl. "We'll see about that."

CHAPTER SIXTEEN

They easily found great seats because much of the audience took a break during barrel racing to visit the restrooms, grab some food, or wander through the vendors on the concourse that ringed the facility before the next, more popular event, like bronc and bull riding or steer wrestling.

They'd hurried back to the arena just in time to watch the terrier races, one of Wil's favorite feature events that entertained the audience while the floor was prepared for the barrel racers.

Many ranches had terriers—mixes and purebred—around to keep the mouse population down in the barns. Most had barn cats, too, but cats hunted when a mouse caught their attention and they weren't too comfortable to rise and give chase. Small, feisty terriers, driven by scent, were relentless in their pursuit once they detected a trail. So, some brought their little dogs along and entered them in the race, where the dogs chased a fake fox tail the length of the arena and through a gap left in a wall of hay bales. First dog through the hole wins.

"Do you have a dog at the ranch?" Lacey asked.

"We raise some cattle as a side venture and have a couple of border collies to help herd them, but they really belong to our foreman, Jimmy. They sleep in the bunkhouse with him. Mom used to have a terrier mix, but it was old and died the year before she did." Wil bumped Lacey's shoulder to let her know she was okay with the question. "How about you?"

"No. My aunt, the one I lived with until I got out of high school, had a Jack Russell terrier. It was really smart and fun. Sometimes,

I've thought about getting a puppy, but I never have. Maybe one day, if I ever give up the nomadic life."

"Excuse me." A slender woman, dressed in crisp, new Western wear, stood a few seats away from Lacey. "You're Lacey Bishop, right?"

Lacey looked wary, so Wil also stood when Lacey did to greet the woman.

"Yes. I'm Lacey."

The woman stuck her hand out. "Hi. I'm Amanda Greene. I work for an Australian clothing manufacturer that is trying to establish a new line of Western clothing here in the United States. We're branding it Saddle Up and are looking to sponsor a couple of women who will be at the national finals. Could I interest you in that?"

Lacey seemed frozen as she stared at the woman, so Wil took the woman's hand. "Hi. I'm Wil Rivers. We'd like to hear more about what you're proposing. Would you care to sit down?"

"Thank you." Amanda hesitated. "If that's all right with you," she said to Lacey.

A touch to Lacey's back apparently woke her up. "Yeah, sorry." She belatedly offered her hand and shook Amanda's. "Please join us. We were waiting for the barrel racing to start."

Amanda nodded. "You turned in a really good time this morning. We've been tracking your progress because we want a fresh face, someone who has put in the work to get to the finals. Our clothing line, while very attractive, is designed to be tough and is manufactured in an ecologically friendly factory. No foreign sweatshops for us."

"We'd have to check what you're telling us," Wil said.

"Of course. While our company might not be well known in the US, our reputation is solid in Australia and Europe."

"What exactly would you want from me?" Lacey asked.

"To wear our clothing line…basically shirts, jeans, and jackets with our logo on them. Later, we plan to add a line of Western boots and belts, as well as some dresses and skirts."

Lacey made a sour face. "I don't wear dresses."

Amanda smiled. "Noted. But you do wear shirts and jeans. We'd, of course, provide you some samples to try on before we asked you to sign a contract—to make sure you find the clothes comfortable."

"What's your timeline for this?" Wil asked.

"I can have a box of clothing sent to Miss Bishop's home within the next two weeks."

Lacey's face reddened. "That might be a problem."

"Why is that?" Amanda appeared surprised.

Wil jumped in, knowing how sensitive Lacey was about not having a permanent home. "Well, she's on the road until the Thanksgiving break, then headed for the national finals. But you could ship the box to my ranch, the Double R, outside Bowie. I could make sure she gets it." Wil paused. "If that's okay with Lacey."

Lacey cleared her throat. "Uh, yeah. That would work. Thanks."

Amanda accepted the Double R's business card Wil held out to her. "Excellent. If everything works out to the satisfaction of all, then we'd also pay your entry fee to the finals. You would still be responsible for your other expenses, but we'd spell all that out in a contract beforehand." She stood, and they stood again. "Good luck on Sunday, Miss Bishop. Looks like the barrel racing is starting, so I'll leave you to it." She handed Lacey a business card. "Miss Rivers, so nice to meet you."

Lacey stared at the card as Amanda retreated. "Wow." She looked up as Wil guided her to sit again. "I might have a sponsor."

Wil grinned. "Cool, huh?" She was glad she'd decided to spend the afternoon with Lacey instead of talking up clients. "If you don't have a lawyer, I can get the guy that handles contracts for the ranch to give their offer a look-see."

Lacey seemed relieved. "That would be great, because I don't have one." She stared down at her hands. "A lot of things are overlooked when you don't have a permanent address."

Wil tugged one of Lacey's hands into her lap, not caring who might see them, and held it in both of hers. No words were needed.

❖

"Next up is Brittney Abbott. Ranked in the top ten nationally, she's riding Dash of Charm." The announcer's deep voice still echoed in the stadium when Brittney and Dash hurdled into the arena. She took the first two barrels perfectly but kicked her heels against Dash's sides when he slowed his approach to the third barrel. His feet nearly went out from under him, and his shoulder skimmed the barrel, but he recovered to sprint out of the arena.

"Damn her. That stumble was entirely her fault and probably cost her a half second at least," Wil said. "I swear I'll never sell that woman another of my horses. Dash deserves a better rider."

Lacey's heart jumped when Brittney's time posted on the scoreboard. "Shit. She would have beaten my time if her horse hadn't slipped."

"She would have if she'd listened to me…hell, if she'd just listened to her horse. Dash knew he needed to slow to make the turn."

Lacey frowned. "Hey, exactly who are you rooting for to win?"

Wil froze for a second, her eyes widening as she appeared to realize how her tirade against Brittney could be misconstrued. "No. I want you to win, of course. It's just—"

Lacey waved a dismissive hand and smiled. "I'm messing with you. I know what you meant."

"I only want Dash to reach his full potential. I raised him on the ranch from a colt, and how he performs reflects on the Double R." She took Lacey's hand again. "But I definitely want you and Denver to win."

Lacey smiled, and Wil appeared relieved when she squeezed her hand. Trouble was, while she worked to assuage Wil's doubts, her own flared. She and Denver would need to run their best in Sunday's final if she hoped to take first place.

❖

"You sure you're okay with this?" Wil asked the question for the fourth time.

Lacey captured Wil's face in her hands, forcing her to look into her eyes. "Stop asking. I'm fine doing this for you."

"I know it's been a while since you roped anything, so I don't want you to worry if you miss. It's all good, okay?"

Lacey dropped her hands from Wil's face but held her gaze.

"I won't miss. I've worked as a day wrangler at ranch roundups for more than ten years to make extra money. I know how to lasso a calf." She turned to mount Denver. "So, let's go. We're up next."

Wil swung her leg over Buckeye's back and settled lightly in the saddle. Lacey envied her long legs and the way she moved with smooth grace. In fact, Wil did everything with grace. She seemed to make friends easily, and business clients treated her with respect. Even the most difficult horses calmed under her steady hand.

A collective groan came from the arena audience.

"Whoa. That's one smart calf, ducking just in time to slip the noose from his horns." The announcer's deep voice boomed over the arena. "That'll be a no time this go-round for the current leaders, Brett Olsen and Rick Simpson. Next up, the Double R Ranch, represented by Wiloree Rivers and Lacey Bishop."

Lacey backed Denver up into position to the left of the calf chute. Her nod would release the calf into the arena, and her lunge to pursue would start their timer, so she had to be precise when a hundredth of a second could mean the difference between first place and no place. She glanced over at Wil, positioned on the other side of the calf chute. A very slight nod told her Wil was set to go. She gave the steward a firm nod, and they were off!

Lacey was already beginning the first swing of her lariat over her head as Denver jumped forward to position them near the left hip of the calf. Wil and Buckeye were also in pursuit on the other side of the calf. Buckeye had to get close enough to keep the calf running forward and not veering away from Denver, but not so close they might interfere with Lacey's rope.

One swing overhead and she released the second one to settle her loop over the hat of fake horns strapped to the calf's head. Denver began sliding to a stop the second Lacey launched her throw, expertly tightening the noose and jerking the calf around when the rope went taut. Wil stood in her stirrups to cast her lariat at the calf's heels, and Buckeye executed a sliding halt before Wil sat again to secure the rope around both hind legs. The second the calf was stretched on the arena floor between them, they released their nooses so the calf wouldn't be hurt.

"And that's the way to do it," the announcer said. "Five-point-four-five seconds for Bishop and Rivers, which moves them into first place."

They grinned at each other as they gathered the loops of their lariats and moved toward the gate to give the next team the arena.

"Way to rope, partner," Wil said. "I only intended to show off Buckeye's talent, but you might have put us in the money."

Lacey laughed. "A bunch of teams haven't run yet, you know. We'll probably get bumped down before the day's over."

"Doesn't matter. Buckeye did his thing perfectly. Ross is probably writing a check right now."

Lacey turned them toward the stabling area, where they'd walk the horses around the warm-up ring a few times before putting them to bed. "He'd be crazy not to."

Wil eyed her. "Why are you entering only barrel racing? The purses are a lot higher in the roping events, even the breakaway roping for ladies."

She shrugged. "I don't know. Barrel racing is what I do. I have no desire to wrestle a calf to the ground in open roping and have no partner for team roping. Plus, the breakaway roping isn't that much more money than barrel racing."

"I'm just saying…it'd be easy money for you."

"I'll keep that in mind."

❖

"You weren't kidding when you said that horse seems to anticipate what comes next," Ross said, smiling at Wil as he pulled out his checkbook. "My boy has always favored buckskin horses, so he'll be happy as a tick on a hound's ear when I bring this one home. Eight thousand, right?"

"I'll give you ten."

Wil turned to the deep-voiced man behind her. "That's tempting, but Ross and I shook on eight thousand yesterday, Mr.—" His eyes seemed familiar, but Wil couldn't quite place or name him.

"Judson Chandler, Sierra Canyon Ranch."

Wil shook the hand he held out to her. She recognized the ranch as a very large operation in New Mexico. "My father is currently training two more ropers we'll have for sale soon. I'll be happy to give you a call when he decides they're ready."

"Thanks, but I need a horse this weekend. One of our roping horses has come up lame, and I need a replacement. Our SCR team is in the top five, and we'll have to forfeit if I don't find a replacement. My boss will give you twelve thousand."

"That's very tempting, Mr. Chandler," Wil said. "But I gave my word to Mr. Martin, and I always stand by our word. It'd be bad business if we didn't."

Judson sneered at her. "Letting a woman do a man's negotiating is bad business. You're an idiot for turning down an additional four thousand." He turned to Ross. "How about this—you give her a check for eight thousand, and then I'll write you a check for twelve. No man is stupid enough to turn down a four-thousand-dollar profit made that quick."

Ross ignored him and finished writing his check for Buckeye. "Here's my check, but don't cash it until after you compete in the team-roping finals. I'm figuring you and your partner have a good chance of placing in the money, and I don't want to stand in the way of that. Maybe you'll earn enough to make up what you're turning down from this guy."

"I appreciate that, Ross."

"Are you deaf, man?" Judson's face was red. "I just offered you a chance to make four thousand dollars."

"And I just listened to you insult Miss Rivers's integrity. I'd much rather do business with her than some jackass who thinks money can buy anything. This horse is the perfect birthday gift for my son, and I'm not selling him to anyone, especially not you." He tore off the check from his book and handed it to Wil.

"You're as stupid as she is." Judson stormed off to where the Sierra Canyon horses were stabled on the other side of the huge building.

"I wrote it for ten thousand to split the difference," Ross said.

Wil glanced at the check. "You don't have to do that. We agreed on eight."

"I know, but the extra two thousand is for not selling to the higher bidder. A lot of people would have. Just do me one favor."

"I will if I can."

"Beat the pants off that guy's team in the finals."

Wil smiled. "I'll do my best."

❖

Lacey lifted the handles on the wheelbarrow, loaded with two bales of hay from her trailer, and guided it toward the stabling building. Cowboys, horses, and trailers were coming and going. The rodeo competitors had been winnowed down to those who would compete in the finals, so a lot of the losers were leaving early for the next rodeo on their schedule. She slowed once she cleared the area where trucks and trailers were parked and had to contend with only foot traffic.

"Well, well. If it isn't Wil Rivers's flavor of the month." Brittney reined Dash in to walk a little too close beside Lacey. "I see she has you doing her sweaty work already."

"For your information, this hay is for my horse." One of the two bales was, but Brittney didn't need to know that.

"So, where's Wil?"

"She's removing the leg wraps on both of our horses while I go for hay." Lacey didn't see any reason to refuse to answer. Brittney could easily go into the stable building and see Wil was there. "I don't think she's keen on seeing you, though."

"Really? She was happy enough to spend the past two weeks with me." Brittney made a dramatic show of covering her mouth with one hand. "Oh. I wasn't supposed to say anything about that."

"Cut the crap, Brittney. Wil and I talked every night before we both went to bed. I knew you were there. I also know about the extra locks Wil installed on her bedroom and bathroom doors to keep you out."

Brittney's smug smile faltered, then grew again. "Every night?"

"Yes, every night." Lacey pushed the wheelbarrow through the wide door.

"You might want to think hard about that."

Lacey ignored Brittney's taunt and turned her wheelbarrow up an aisle to the right, but Brittney got the last word before she guided Dash straight ahead. "I guess that makes you flavor of the week, not the month. It seems Wil likes to go back for a convenient second serving. In the end, she always comes back to me."

CHAPTER SEVENTEEN

First place in this year's team roping goes to Buck Johnson and Kevin Segal, second place to Wiloree Rivers and Lacey Bishop representing the Double R Ranch, and third place to Les Long and Baron Dun of the Sierra Canyon Ranch." The announcement followed Wil and Lacey as they walked the horses back to the stable.

"I'm glad you talked me into team roping," Lacey said. "The second-place cash is nearly as much as a first-place check in barrel racing."

"I can't believe you've been ignoring the roping events," Wil said. "You throw a lariat like you were at a roundup yesterday."

"Well, breakaway roping doesn't pay nearly what the other roping events do. Probably because only women enter breakaway. And, in case you hadn't noticed, I need a partner to enter team roping."

Wil smiled. "Maybe you've found one."

Lacey snorted and shook her head. "You've just sold your roping horse, and I heard you say your father doesn't have any more ready right now. Plus, you can't spend every weekend on the rodeo circuit like I do. You have a ranch to run."

"I know." Wil sighed dramatically. "But a woman can dream, can't she?"

They walked in silence for a while before Lacey noticed Wil was lagging nearly behind her and Denver. She turned in the saddle, but Wil waved for her to keep going. They were almost at the stable entrance when Wil kneed Buckeye to catch up.

"I think you were right the other day when you said Denver didn't seem a hundred percent. She looks stiff."

"Damn. I thought maybe it was me who was sore since I haven't thrown a lariat much lately." She hurried to dismount, and Wil did the same. They took turns, with one walking Denver and the other watching for signs of lameness.

"I think you should get the rodeo vet to take a look. She seems to be favoring that left front a little, but she also looks a bit stiff in her rear."

Lacey bit her lip. "Yeah. It looks like that to me, too."

"I'll track down the vet," Wil said, remounting Buckeye and starting down the long aisle between the stalls.

"Okay. Thanks." While Lacey acknowledged Wil's departure, her mind was on Denver. Would she be even stiffer tomorrow? Should she pull her from the competition? She already had a check from the team-roping competition. Maybe she should be satisfied with that. Had participating in the roping event caused an injury? Nah. Roping was much easier on the horses than barrel racing. If Denver was lame, where would Lacey go from here? She had already won enough money in barrel racing to pay her expenses at the national finals, but it was too late in the season to earn enough points to enter as a team roper. Besides, she didn't have a team. This gig with Wil had been a one-off deal to help her sell Buckeye. Even if she had enough time before the finals to climb the ranks in team roping, Wil couldn't travel the rodeo circuit with her. She had a ranch she was struggling to keep in the black.

She removed Denver's saddle and bridle, sponged off her sweaty spots, then carefully checked each hoof for tenderness or some foreign object wedged between the shoe and the underside of her hoof. All clean, but the mare shifted uncomfortably when Lacey lifted her left front leg to inspect the hoof. She ran her hands along Denver's shoulder and down her leg to feel for heat that would indicate inflammation. The knee was a bit warm. She started a massage of Denver's left shoulder, but the mare shifted away as Lacey moved lower to her chest.

"Vet's on his way."

Lacey started at Wil's voice coming from the aisle. She hadn't even heard her ride up on Buckeye.

"Sorry. I wasn't trying to sneak up on you. I thought you would have heard us coming up the aisle." Wil spoke from the stall next to Denver's while she freed Buckeye of his saddle and bridle. "The doc was at the livestock pens looking at a calf with a bruised sole. He'll be here in about twenty minutes."

"She's sore on the left side of her chest, and her knee in the left front feels warm," Lacey said.

"Well, you couldn't tell she wasn't a hundred percent when she went after that calf," Wil said. "She was fast and her timing great."

"That's what I love about this mare. She has a lot of heart. I think she'd try to run even if she had a broken leg."

Wil left Buckeye's stall, came into Denver's, and hugged Lacey to her. "I'm sure it's not that serious. Let's wait to see what the vet says."

❖

Doc Baker clicked through the X-ray images on his laptop screen while Lacey and Wil watched over his shoulder. "You see this? Inflammation of the fetlock is the most common injury for barrel racers, and you usually see it on the left front like the injury you've got here. That's because the horse has to make one right turn and two left turns around the barrels."

Lacey frowned. "Denver's never shown any signs of injury or inflammation before. I check her over thoroughly before and after each competition."

Doc Baker nodded. "This isn't an injury in the purest sense. It's simply wear and tear. How long have you been racing her?"

Lacey ducked her head, reluctant to answer the question. "Pretty much nonstop for five or six years. I got her cheap at the auction over in Bowie and trained her myself. I've also used her to work roundups for extra money before she got good enough to start winning at rodeos."

"You're either really lucky or have a very good eye for horseflesh." He stepped just inside the stall and appraised Denver, who was munching her sweet feed. "How old is she?"

"Eighteen. I have her papers. She's registered as half Arab. Her dame was Arabian and her sire a registered Quarter horse."

He nodded. "How are you doing in this rodeo?"

"I'm in first place right now."

"You have another horse you can ride tomorrow?"

Lacey scowled because, if she didn't, she was going to cry. "No, sir. I don't."

He lifted his hat to scratch his mop of white hair, then smoothed it back to reseat his hat. "Well, this type of injury normally needs three months to fully heal to race again. We can do a couple of things to get through the final round, but don't expect to get your best time from her, and running her will aggravate this injury for sure."

"I'm not going to run her hurt."

"You can ride Pepper tomorrow." Lacey and Doc Baker turned to stare at Wil, who had been quietly listening, but stepped closer to make her offer. "Our ranch is only two hours away. You're pretty far down in the lineup. I can leave in the morning and be back with her before you have to run."

"I can't compete on a horse I've never ridden before."

Doc Baker spoke up. "I have a client who teaches youngsters how to barrel race. She lives about fifteen minutes from here and has an outdoor ring permanently set up with barrels. I could give her a call to see if you could do a few practice rounds there tomorrow, if you can get that horse here sooner."

Lacey was skeptical. She wasn't used to people offering help. She'd always kept to herself and been on her own. Well, except for Joel and Maggie. They were different. And as infatuated as she was with Wil, they'd known each other only a short time. "I don't know." She looked at Wil. "What if something happened, and Pepper got injured? I know you were looking for a buyer for her."

"She's insured, but nothing's going to happen except you winning. It'll be good exposure for her." Wil's face lit up. "Hey, if you finished out the season and placed in the national finals on Pepper, I could add another ten or twenty grand to her price. You could bring Denver to the Double R to heal and take Pepper to Big Spring, then the national finals."

Was Wil asking her to move in with her…at least for the next month or two? She'd not only be driving the old lesbian-clichéd U-Haul, but she'd also be hauling a horse trailer behind it. This was happening all too fast. Her hopes of winning a big payoff at the national finals in six weeks had ended when Doc Baker said Denver would need three months to recover. And he'd warned that, after recovery, she might never reach her peak times again. So, what would happen after the national finals? Would she feel trapped there? She'd always been a free-wheeling nomad and never thought about settling down. Was that what Wil was offering? Was that what Lacey wanted? She didn't have time to think about it now. She couldn't afford to turn down the use of Pepper tomorrow. She was one ride away from a first-place prize of five thousand dollars.

"Okay," Lacey said. "But maybe you should leave tonight, so you can get back earlier and give me time to try out Pepper in the morning."

"We'll figure that out if Doc can arrange that place to practice."

"I'll call Trina soon and text her address to you if her facility is available," he said.

❖

"Next up is Lacey Bishop, currently ranked sixth nationally in barrel standings."

Lacey had mixed feelings about Pepper. She'd proved very fast when they'd practiced together that morning, but Pepper was bulkier than the very slim Denver and had a longer stride because of her height. Although both had the short backs required to make agile turns around the barrels, Pepper had the beefy rump that made Quarter horses the top sprinters of the equine breeds. Lacey had to rethink her usual timing on turns. The divergent personalities of the two mares also had her feeling off-kilter. She'd ridden Denver exclusively for the past six or seven years and had become accustomed to her prancing and twirling with excitement when they entered the chute for a run at the barrels, then launching from one last twirl like she was the rock in a slingshot. Pepper walked calmly into the long chute, and she preferred to come to a full stop before breaking out of the chute like a racehorse from a starting gate.

They stopped several feet from the end of the chute, and Lacey felt Pepper tense under her. She bent close to the mare's neck and whispered. "Wings on your feet, sweet girl. Wings on your feet." Then she clapped her legs against Pepper's flanks, and they rocketed out of the chute.

Denver's turns were tighter, but Pepper's sprint to the next barrel was so fast, Lacey had to hold on when she came out of each turn. Their pace was blistering, and she was breathless when they flew past the electronic eye of the timer.

Lacey reined Pepper in and swung around. Obviously invigorated by the run, Pepper slowed only to a ground-covering trot to return to where Wil waited at the outside end of the chute.

"Wow. She really flew with a lighter rider. Could you feel how fast you were going?" Wil asked.

Lacey was about to answer but held up a finger when the results of her run came over the loudspeaker.

"Miss Bishop's time of thirteen-point-nine-oh sets a new record for this arena and keeps her in first place, with five more riders still to run."

She felt her eyes go wide and sputtered. "I knew we were fast but didn't expect such an amazing time."

Wil beamed at her. "I train only the best."

Lacey smiled back. "You *are* the best."

They stared into each other's eyes for a long moment until the next rider was announced for their run.

"Brittney's turn is coming up soon," Wil said. She flagged down a teen Lacey recognized as one of the junior competitors and dug her wallet out of her pocket. "Hey. I'll pay you twenty dollars to cool down this mare while we watch the next barrel racer. Just walk her around the warm-up area."

The kid, who Lacey judged to be around twelve or thirteen years old, was clearly eager for the easy money. "Yes, ma'am. I can do that." He took Pepper's reins from Lacey.

Wil handed him the money. "Thanks, buddy. We won't be long."

Lacey frowned. "What's keeping him from running off with your horse and your money?"

"I know his father, and he's a good kid. Dad trained the horse he's riding this weekend in the junior team roping."

"Okay then. Let's find a good seat."

They hustled back into the arena and found third-row seats as the current barrel racer was finishing her run. Among the four riders left to run, only Brittney had a good chance of stealing the big money from Lacey.

"Next rider is Brittney Abbott, running a close second behind Lacey Bishop in both fastest single score and top cumulative time."

The crowd, which had been milling about and finding their seats for the bronc riding that would follow, seemed to pause in place and hold a collective breath. A long second later, Brittney and Dash burst into the near-silent arena. Their first turn was excellent, as was the second. Brittney appeared to be taking Wil's advice to let Dash judge the turns. Now they approached the third barrel, which was Brittney's kryptonite.

"Don't push him. Let him take the turn." Wil muttered the instructions through gritted teeth. "Don't push. He knows what to do."

Lacey kept her gaze fixed on the third barrel. Would Brittney knock it down as she had so many times in her eagerness to sprint for the timer? Damn, she was running fast. Her lessons with Wil had obviously paid off.

Brittney urged Dash toward the barrel, but at the last minute, she sat back and let him slow. Her foot tapped the barrel, and it tipped but didn't fall.

"Go, go, go," Wil yelled.

The applause was deafening. Had people clapped that hard for her run? Even Wil was nodding her affirmation of Brittney's ride.

"Fourteen seconds flat for Brittney Abbott. A fantastic run, folks, but not fast enough to steal first place."

"Let's go retrieve Pepper." Lacey stood and headed out of the arena without looking to see if Wil was following. She understood that Wil had trained Dash and some of her reputation was riding on Brittney's success, but, damn, Wil's enthusiasm rubbed her the wrong way.

CHAPTER EIGHTEEN

Wil woke slowly, savoring the warmth of Lacey, naked and half sprawled on top of her. She smiled without opening her eyes. She wished she could freeze time and that moment forever. She'd decided to stay at the Abilene rodeo facilities another night so she could deliver Buckeye on Monday, the actual birthday of Ross Martin's son. A little persuasion—takeout from a local steakhouse and streaming a movie—had convinced Lacey to stay the extra night, too. Wil chuckled to herself. A few heated kisses—a promise of what would come after the movie—sealed the deal.

"Why is my mattress shaking?" Lacey's voice was hoarse with sleep, and she nipped at Wil's nearest nipple. "Bad mattress. Go back to sleep."

"Ow." Wil waited for a heartbeat. "Do that again."

"Sleep."

"I thought you were an early riser."

"I am when I don't have any reason to stay in bed." Lacey flicked her tongue against the still-hard nipple.

"Ah. We can stay in bed another hour," Wil said, flipping them so she hovered over Lacey. "But I don't plan to spend it sleeping."

❖

Lacey glanced around to see if anyone was watching them, then gave Wil one last kiss. "I'm going to miss your mouth."

"Only my mouth?" Wil was headed for Jacksboro to drop off Buckeye, then on to Bowie to check on things at the Double R. She was to rejoin Lacey in Sweetwater on Thursday.

"Nope. I'll miss your delicious body, too."

"I see how it is. You just love my body." Wil's tone was teasing, but her smile was tentative.

Lacey brushed her lips against Wil's. "No, silly. I'll miss all of you."

Wil's smile widened. "Good. Because I might start feeling objectified and not show up in Sweetwater."

She bestowed one more feathery kiss. God, she loved Wil's lips. "I'm not worried." Her smile was smug. "I've got your horse." Lacey planned to drive in the opposite direction to the Sweetwater rodeo, with both Denver and Pepper riding in her trailer.

Wil laughed. "Yes, you do. Drive careful."

"You drive safe, too. You have a lot farther to go."

Wil sighed. "Then I guess I need to get going."

"Call me tonight?"

"Wouldn't sleep if I didn't," Wil said. "Now get out of my truck."

Lacey laughed and climbed down from the big dually. She stepped back and waved. "See you soon."

❖

Ray Rivers strode toward Wil's truck as she pulled in and parked it alongside the main barn. "Hey, we missed you around here. Need some help unloading?"

Wil stepped down from her truck and snagged her duffel from the back seat of the crew cab. "Nothing to unload." She pulled Ross's check from her pocket and handed it to her dad. "I sold Buckeye to a fellow named Ross Martin and delivered him on the way home."

Ray's eyes widened when he looked at the check. "You sold him for ten thousand? I was afraid I'd have to take less than eight since a lot of people like us are still trying to catch up financially."

"Actually, I was offered twelve thousand, but I already had a handshake deal with Ross for eight."

"How'd you end up with ten?"

"I refused to break my deal with Ross, so he split the difference. He didn't like the guy offering twelve either and was buying Buckeye for his son's birthday. I think Ross was as excited as his boy when I delivered that horse."

Ray nodded and grinned. "That's really good. Every kid remembers their first horse fondly. Who was the other guy?"

"Didn't know him. Said his name was Judson Chandler from Sierra Canyon Ranch."

Ray scowled. "He's got to be near my age. He was around when I was riding in rodeos."

"He wasn't competing. He said he was there to supervise a team of cowboys riding for the Sierra Canyon in various events."

"Last I heard, that ranch was trying to make a name for itself raising bucking horses and bulls for stock contractors. I guess having some of their boys on the circuit helps that goal. I don't like how they treat their animals, but the rodeo inspectors always keep a close eye on them because of their reputation."

"He wanted Buckeye because one of their horses was injured, and his team was among the contenders to win team roping. They dug up a horse from somewhere because they came in third in the finals."

"Well, I'm glad he didn't get Buckeye, and I don't want to ever sell to them."

"I totally agree." Wil hooked her arm in her dad's as they walked into the barn for a couple of brooms to sweep out the trailer she'd just used. "We won't miss the extra two thousand, though." She pulled the second check from her pocket and handed it to him. "Lacey and I came in second in team roping."

Ray took the check and laughed. "Did you now? That's my girl. Maybe I should put you out on the rodeo circuit instead of training horses here at the ranch."

"I'm glad you said that."

His smile faltered, and he stopped at the barn's entrance. "Wait. Where's Pepper? I thought you maybe swiped her in the middle of the night because you had a buyer for her. Do you have another check you want to whip out?"

Wil pointed at him. "Good question." She grabbed a couple of brooms from the tack room, then began explaining the plans for Lacey to ride Pepper through the National Finals Rodeo.

❖

Wil growled when her iPad froze again as Lacey was mid-sentence. She picked up her phone and texted. *Calling because the storm here is getting worse and our internet keeps cutting out.* She waited for Lacey to answer.

"Hey," Lacey said. "What's the last thing you heard before your internet crapped out?"

"You were saying something about Brittney."

"Oh, yeah. She's entered here in Sweetwater. She never goes to rodeos this small."

"I'm not surprised. She was pissed that you beat her in Abilene. She's looking to get back at you."

"Dash is pretty good."

"I know. I trained him, remember?"

"You also trained Brittney." Lacey paused at her accusatory tone. "I'm sorry. That was unfair."

"She'll never be the rider you are. She had a great horse and two weeks of coaching from me, but she still couldn't beat you and Pepper."

"Sweet talker."

"Just stating the obvious," Wil said.

"Did you want to—" A huge boom of thunder drowned out Lacey's next words.

"Say it again. I couldn't hear you over the thunder."

"I asked if I should register us for team roping, too."

"Yes. Definitely. I'm sure the payout here isn't as large as in Abilene, but it'd be good practice for Big Spring." Lightning flashed, and thunder boomed a mere second later. Wil flinched. "Damn. That one was close."

"Wil, we should hang up."

"This isn't the old days when lightning could travel inside on electric or phone lines."

"I know, but I can hardly hear you over the noise. You probably should check on the horses in your barn. They might be freaking out."

"You're right. Wait." Her father was shouting from the front door. "Dad's yelling about something."

"Go see what he wants. But be careful if you go out in that storm."

"I will. See you Thursday?"

"I'm counting on it," Lacey said. "Talk to you soon."

Wil wanted to say more. "I love you" was on the tip of her tongue, but Lacey was gone. Thank God. What was she thinking? Actually, she wasn't thinking with her head. The declaration was too soon and would likely scare Lacey into running. "Bye," she said to the severed connection.

"Wil, Wil..." Lightning flashed, and thunder shook the house a second later. "...fire!" The word dreaded on any farm or ranch jerked her into action. Before she could think, she threw her phone onto the bed and was in the living room with her father. Then they were running out into the downpour.

They sprinted to the main barn, relieved to see the horses restless and spooked by the thunder, but safe in their stalls.

"Jimmy said...the barn...was on fire." Ray panted out the words, his lungs still suffering.

They turned toward the bunkhouse and saw Jimmy running toward them. He stopped and pointed to the huge old barn a hundred yards behind the bunkhouse. Flames shot up from the top, and one end of the roof collapsed into the structure.

"The hay barn. It's the hay barn that's on fire," Jimmy shouted. "Lightning hit the roof. I called the fire department."

Sirens sounded in the distance, but they all knew it was useless. Those old barns went up in minutes, the heat so intense no one could get within twenty yards of it. Plus, that barn was filled with newly cut bales of hay so nitrogen rich, many were exploding in the heat. Not even the storm's downpour could quench the inferno. The firefighters' only job would be to soak the surrounding grass and closest structures to prevent the fire from spreading. Wil saw the dozen feral cats that lived in the barn running through the field to safety. She hoped they all were able to escape.

The fire trucks arrived, and men ran to lay hoses that would suck water from the manmade pond nearby to spray the ground and bunkhouse, since the storm moved through fast and took its rain with it. Ray, Wil, and Jimmy stood by helplessly.

"Dad? How bad is this?"

"This summer's high temperatures hurt our yield some, but we had two cuttings already put up—about two thousand bales. All that's ash now. We might get a third cutting if we have a little more rain in the next month, but it won't be good enough for the horses. We'll feed it to the cattle."

Wil nodded. The barn and its contents were insured, but there would be a thousand-dollar deductible, a new barn would cost significantly more than the insured value of the old structure, and the policy wouldn't pay enough to replace several thousand bales at the current prices. Also, finding enough quality hay for sale this late in the season would be tough. Smaller ranches that didn't have enough land to grow their own usually contracted with hay growers at the first of the summer to buy a set number of bales. Hopefully, the growers had baled more than they contracted.

❖

Wil rubbed her eyes and dialed one more number. "Hey, could I speak to Thurmond Dunst?"

The man on the other end of the call barked a big horse laugh. "Honey, nobody but my mama calls me Thurmond."

"I'm sorry, Mr. Dunst. This is Wiloree Rivers at the Double R. I was calling because I heard you have some horse-quality hay for sale."

"Butch. Just call me Butch. Are you Ray Rivers's kid by any chance?"

"Yes. He's my dad."

"Knew him back in the day when he was still rodeoing, but I'm sure you weren't calling me about that. I thought Ray cut his own hay."

"We do, but lightning hit our hay barn last night, and we lost it all. I'm trying to contract enough to get us through the winter."

"Well, you're in luck. A couple of the smaller farms that usually contract with us had to call it quits, so we have some extra to sell. How much do you need?"

"A thousand bales. What's your price? And do you have any left from your second cutting?" The second cutting in the spring would be the tenderest and have the highest protein content.

"About two hundred bales of first-cut Bermuda are left, at eight dollars a bale. I can sell you another six hundred of second-cut Bermuda at the same price, and two hundred of second-cut premium alfalfa for ten dollars."

Wil did quick calculations in her head. At eighty-four hundred, his prices were better than fair compared to what she'd agreed to pay for the first thousand she'd already secured. "I'll take that deal."

"It's an extra eight hundred if you want it delivered."

"Nope. Dad and Jimmy will drive some trailers up to retrieve it. Do I need to send workers to load it?"

"Got you covered there."

"Thanks, Mr. Dunst, er, Butch. We appreciate it. I know you could have gouged us since it's so late in the season and most hay's already sold."

"Now, that wouldn't do much for my reputation, would it?"

"No, sir. It wouldn't, but that doesn't stop a lot of people. I appreciate your integrity. Dad will get a cashier's check and pick up the hay next Tuesday, if that's okay."

"That'll be fine. You have a good day."

"Same to you."

Wil was exhausted. She'd watched the fire until dawn, then provided ham biscuits and coffee to the firefighters before catching three hours of sleep, then hitting the phones. She had to arrange for the insurance adjuster to come out, then haggle with her dad over whether they should go with a metal building or build another wooden barn to replace the burned one. Ray liked the tradition of wooden barns, and the cost of wood had come down since the recent high prices, but there was still a shortage, which could have them waiting on timber more than a month. A metal building would reduce the chance of another fire, was available immediately, and could be erected before materials for a wooden barn would be delivered.

She had only a moment because she still had horses to train, groom, and feed, but she relaxed into the tall-backed leather office chair and closed her eyes. The ruins of the hay barn wouldn't be cool enough to poke through until tomorrow. She woke with a start.

Lacey's ring tone was going off somewhere in the house. Damn it. She didn't mean to fall asleep. She looked around the desk in confusion, then realized the last time she'd had her cell phone was in her bedroom, talking to Lacey the night before. She dashed down the hall, but the ringing had stopped. She tapped her cell phone to wake it, surprised to see her unintended nap had lasted ninety minutes. Her notifications showed a dozen texts from Lacey before she finally called a moment ago. She hit redial.

"Hey. I was leaving a message. Are you okay?" Lacey sounded frantic.

"I've been better." She blew out a breath and was about to elaborate when Lacey jumped in with a barrage of rapid-fire questions.

"Where are you? You're not in the hospital, are you? Is your dad okay? Is the ranch okay?"

"Whoa. Lightning hit our hay barn last night, and it burned to the ground with all of our hay for the winter, but no one was hurt."

After a few seconds of silence, Lacey responded, her voice tight. "Local news is reporting several tornadoes touched down in that area last night, and two people are dead. When I couldn't get in touch with you, I was scared to death something had happened."

"I'm sorry. I didn't know that. No tornado here, but we were up all night with the firemen, making sure sparks from the hay barn didn't catch on any other structures on the ranch."

Lacey's tone turned from worried to irritated. "I wish you'd phoned, or at least texted to let me know you were okay. Last night's call ended with your father yelling something at you. All kinds of things have been running through my head today when you didn't answer any of my texts."

"Sorry. I left my phone on the bed last night when I ran out to see what Dad was yelling about and forgot about it until I heard your ringtone going off somewhere in the house." Wil was too tired to listen to a lecture, but Lacey was on a roll.

"You should always keep your phone with you—especially during a storm. You didn't even get the tornado alerts. Those two people reported dead could have been you and your father."

She understood why Lacey was so upset, but she was too sleep-deprived to stop her own irritation. "I had about three hours of sleep and have been in the office since ten this morning, trying to find enough hay to replace what we lost and get bids on a new barn so we'll have a place to store what hay I could find this late in the season. With everything else I have to do, checking my phone for texts isn't a priority." She regretted the words as soon as they left her mouth and Lacey went silent on the other end of the call. She was about to apologize again, when Lacey finally spoke.

"I'm sorry. I won't take up any more of your valuable time."

"Wait. I didn't mean that. I'm just beyond tired and stressed."

The only answer was a beep, indicating the call had been ended. She pounded the side of her fist on her forehead. "Stupid, stupid, stupid." She tried to reinitiate the call, but voice mail immediately picked up, so she fired off a text.

I'm so sorry. I absolutely didn't mean that when it comes to you. I'm exhausted, but that's not a good excuse. I have to go work horses right now, but please answer when I call tonight.

Lacey was stunned and speechless. She ended the call without thinking. The woman on the phone wasn't the sweet, thoughtful Wil she'd been dating. But didn't everybody have moments of being too stressed? Yeah. Her father had disappeared when supporting a kid and her mother became too much for him. And her mother drank away the stress of being stuck with a kid without a man to help support them. Hell, her aunt probably died just to get away from her, too. But, God damn it, she was her own person and would not be anybody's whipping boy.

She ignored her phone when Wil's ringtone sounded immediately after Lacey had disconnected the call, then powered down her phone. She needed time to think before she talked to Wil again…if ever.

She walked into the night, to the building where Denver and Pepper were stabled. Her mare was the only one who never let her down. She ran her heart out in Abilene, even though she was injured. Denver would have done the same in the finals of that rodeo, if she'd asked it of her. Had she let herself be sucked into believing Wil's heart was like that, too? No. Everybody had bad days. Wil was suffering from an immensely bad day. With her father physically compromised, so much rested on her shoulders. She didn't deserve to shoulder Lacey's insecurities, too.

She reactivated her phone and read Wil's text. The message sounded a lot more like her Wil. She answered with a text.

❖

Wil laid her forehead on the desk. She hadn't cried since her father was at his lowest with the virus and she thought she'd be orphaned. But she cried now. She didn't know if she could manage one more crisis in her life.

"You okay, short-stuff?" Her dad hadn't used her childhood nickname since…well, since she was a child. She had nearly matched him in height since she was a teen.

She didn't look up as she swiped her sleeved arm across her face as though she was wiping away sleep, not tears. "Yeah. I'm just really tired." Still refusing to look up, she took a deep breath. This was no time to indulge herself as Daddy's little girl again. Back to business. "I've called around and found two thousand bales of hay. It's going to cost us, though. I told them we'd come pick it up to save delivery costs. You and Jimmy can haul it on the flatbeds."

"I need to stay on the ranch. Jake Meadows is coming to look at Blue Cat. I think I can get $30,000 for him. Jimmy can talk to Nora Hansen. Her boys are seventeen now and strong as bulls. If she'll give permission for them to miss a little school, I know they can use the money."

"Dad, you can't use the money from Cat to replace the barn and hay. We need it to buy horses you can train to sell next year. If we don't, we'll be in the same financial fix we're in now."

"I know. I've been thinking about that. I'm going to put Diamond up for sale."

"No, Dad. We'll figure something else out. You've been training him to be your personal horse on the ranch. Old Barback needs to retire."

"I need to semi-retire, too, but we both have a few more years left in us. I'll find another prospect to replace Barback. Take

Diamond with you to Sweetwater to give him some exposure in the team roping. Lacey is entering that with you again, isn't she?"

"Yeah. At least I think she is." Her eyes teared with fatigue and uncertainty. This was ridiculous.

Her dad knelt next to her chair and took her face in his big, rough hands. "Hey, short-stuff. What's this about?" He pulled a bandanna from his pocket and dabbed her eyes.

"I'm just tired, and we have so much to do. And when Lacey called a little while ago, I was a jerk. She said it was on the news that several tornadoes had touched down in this area and two people were killed. She was worried it was us."

"Oh, good Lord. I hope it wasn't anyone we know. Your mama must be looking out for us. Instead of us losing a hay barn, a tornado could have taken out the house and main barn, too. We'd be homeless and out of business."

"I was just too exhausted to think of all that, and I snapped when she started to lecture me about keeping my phone with me at all times."

"She's right. Working with cows and horses can be dangerous. With us spread out all over this big ranch, one of us could get hurt with nobody else around." A sudden panic flashed in his eyes. "One of your racers could slip and fall on you, breaking your leg or worse. If you didn't have your phone to call us, it might be most of the day before one of us realized you were missing and go look for you."

She took his hands and calmed her voice. "Dad, what happened to Mom was a freak accident. I swear I'm careful." The tables had turned, and she was consoling him.

"Your mother wasn't reckless either, damn it. And you better keep your phone on you."

"I will. I promise."

He nodded and seemed to collect himself. "Good. Did you make the same promise to that sweet girl you're courting?"

Wil shook her head and blinked back new tears as her throat tightened around her answer. "She said she wouldn't take up any more of my time, then hung up on me."

He gave her a half smile. "I swear the fire in that girl reminds me a lot of your mother. You called her right back, didn't you?"

"Yes." She explained what had happened.

"Okay. Help me stand up." He braced one hand on the desk, and she held on to his other arm to help him rise from where he'd knelt next to her. Then he took her phone and looked at the text she'd sent. "I reckon that's better than I could have done with your mother. I finally figured out that I needed to give her time to cool off before I crawled on these bad knees to her." He was still holding her phone when it signaled a new text. "Speak of the devil."

Wil stood to grab for the phone he snatched up, but he held it out of her reach and read the incoming text.

I'm sorry. I was freaked out with worry for you and had no idea you'd been up all night with a barn fire. I'm still learning how to care for someone other than Denver and me. I'll answer when you call tonight.

He handed the phone to her. "See? She just needed to step back and calm down."

Wil read the text several times as relief flooded her. When she looked up again, Ray was studying her.

"You really care for that girl, don't you?" he asked.

"She's not like any woman I've ever dated." She looked into her dad's eyes. "She might be the one. We still need time to really know each other, but I'm pretty hooked already."

"Well, I'm no expert on women, but your mother spent a lot of years training me in what to do and not do. So, if you need an ear or a shoulder to lean on, I'm always here."

She stepped closer and laid her head on his broad shoulder. "I know, Dad. I've always known that shoulder was there when I needed it."

He pulled her into a tight hug. "And don't you forget it." He released her, took her phone, and tucked it into her pocket. "Now, you keep that thing with you, or I'll put it in a pouch and tie it around your neck."

She smirked. "How about I get one of those phone holsters you put on your belt instead?"

"See, I knew you were the idea person around here. I'm the planner, and here's today's plan. Jimmy's in the bunkhouse right now making bacon-and-tomato sandwiches for all of us. You're going to eat some lunch, go work that crazy racehorse, then come back to the house for a long nap. But you're going to turn that phone all the way up and leave it right by your head so you don't sleep through it if that girl calls you."

"You need to sleep, too, Dad."

"I'm good. I had six solid hours. You're the one who got up so quick and started making calls about the barn and hay." He steered her out of the office and toward the bunkhouse.

"I think we should go with a metal building." She put a hand up, palm out, to stop his reply. "I called around, and so much of the wood we'd need is on back order, it could take months to finish a new barn."

"Okay."

"Okay?" She'd braced for a fight to get him to accept metal.

"That's all I was going to say when you put your hand out like a traffic cop."

She shook her head. "I think a tornado did come through here and landed us in an alternate universe."

CHAPTER NINETEEN

Lacey was nervous as she watched Wil climb down from her truck. They'd both apologized in video chats several times, but both were cautious after having their first fight. Wil had been a myopic jerk. Lacey had hung up, fled, at the first sign of trouble. Would their kisses be as passionate? Would their touches feel the same?

They stood ten feet apart, eyeing each other cautiously.

"Hey," Wil said, sliding her hands into the pockets of her jeans.

"Hey." Lacey wiped the back of her hand across her mouth when she realized she was chewing her bottom lip. It was her worst nervous tell. "Who do you have in the trailer?" Horses were always a safe subject between them.

"Diamond Jack. Dad was planning to keep him but decided we needed to sell him to help pay for the barn. I brought him for the team roping this weekend and at Big Spring so we can show him off some. Then Dad's going to take him to a reining competition to push his price up."

"Good idea." Lacey followed Wil to the back of the trailer to help unload Diamond and stared when they lowered the trailer ramp. The stocky sorrel stallion was the spitting image of one of the greatest Quarter horses on record. "Jesus, he's Two Eyed Jack reincarnated."

"He's from that line. Dad originally wanted to keep him as a breeding stallion. We don't currently have one on the ranch. But this horse is so gentle and trainable, he planned to also claim him as his personal ride. Come in and check him out."

The two-horse, slant-load trailer was roomy, and Wil ducked

under the stallion's neck to his other side while Lacey approached the horse cautiously. Stallions could be temperamental, and Sweetwater was the first noisy, chaotic rodeo for this guy. He turned his head to look at her and nickered. She let him sniff her hand, and the whiskers on his nose tickled her fingers. Assured of his acceptance, she ran her other hand over his back and large rump. His coat shone like silk.

"Wow. I can see why your father wants to keep him for breeding. He's gorgeous." She looked up at Wil. "Can't you sell some other horse?"

Wil sighed. "No. He and Pepper are all we have left that are ready. I'm sure Dad will negotiate to get several breedings from him as part of the deal."

Lacey ducked under Diamond's neck to join Wil on his other side. She clasped Wil's forearm. "I'm so sorry you have to get rid of him because the barn burned down."

Wil stared down at her hand. "Is it okay if I kiss you? I've been dying to since I got out of my truck."

No further invitation needed, Lacey moved closer and grasped Wil's nape to pull her down to her ready lips.

❖

Though Pepper's calm control and physical cues were becoming more familiar, Lacey missed Denver's whirlwind of energy indicative of her hot Arabian blood when they approached the arena for a run around the barrels. Pepper barely pranced, but Lacey knew to hold on when she brought her to a stop. She felt Pepper gather under her like a coiled spring, then clapped her legs against the mare's sides. They were a controlled missile, blasting into the arena with the first barrel in sight. Also trained in reining, Pepper responded quickly to leg pressure and the slightest touch of the reins against her neck.

They rounded the first barrel cleanly with a perfect trajectory to the second one. Whereas Denver's turns and accelerations between barrels were one smooth run, Pepper's turns were wider and slower, but were followed by powerful, warp-drive sprints to the next barrel or finish line.

They broke the timer's beam before Lacey had barely drawn a handful of breaths. Her time flashed on the scoreboard.

Damn, this horse was good. But was it the horse or Wil's training that made her that fast?

Wil met them at the chute. "Dang. You guys rocked that run."

"Thirteen-point-eight-nine. That wraps up the barrel-racing with Lacey Bishop solidly in first place, a half second ahead of Brittney Abbott. Third place goes to Lisa Newman. We'll have a twenty-minute break, and then saddle broncs are up."

Lacey returned Wil's grin. They'd won second in the team roping again, and that celebration, along with this moment of exultation, felt like the old chemistry that burned between them.

Even though apologies had healed their earlier rift on the surface, a few deep cracks in their trust had remained. Lacey could feel Wil cautiously measuring her words as if uncertain how Lacey would respond to a conversation or situation. And, honestly? Lacey was still unconsciously expecting to find out there was an alternate Wil under the charming woman who was courting her. Would her sweet Wil turn into a different person if they proceeded down this path to some type of commitment?

People often did that. Her father no doubt was a charming suitor until her mother became pregnant, before he changed into a jerk and disappeared. Good thing Wil couldn't get her pregnant. Lacey chuckled at that thought, and Wil looked at her quizzically.

"What?" Wil asked as she rode Diamond alongside while Lacey cooled down Pepper.

"Nothing." She looked at Wil. "Just happy." And as Wil gazed at her with a soft smile and open affection, she pushed away her doubts for that moment and let herself be truly happy.

❖

Though Diamond's coat already gleamed under the stable building's light, Wil continued to run the soft brush over his back. Her strokes were a calming therapy for both her and the horse, even though Diamond didn't need to be calmed. He was nearly comatose, head lowered and bottom lip hanging in relaxation, from her gentle ministrations. The repetitive motion, however, had helped her think through a myriad of problems and situations since she was tall enough to reach the backs of the horses in the Double R's barn.

Today, she was pondering her growing feelings for Lacey and, well, worrying she could disappear from her life in a blink. The thought nauseated her. Nothing other than the loan of Pepper was keeping Lacey on the rodeo circuit. Would their blossoming romance be enough to keep her in Wil's life if something happened to that arrangement? The uncertainty nagged at her. Lacey's past experience with relationships—her father, her mother, and the other women on the rodeo circuit—made her a flight risk. Wil had so much other stress in her life, was she willing to gamble with her heart in this tenuous situation? Trouble was, she was already irrevocably hooked. Despite her mental machinations, she smiled to herself at the memory of Lacey shining with excitement over her successful runs with Pepper. She lived for the moments that Lacey looked into her eyes with lust and affection. Yeah. She was hooked.

"Ms. Rivers, isn't it?"

Wil turned to find an unwelcome visitor standing in the doorway of Diamond's stall. "Yes." She stilled her brush but kept a hand on the stallion's withers. "And you're from Sierra Canyon Ranch, if I remember correctly."

"Judson Chandler."

She remembered who he was but nodded at his confirmation. His macho demeanor rubbed her wrong, but something more, something familiar disquieted her. "What can I do for you, Mr. Chandler?"

"I don't see your roping partner around."

"Were you looking for her?" She didn't think it was any of his business that Lacey had gone to pick up dinner for both of them.

He eyed her for a second. "No, but I *am* still looking for a new roping horse. The one that was injured in Abilene is done on the circuit. My boss is interested in that stallion you have there. What's his asking price?"

"More than you want to pay for a roping horse. I brought him here mostly to get him used to the noise of a rodeo. He's also trained for reining and left ungelded because—as you can obviously see—the Two Eyed Jack bloodline is strong in him. My father plans to campaign him at a few reining competitions before setting a price, but it will be well into five figures."

"Sierra Canyon is always looking for good investments. You tell your father to give my boss a call."

Wil stepped away from Diamond Jack and straightened to her full height to look the man directly in the face. "You need to understand a few things, Mr. Chandler. One, my father and I are fifty-fifty partners in the Double R. We make our decisions together. Two, I spoke with him about what you tried to pull in Abilene with Buckeye. We agreed that neither of us is comfortable doing business with you." She didn't think it was necessary to tell him she hadn't told her father how Judson had spoken down to her before. She didn't need Ray to fight her battles for her or to have to bail her father out of jail.

"Now, hold on. I was just doing what any savvy businessman would do."

She interrupted his interruption. "Third, the entire rodeo circuit is aware of Sierra Canyon's injury rate. My father and I will not sell our highly trained horses to any organization that disregards the health and care of its stock."

He stepped forward, placing his face inches from hers, and sneered. "Don't you turn your nose up at me, you pussy-sniffing pervert. Yeah. I know all about you, so you and your high-and-mighty father might want to consider whether you want the rest of the rodeo circuit to know who you munch on in that camper at night."

Wil blinked, his threat blindsiding her. Then her shock turned to seething. She poked him in his chest as she spoke. "My sexual orientation has no bearing on Double R business or our success."

He pushed her finger away. "We'll see about that, dyke. Folks might not care about the trash you're hitting now, but Mac Abbott might have something to say when word gets around about you and his daughter."

Wil saw red and moved to hit him, but he caught her forearm in time to hold off the blow.

"Careful," he said. "You wouldn't want to damage the father of your current slut."

Shock immobilized her as she stared at his features. So that's why he seemed familiar.

❖

Lacey parked her truck and gathered the bags of take-out food for her and Wil's dinner. She opened the driver's side door and hopped out, only to find herself face to face with Brittney. A very angry Brittney.

"You better reel in your white-trash family, bitch, before my daddy crushes your slimy cockroach of a father."

Father? Food bags in her hands and the truck at her back, Lacey was practically helpless to fend off the furious woman. "I don't know what you're talking about. My sperm donor took off before I was born. I've never even seen a picture of him, so I wouldn't know him if I bumped into him."

"Well, that Judson Chandler guy says he's your father, and he's drunk at the Watering Hole right now and gossiping about Wil Rivers's conquests—especially me!"

"Hold on." Lacey put the food back onto the truck's bench seat. This had to be a mistake or someone's idea of a joke. Because her father and mother weren't married, she had her mother's last name, and her mother had only ever referred to her father as the big turd. "Who is Judson Chandler?"

"Some homophobic old bigot who looks suspiciously like you."

Lacey put her hands on her hips. "Are you saying I look like an old man?"

Brittney snorted. "You do *act* like a grumpy old man, but I meant like kids resemble their parents."

Lacey let the "grumpy" remark pass because she was trying to remember everything, anything her mother had mentioned about her birth father. This didn't make sense.

"He says he's in charge of a group of riders from Sierra Canyon Ranch," Brittney said.

Lacey shook her head. "I've heard of that ranch, but isn't that out of New Mexico? I don't know anybody from there."

"He apparently knows everything about you and Wil." Brittney pointed at Lacey. "And I'm figuring you must have told him about me and Wil. I'm getting engaged to Bart Roberts right after the national finals and don't need that white trash spreading stories about me being with Wil."

It was Lacey's turn to snort. "Haven't you spread enough of those stories yourself? Every time I turn around, you're hound-dogging after her."

Brittney looked smug. "I assure you that Wil Rivers is no angel. I have plenty of other options, so I wouldn't be keeping the door open if she wasn't popping back in for another drink of this water every now and then." She pointed to herself.

"Liar."

Brittney tapped a few things on her phone, then held it up for Lacey to see. Wil appeared in the foreground of the photo, lying on her side with one shoulder bare above the sheet tucked under her chin. Spooning behind her was an obviously naked Brittney, grinning at the camera as she shot the selfie. "Note the time stamp."

Lacey felt sick. "That's a doctored photo. Wil and I FaceTimed every night."

"Every night?" Brittney put her hand to her cheek, her mouth forming an O in an overly dramatic expression of surprise. "She used the migraine story." She nodded. "That's her go-to."

"I don't believe you. Wil wouldn't do that."

"How long have you known her?" Brittney was smug before her expression turned into a scowl. "Doesn't matter. You need to go to the Watering Hole and shut up that old man of yours. My daddy and Bart know I'm a healthy, sexual woman, but they won't tolerate some yahoo smearing my reputation around the rodeo circuit. If your daddy keeps spreading stories about me and Wil, my daddy might have to find somewhere other than the Double R to buy his horses."

"That guy is not related to me." Lacey didn't know what else to say. Her mind was running in a dizzying loop between the photo Brittney had shown her and her insistence that this drunk at the Watering Hole was her long-absent father. "So, you can just get the fuck out of my face and leave Wil alone."

"You should leave Wil alone before your trashy family bankrupts her business."

"What Wil and I do doesn't concern you." Lacey grabbed the take-out bags from the truck again and stepped around her. All she wanted to do was make it to her trailer and shut herself inside.

Brittney wasn't giving up. "No matter what you think of me, I do care about Wil. She has worked her ass off to keep that ranch afloat after her mother died and her father got so sick. If that Chandler drunk starts hurting their business, who do you think she'll choose—you or the Double R?" She glared at Lacey. "Her mother is buried on that ranch."

Lacey pushed past her, ripped the camper door open, then went inside and slammed it behind her.

❖

"Hey, Dad. Did you see my text? Second in team roping and first in barrels. Brittney clocked a personal best time on Dash, but still second to Pepper."

"So, Pepper's turning in good times?"

"Thirteen-point-eight-nine."

"Whew. That's fast."

"I already got an offer on Diamond, but I turned it down." Her ear to her phone, Wil put her manure fork away, double-checked that the stalls on their three horses were properly latched, and walked toward the building exit.

"Not a good offer?" Ray asked.

"It was that Chandler guy again, still looking to pick up a new roping horse. I told him Diamond was primarily a reining horse and would go for a lot more, but we never talked money since we're not going to sell to that ranch anyway."

Her dad paused, a long second of silence hanging between them. "Look, kiddo. I know you were counting on letting Lacey take Pepper to the national finals, but we have a very good offer for her we shouldn't turn down."

Wil's heart dropped. She stopped and leaned against the doorway, the building illuminated behind her and darkness gathering outside before her. "How good is it? If Lacey places well in Vegas, we could ask even more. Tell the buyer Pepper's not available for sale until after the finals."

"Can't do that, Wil. He's our biggest client."

"Mac Abbott? He said he wouldn't buy Brittney another horse."

"Apparently, she went over his head to her grandmother, his mother-in-law. Mac built his oil empire up from one well, but the grandmother's family money got him started. She doesn't interfere much, but when she does say jump, Mac still asks how high."

"Brittney's doing this just to get Lacey out of her way."

"Doesn't matter, Wil. I'm sure Lacey will understand that business is business. A couple of times I had to make decisions that didn't set right with your mother, but she knew it was what we had to do."

"The barrel horses are my deals to make. I trained them." She'd never challenged her father on a business deal, but, damn, she'd promised Pepper to Lacey through the national finals.

"That's why I called. I'm texting you Mac's number. The deal is yours to wrap up."

"I'll call Mac now."

"You need to know something else," Ray said.

Wil took a deep breath to brace herself. This day had started out so good with Lacey's win. How could it be ending so wrong? "What is it?"

"The estimates on the metal barn you want to build came in. The lowest bid is forty thousand more than the insurance on the old barn."

"I thought the base price was forty thousand."

"Apparently, the price they advertise is just a bare hull of a building…no doors, ventilation, plumbing, or wiring, and the foundation, taxes, and permit fees are extra."

"Maybe we can rent a warehouse somewhere to store hay until we can get a new wood barn built." Her father's silence was his rebuke. Crap. Paying rent would be throwing away money, and the current price of wood might end up costing as much as a safer metal barn.

Ray finally spoke. "I'm not going to tell you what to do, Wil. Talk to Mac, and then make your decision. I'm confident you'll make the right one because this is your future we're investing in."

"I know, Dad. I'll let you know something after I talk to Mr. Abbott." Wil ended the call. Her decisions now also could secure or endanger her father's retirement. Ray's text message came through, and she clicked on the number he sent. Mac answered on the second ring.

"Mr. Abbott, this is Wil Rivers."

"Hi, Wil. I was expecting your call."

"Dad says you want to make an offer on Red Pepper."

"The women folk have ganged up on me, and Pepper's win over Dash today sealed the deal."

"With her bloodlines and breeding potential, I would have asked thirty thousand when you were at the ranch to buy Smarty. But since then, she's proved she has the potential to beat any barrel horse in the state…maybe any that show up for the National Finals Rodeo. That's doubled her price to sixty thousand."

"That's pretty steep for a barrel horse who hasn't won any major rodeos."

"I'll be happy to guarantee sixty thousand if you'll wait until after the national finals just because you've been a great client for the Double R. I've got a rider who's doing great on her, and I want to see if they can compete on a national level."

"Seventy thousand is my last offer, and for that price, I want you to haul the horse to Big Spring and help Brittney settle in on her. That's money in your pocket now, and it seems this horse might also give you the best chance of cashing in on that bonus I promised if Brittney places in the money at the national finals."

Wil closed her eyes. That price would pay for the new metal barn and help her start building a financial buffer for the ranch in the event of another disaster like the unexpected pandemic. "Sixty thousand and sign Dash back over to me, and then you've got a deal, Mr. Abbott."

"I paid a lot more than ten thousand when I bought that horse from you."

"He was the best horse I had when you made that purchase. Now I have a better horse. Your daughter wants to win races, not place behind a better horse. And since he's gelded, he has no value as breeding stock."

"You drive a tough bargain, but I'm ready to get these women off my back. You've got a deal."

"Good. You can transfer the money Monday."

"No need. I'm at the hotel having dinner with Brittney. I've got to go, but you can come over and pick up a check from her."

"I'll be there in a few minutes, and we can settle on when she wants Pepper delivered to Big Spring next week."

❖

Lacey walked through to the stable building, entangled in an emotional net of disappointment, possible betrayal, and a past she apparently was unable to escape. She had waited until Brittney had left, then went to find Wil. She couldn't trust anything Brittney said. Even if it was true that Wil had lied and succumbed to Brittney's beauty and money, she had to give Wil the chance to admit it. Then she couldn't doubt whether she'd been right all along. People always let her down.

She spotted Wil standing in the cavernous entrance to the warehouse-type building, her phone to her ear. Who was she talking to? The night was starless, moonless under a cloudy sky, and she realized Wil couldn't see her as she approached, so she lightened her step.

Many of Wil's words were too low or muffled for her to distinguish, but she managed to catch enough to understand the gist of her conversation— "...barrel horses are my deals to make... let you know something after I talk to Mr. Abbott...you've got a deal, Mr. Abbott...settle on when she wants Pepper delivered to Big Spring next week."

Lacey turned and quietly headed for her truck, numb inside and out. She'd gotten sucked in because she wanted to believe she was important to Wil, but perhaps she was a convenience rather than a commitment. And now she was an inconvenience, like she'd been to her mother and absent father. Was Judson Chandler really her father? It was of no consequence now, but some part of her still wanted to know.

❖

Lacey parked in the crowded lot and watched two cowboys come out of the Watering Hole and head for a truck with a Sierra

Canyon Ranch logo on the door. A drunk man staggered out after them.

"Come on, boys. Gimme a ride back to the hotel."

The tall cowboy turned and laughed at him. "Hell, no. Find your own ride. Anyway, the boss says today was your last chance to get that horse he wanted. Your room is canceled after tonight because you're fired."

"I told him I'd have that horse by the time he got to Big Spring. That's next week."

The shorter, wiry cowboy spat tobacco juice onto the parking lot's gravel. "I reckon he found out you were telling everyone that you were in charge of us after he hired you to shovel shit and clean saddles for us."

The drunk lifted his chin in an indignant display. "You idiots. The high and mighty Ray Rivers don't do horse deals with stable help. I was settin' him up." He made a sweeping arm gesture that knocked his hat off his head, then nearly fell over when he bent to pick it up.

"Judson, I don't think you ever knew Ray Rivers," the tall cowboy said.

"We rodeoed on the same circuit. We was friends."

"You might have been on the circuit at the same time, but I heard you ate a lot of arena dust and chased whores while he was busy winning championship buckles." The two men laughed. "I can't believe the boss thought you could get a Rivers-trained horse for him," the tall one said.

"You won't be laughing when I turn up at Big Spring with that horse."

They climbed into their truck, but the shorter man lowered his window and threw a twenty-dollar bill on the ground. "Call a cab and go sleep your liquor off." Their tires spit a cloud of gravel and dust as they drove off.

Lacey waited until they were gone and climbed down from her truck. Judson picked up the money, stumbled past a few vehicles, then stopped to piss on the dual rear tires of one truck. She waited until he was mid-stream before she spoke from behind him. "I heard you're going around telling people you're my daddy."

He jumped when she startled him, then cursed when he splashed urine on his boots. "God damn it, girl. Don't you know better than to walk up on a man when he's relieving himself?" He finished and zipped up before he turned to face her.

"I always wondered about men's infatuation with peeing outdoors, but I guess it's just that some fuckers tend to piss on everything and everybody they can." She studied his face. His eyes were the same color as hers, but a lot of people had brown eyes. His brow was a bit fine for a man, and his long jaw tapered to a slight cleft in his chin identical to the indentation in hers. She could imagine he was handsome when he was young and cleaned up. The man who stood before her now had tobacco-stained teeth, skin wrinkled and leathery from too much sun, and beard stubble too unkept to be fashionable. He reeked of alcohol. She felt contempt, not compassion, when she looked at him.

He straightened and stared down at her. "Well, look at what the dog finally dragged up. Yes sirree. I reckon my swimmers did find their mark. You've got your mother's pretty brow and nose, but that jaw and chin are all mine." He spread his arms in a grandiose gesture. "It's your lucky day. You done found your long-lost daddy."

"I don't have a father. Fathers provide for their children…make sure they have a home and food to eat. Real fathers don't impregnate teenage girls, then skip town."

"If she didn't want a baby, she could have had an abortion."

"There were times when I wished she had because she was passed out drunk with no food in our ratty trailer for more than a week."

"I reckon she didn't beat you like my daddy did me." He paused at this admission and seemed to sober a little, but then his expression grew hard. "So, if you ain't interested in getting to know your dear old daddy, why'd you come looking for me?"

"I want you to shut your big mouth and get the hell out of Texas. I don't know where you've been all these years, but you need to take your sorry ass back there. Leave me alone, leave the Rivers family alone, and quit spreading stories about Brittney Abbott."

"I've got the same freedom of speech every American has. I can say anything I want about anybody. Besides, it's not like I'm telling lies. Everybody knows that Rivers girl is a dyke and that Abbott girl will hump anything." His quick move belied his level of intoxication. Before she could dodge away, he wrapped his big hand around her bicep and jerked her almost to her toes. "I also hear you need someone to teach you how to fuck a man so you don't have to munch on Rivers's pussy."

This vile, crude man was likely her family. She could see herself in his features. She would never be worthy of decent company. She came from trash and would not taint the Rivers family with her garbage, even if Wil had slept with Brittney again. She swung her left fist up and punched him in the throat, causing him to release her arm and stagger backward. "You touch me again, and you'll be picking your balls out of your teeth." She moved a step back out of his reach. "If you know what's good for you, you'll find your way back to wherever you're staying, pack up your stuff, and hightail it out of Texas as fast as you can."

He rubbed his throat and coughed. "What are you going to do about it if I don't?"

She took another step back in the direction of her truck. "I won't have to do anything once Mac Abbott sends some of his oil-rig roughnecks looking for the man talking shit about his daughter. All I have to do is sit back and let them take care of you."

Judson cursed and shook his finger at her. "This ain't over, you little bitch."

She climbed into her truck but lowered her window. "Yes, it is."

CHAPTER TWENTY

Wil slowed as she approached Lacey's camper. Would Lacey understand why she had to switch horses? Even if she did, Wil could still find herself in an uncomfortable situation. Pepper was a better, faster horse than Dash, but Lacey's skill as a rider was far superior to Brittney's. If Lacey and Dash placed higher than Brittney and Pepper in the National Finals Rodeo, would Mac think she'd cheated him and stop buying horses from the Double R? She shook her head. This mental tail-chasing was useless. She needed to focus. Keeping the Abbotts' business was important, but keeping Lacey in her life was essential. She hoped Ray was right that Lacey would understand like her mother had understood the hard decisions her parents had to make over the years.

Lacey's truck was still gone, so Wil was surprised to find their take-out dinner on the table in the camper. Where was Lacey? She peeked into the bag, then shrugged. Maybe the restaurant forgot something, and Lacey had gone back to get it. No matter. Italian takeout was easy to reheat. In fact, this would be a good time to go pick up that check from Brittney. When she got back, they could talk, have dinner to celebrate Lacey's win that afternoon, and spend the evening together before hauling both of their trailers to Big Spring. She took a napkin from the take-out bag and wrote a note to Lacey.

Got to pick up a check for another horse sale, but I won't be long. The rest of the evening is ours. Wil

❖

Lacey again stood in the dark behind another camper-trailer while she watched Wil leave, then slipped into her camper to check that everything was secured for travel. She read Wil's note. Yeah. Seemed she couldn't wait to get that check for Pepper and make plans with Brittney. She barely looked at the bag of takeout before snatching it up and tossing it in the refrigerator. Her stomach felt like a hollow pit but roiling with nauseating emotions she didn't have time to sort at that moment.

Ten minutes later, the trailer was hitched to her truck, and she was pulling up to the stable building to load Denver and get the hell out of there before Wil returned.

The building was nearly empty. Most people had already packed, loaded horses, and left to return home or head for the next rodeo. A few with long distances to travel had opted to wait until morning. That had been her and Wil's plan, even though Big Spring was only a few hours away. They'd loaded everything for Denver, Pepper, and Diamond into the trailers except overnight essentials, so she unloaded Pepper's equipment from her trailer, then gathered Denver's remaining things and led her into the trailer. The routine was so ingrained, she was ready to go in fifteen minutes. Her throat tightened when she hung Wil's duffel, stuffed with the clothes and toiletries that had been in her camper, on the latch of Pepper's stall door. Deciding what to write in a note would take too much time. Did she even owe Wil an explanation? She was sure Brittney would tell her everything after Lacey was gone.

The night remained as dark as her mood when she drove away from Sweetwater. She didn't worry about Wil following, because she would be driving west to Big Spring while Lacey headed southeast. Now that she'd made a clean escape, she realized she was emotionally and physically exhausted. She blew out a breath. She'd get an hour or so away, watch for a brightly lit truck stop to maybe catch a few hours of sleep, then grab some coffee before she got back on the road.

Yeah, she was hanging up on Wil again, figuratively, and turning off her phone, literally. The photo Brittney had shown her flashed through her mind. The stabbing pain in her chest felt as real as a knife. She couldn't deal with that right now. She was doing what had always helped her survive in the past.

Act first, think later.

❖

Wil pushed down her peeve at Brittney's manipulation to get Pepper out of Lacey's hands. It was strictly business. Brittney's goal to win or place at the national finals was the same as Lacey's, and she was using all her resources to secure the horse most likely to ensure her success.

She knocked, and when Brittney opened the door to her hotel room, Wil was happy to see her usual entourage of groupies absent because she didn't have time for their snide comments and childish taunts. She also was relieved to see Brittney was clothed. Maybe she'd finally given up her mission to get Wil naked one more time. Her long blond hair draped attractively about the V-neck of her soft gray, feminine sweatsuit. It was a shame such a beautiful woman was marred by an ugly, narcissistic personality.

"Your father said he'd leave a check with you."

Brittney stepped back and motioned for Wil to enter the suite. Not a room, but a suite. What a waste of money. But then, the Double R was about to benefit again from the Abbotts' free spending. Wil followed her to a desk where Brittney picked up a long white envelope with Wil's name written on it. Well aware of Brittney's penchant for trickery, she checked the contents of the envelope.

"I keep telling Daddy that people don't write checks anymore, especially for huge sums like this. For some reason, though, he likes to write them when he buys horses."

Several of the old horsemen felt the same. They said it was easier to stop a check if something went wrong with the vet report or transfer of the registration than to refund a bank transfer. Unlike most men's scrawl, Mac's penmanship was careful and precise. Sixty thousand, as promised, with a notation that the money was for the purchase of Red Pepper, Quarter horse mare.

"Thanks," Wil said. "I saw Gabe drive out earlier with your trailer, so I guess we'll swap Pepper for Dash in Big Spring."

"Daddy said he'd sign over Dash's papers when he gets home. I'll bring them with me to Big Spring."

"It's only a few hours west. You're headed four hours east to go home first?"

"In exchange for her interference to get Daddy to open his wallet, Nana demanded that I attend a meeting on Tuesday to plan my engagement party."

"I didn't know you were engaged."

"To Bart, of course. He hasn't officially asked yet, but I suppose they'll plan the timing for that as well. His father has demanded he settle down and get serious about the family business." Brittney tossed her hair and walked over to the small bar, where she refilled her nearly empty wineglass. "I hope they don't think I'm going to let them plan when we have babies, too."

Wil didn't want to think about the poor child who'd get Brittney for a mother. "When can I expect you in Big Spring? I need to arrange some practice runs for you and Pepper to get acquainted before the competition on the weekend."

"I'll be there by lunch Wednesday. Daddy's jet is free, so I'll fly out instead of drive almost five hours from Denton."

"I'll see if I can arrange something for Wednesday afternoon and on Thursday."

"That sounds good." She held up the bottle of wine. "Have a drink with me to seal our transaction?"

"No thanks. Lacey and I were about to have dinner, so I need to get back." Wil started across the room to leave.

Brittney raised an eyebrow. "She's still speaking to you?"

Wil stopped. "Why wouldn't she?"

Brittney shrugged.

"What did you do?" Wil took a threatening step toward Brittney. "So help me God—"

"Her white-trash drunk of a father is down at the Watering Hole running his mouth about you and me in the worst kind of language to anyone who'll listen because you wouldn't sell a horse to his boss. I paid your little girlfriend a visit to tell her to go shut him up or my father would do it for her."

Wil's heart began to pound. "Jesus, Brittney. She doesn't even know that guy who's suddenly claiming to be her father. And there's no proof he is."

"She looks like him enough to be his daughter. Besides, nobody cares about proof anymore. Any slander is good enough to pass around as truth."

"She's never even met him. She wasn't with me either of the two times he tried to buy one of our horses." Crap. Was that why Lacey's truck was missing? Had she gone to that bar rather than back to the restaurant?

"Doesn't matter. It's not her he's spouting off about in graphic imagined detail. He's going after you and me. I told Lacey that her trashy family would be the end of your ranch because nobody would want to be seen doing business with you."

She practically ran for the door. "I need to find her."

❖

Wil stared only a few seconds at the empty space where Lacey's horse trailer had been parked next to hers, then drove as fast as was safe up to where the horses were stabled. No trailer there either. She slammed her gearshift into park and ran inside. She knew Denver was gone the moment she spotted her blue duffel hanging on the door to Pepper's stall.

"Son of a bitch." She paced in front of the stalls, phone pressed to her ear as she prayed Lacey would answer. It went directly to voice mail so she ended the call. "Damn it." Lacey had turned her phone off. She called again but this time left a message.

Lacey, sweetheart, where are you? Brittney said she talked to you about that guy claiming to be your father. Please don't shut me out again. Let's face whatever together. I want to be there for you. Please, please call me. Please come back.

Wil sagged against the outside wall of Pepper's stall. What should she do? It was late. Her dad would already be asleep. Shit. Her trailer didn't include a camper. She needed to find a place to sleep. Might as well find one here since she wouldn't have any place to stable the horses if she arrived in Big Spring in the middle of the night. She had no idea where Lacey might have gone. She wouldn't be headed to Big Spring without a horse to ride, and it was unlikely she knew Wil was getting Dash back for her. Pepper stuck her head over the half door of her stall and snuffled at her hair, so Wil turned and wrapped an arm around the mare's neck, resting her forehead against her coarse mane for a few minutes. Hell, she'd just sleep in the back seat of her truck, then pull out early in the morning for Big Spring. She patted Pepper's neck and trudged toward her truck. The weight on her shoulders felt heavier than ever…more than taxes owed, more than late mortgage payments, more than a destroyed hay barn.

❖

The bright sun and cloudless sky did nothing to lift Lacey's spirits out of their downward spiral. Not even driving through the gates of the J&M Family Campground. She'd completed half of the four-hour trip before finding a suitable truck stop, where she'd loosed Denver in the roomy trailer compartment and set out a bucket of water to make her comfortable for several hours. Then she shed her boots and climbed into her bed in the camper compartment. To her surprise, she was so mentally exhausted that she slept for nearly four hours before waking, grabbing fresh coffee from the truck stop, and preparing Denver to resume travel. Two hours later, she was arriving just in time for breakfast with Joel and Maggie.

Maggie stood at the stove flipping pancakes when Joel opened the door. "Baby girl," he crowed. "Look who's here, Maggie."

Lacey burst into tears when he wrapped his arms around her and hugged her close. Damn it. She never cried. Not when she'd hid under her bed because the men who paid to visit her mother began to look at her with interest. Not when her great-aunt died and she found herself basically homeless. Not the times when she had to buy feed for Denver rather than groceries for herself. But she was emotionally lost and road weary, with no plan for her future.

Joel stroked her hair and tightened his hug. "Oh, honey. Whatever this is, we'll fix it. You're not sick, are you? Did somebody hurt you? Did someone hurt Denver?"

She managed to shake her head in answer to his questions.

Maggie turned the flame off on the stove and came over to

envelop them both in a massive group hug. "It's going to be okay, sweetie. You just cry it out, and then we'll sit down, and I'll cook your favorite pancakes. That always makes you feel better." Their kindness made her sob even harder, so they all stood there for a long while until her sobs became sniffles. Joel led her to the table and seated her, while Maggie returned to the stove.

"How long since you ate, sweetie?" Maggie asked.

Lacey had to think. "I, uh…a hot dog around lunch yesterday."

"Good Lord. No wonder you're so skinny. Joel, fetch that child some coffee."

"Denver's been in the trailer all night. I need to get her settled."

Joel slid a mug of steaming coffee in front of her, then plunked down the sugar and creamer next to her cup. "I just mowed her pasture, so I'll go turn her out there. Your favorite campsite overlooking the pond is open. Give me your keys, and I'll pull your trailer down there after I take care of Denver."

She only nodded when her throat tightened around the threat of fresh tears and dug her keys from her pocket. She finally managed a mumbled "thanks," then busied herself doctoring her coffee the way she liked it.

Maggie expertly folded pecans into her pancake mix and re-ignited the stove's flame, poured two generous pancakes onto her flat cast-iron skillet, then thankfully eased into the conversation Lacey knew they had to have. "That was some time you clocked yesterday in Sweetwater. You and Denver seem to be getting better and better."

Lacey closed her eyes for a second as she savored her coffee. Maggie's was the best. "I wasn't riding Denver. She's hurt."

Maggie flipped the pancakes. "Oh, dear. Not bad, I hope."

"She'll heal, but running her most weekends every year has put too much wear and tear on her legs. Her knees are full of bone spurs. Vet says she could race again in three months or so, but she's already peaked. Her best times are behind her."

"Then whose horse did you ride yesterday?"

"I rode a Quarter horse the Double R Ranch is campaigning for sale."

"They asked you to ride for them?"

"I've sort of gotten to know Wil Rivers, one of the owners. She asked me to enter some team-roping events with her, so I did it to earn some extra money."

"Wil's a she, huh?"

"Wiloree. It's an old family name." Lacey ignored Maggie's unspoken insinuation. "It was after one of those roping events that Denver came up lame. Her lameness wasn't Wil's fault because it's a cumulative injury, not something that happened while we were roping. Still, she offered to let me ride her horse in the barrels because she's taller and heavier than me. She thought I could get a better time on Pepper than she could."

"Did you?"

"Yeah." She shrugged. "Pepper's a great horse."

Maggie slid the plate of hot pancakes, butter melting and dripping down the sides, in front of her, then placed the syrup next to it. Lacey didn't think she would eat, but the rich, buttery aroma reminded her stomach they'd missed dinner. She dug in.

Maggie sat down at the table. "So, Denver's hurt and needs to recover. That's not worth the breakdown you had when you got here. What are you holding back?"

"Wil offered for me to ride Pepper in the National Finals Rodeo, then sold the mare to my archrival." She almost slapped her hand over her mouth as soon as the words came out. She sounded like a petulant princess...like Brittney Abbott. She began stuffing her traitorous mouth with pancakes to stop herself.

"That's a setback, for sure, but not something you'd cry over." Maggie sat back, sipping her own mug of coffee, and waited patiently while Lacey ate voraciously to avoid explaining further.

She was mopping up her second pancake when Joel returned.

"Beautiful fall day out there. Denver sure was glad to get out of that trailer. She ran around that pasture like a filly, head up and mane flying. I gotta say, though, she seems a little sore in her front legs." He refreshed the coffee he'd left and took his seat at the table.

"Denver's just overworked and needs some time to heal." Maggie's tone sounded suspiciously like the same could be applied to Lacey, but she went to the stove to make him a stack of pancakes rather than elaborate. "Couple more pancakes for you?" she asked Lacey.

"Please," she said around her last mouthful of the tasty treat. She swallowed and gulped down a mouthful of coffee.

Joel laughed. "Slow down. You know she'll stand at that stove and make you pancakes all day if you want."

Lacey shook her head at herself and finally smiled at Joel. "I know." Her throat tightened again. Crap. She refused to cry again. Thankfully, Joel rose one more time and brought the carafe over to freshen her coffee and give her time to regain her control.

Just a couple of country Texans, Joel and Maggie weren't physically attractive, accomplished, or rich. But they were what people called "the salt of the earth" in the biblical sense of healing. They were honest, caring, unselfish, and nonjudgmental. They were better than any parents she could have had. *Shit. Don't cry, don't cry.*

"You resting up for the big rodeo in December? Or is Denver done for the year? Either way, we're tickled that you're back home with us."

Home. Her eyes filled, but she cleared her throat and forced herself to buck up. "Her knees are done racing around barrels, so I might be done, too."

Joel didn't miss a beat. "Now, you listen to me. This is just a bump in the road. You'll figure things out. Just give yourself and Denver some time."

"Thanks, Joel, but I don't want to sponge off you guys too long."

Maggie plated a towering stack of pancakes and brought them to the table for the three of them. "Are you kidding? Joel has a list a mile long of things he could use help with. Besides, you can't sponge off family. Your company alone is worth marking your campsite as unavailable. You know we don't have any children, but we think of you as ours."

This time, Lacey didn't try to hide the tears filling her eyes. "Thanks, guys. I don't know what I'd do without you."

CHAPTER TWENTY-ONE

As it turned out, Wil didn't have to search for accommodations. Brittney texted her with the details of a dude ranch where she'd booked them and the horses through the weekend. She was met by a petite older woman dressed for ranch work when she climbed down from her dually truck at the dude ranch outside Big Spring. The woman held out her hand.

"Hi. I'm Tess. You must be Wil Rivers."

"Yes. Pleased to meet you. Thanks so much for accommodating us."

"No problem. You can stable your horses in the stallion barn. It's empty, and the stalls are ready for you. We don't keep a stallion, but guests are allowed to bring their own horses to ride, and we do get an occasional stallion that we want to house away from the other horses. The Abbotts' man has already dropped off your third horse. His trailer is parked over by the main barn, but he said he was going to spend a few days with his cousin in Big Spring until Miss Abbott needed him."

"Good. Have you received payment from the Abbotts yet?"

"Got the Venmo this morning. They paid through Sunday. Did you change your mind about leaving on Thursday?"

"I'm not sure how long I'll stay. Maybe through to Sunday. It depends on how well Miss Abbott and the mare I've sold her get along. She'll be moving the mare to the rodeo grounds Thursday afternoon, since the barrel competition starts Friday. I'd prefer to keep the other two here until I head back to Bowie, if that's okay. I lost my team-roping partner so won't be competing after all."

"That's fine. I used to barrel race myself when I was younger. Still had the barrels stored in the hay barn. I had one of my wranglers set them up in the pasture behind the stallion barn for you. It's not a professional arena, but it's flat and sandy near the barn, and I had it dragged to get rid of any stones."

"I'm sure it'll be fine. We don't want to be any trouble."

"Honey, you can be all the trouble you want for the price the Abbotts are paying me. I didn't have any space available in the lodge, so I put you in one of the two-bedroom log cabins we built last year up on the hill for guests. They're pretty fancy. Your booking includes meals at the lodge, but the cabin has a kitchen if you prefer to cook for yourself. Or you can order from the lodge menu and take it back to your cabin." She pointed to several cabins that overlooked the lodge and main barn. "You can come down to the lodge after you settle your horses, and I'll get you checked in. You need any help?"

"I'm good. Thanks, Tess."

❖

Joel handed Lacey the smallest wrench he had. "Lucky you showed up. I can't get my hands in that little space and would have had to pull the engine to get at that loose bolt."

"When we leprechauns got our last pot of gold stolen, we found out many jobs are available for small people."

He laughed. "You know it. My hands might be too big for this one, but when I was in the navy, I was the guy they were always calling to crawl into tight spaces because the others were too big or fat." He patted his belly that protruded like he had a medium-sized turtle under his shirt. "Of course, that was before I married Maggie and started eating her pancakes and biscuits. Lord, that woman can cook."

"Amen," Lacey said. She enjoyed working with Joel, and they'd been checking items off his work list faster than turkeys disappearing from the grocery store right before Thanksgiving. Joel and Maggie seemed to understand that she needed to stay busy. That made the days bearable, but the nights were long and soul-crushingly lonely without Wil. Maybe she should have talked to Wil instead of running off, but she'd been too humiliated. If Wil wanted another woman or to be free to date other women, why had she asked that they be exclusive? Maybe she'd changed her mind.

She'd tried to remember the details of that video conversation when they discussed it. She should have recorded those video chats. Yet despite Wil's apparent betrayal, she would have tortured herself by watching them. Wil's absence was a vacuum that sucked every molecule of happiness from her life.

During those dark hours when she was alone, she tried to remember every word of her confrontation with Brittney. She even closed her eyes and attempted to visualize that hurtful photo Brittney had shown her of them in bed. Brittney could have photoshopped the image or the time stamp.

"Hey. I think that bolt is tight enough. I'll have to shear that off if I ever do have to pull the engine."

"Sorry." She glanced at the open door of the equipment barn. "Speaking of Maggie, she's headed this way." She was relieved the distraction would stop him from asking what she was thinking about while she was yanking that nut so tight.

He straightened and wiped his hands on the bandanna he pulled from his back pocket. "You can set your clock by that woman."

Maggie pointed at Joel when she reached the door. "You lose your watch, old man? Lunch is waiting on you two."

He handed his bandanna to Lacey so she could wipe her hands, too. "Nope. I was hoping you'd walk out to get us. I wanted to hold your hand and share this beautiful fall foliage and fresh air with my lovely wife on the way back to the house."

Maggie smiled like a schoolgirl. "Aren't you all sweetness and light." She took his hand. "I'll bet sugar don't melt in that mouth."

Lacey smiled at their antics, but inside she wanted to cry. She wanted Wil's hand in hers. She'd been so stupid to fall for her.

❖

Wil felt a hundred percent better and more clearheaded after a long, hot shower and several hours of sleep.

She'd checked on the horses and turned them out into the small pasture where the barrels were set up so they could stretch their legs after the long stall and trailer confinement of the past week. Diamond was a good stallion. He didn't harass mares unless they were in season, but he kept close to Pepper to watch over her.

Then she'd visited the lodge and ordered an early dinner that she took back to the cabin. She needed to answer several business emails, talk to her father, and let Brittney know their accommodations were good. Most of all, she wanted to figure out where Lacey had gone.

Business emails first. She ate her supper while she worked.

Several were receipts for the hay she'd paid for and had the men pick up. They'd decided to move the tractors and hay-baling attachments out of the equipment barn and temporarily store the hay there. If bad weather came up before the new hay barn was finished, they'd cover the machinery with tarps, which were cheaper than paying rent on a warehouse for a month.

Most of their other bills were paperless, so she was able to pay them online. Her mother always kept the books at the ranch, and even though Wil had been only a teenager, she'd taken over the task after her death because Ray was so devastated, he could barely function.

Dinner eaten and business complete, she picked up her phone to try Lacey's number again. Straight to voice mail. She left another message.

Hey. It's Wil. I'm going to keep calling until you talk to me. Please, please call me back, or at least keep your phone turned on and answer next time. If you're here in Big Spring, I'll find you. I miss you, sweetheart.

If she had to search to hell and back to find Lacey, she would as soon as she finished her business commitment with Brittney. She looked at her to-do list. She had a lot more to take care of, because by the end of this week, nothing would stop her from hunting down the woman she'd fallen head over heels for.

Her iPad rang with a FaceTime request. "Hi, Brittney. I was about to call you."

"Good. How's the dude ranch?"

"Where we're staying is very nice." She took a few minutes to walk around with the iPad so Brittney could see the inside of the spacious cabin.

"Not bad," Brittney said, her tone pleased rather than showing her usual bratty disdain.

"Plus, we've got the stallion barn to ourselves and barrels set up behind it. I'll run Pepper through the course a couple of times tomorrow. Then we'll put you on her Wednesday afternoon."

"If Mother and Nana keep driving me crazy, I might sneak out after the big meeting with Bart's mother and drive all tomorrow night to get there."

Wil laughed. "Ah, the price of being a princess."

Brittney's scowl instead of her usual pouty expression indicated she was genuinely irritated. "Wil. Seriously. I might have made a mistake going around Daddy. He's the only one who can get them to back off, but he's ignoring me. Mother and Nana started in on me when Bart was here for dinner tonight. When I gave Daddy my best please-rescue-me look, he invited Bart to smoke cigars on the patio, and they left me with those two bossy bitches."

"All the more reason for you to focus on barrel racing. If you don't apply yourself and place at the national finals, that'll be their ticket to make you quit the rodeo and your wild parties and become the respectable socialite they intend."

"I'm going to have nightmares tonight."

Wil laughed again. She actually liked desperate Brittney. That side of her was a lot more real than the princess-and-her-entourage act. "Now, I've got more business calls to make. See you soon." She ended the call without waiting for Brittney to say good-bye and typed a text message asking her father to FaceTime whenever he was ready. She threw her dinner container into the trash and had barely finished pouring herself a cup of coffee when her iPad buzzed again.

"Hey, Dad. How's everything at the ranch?"

He frowned. "My ears have been ringing and the horses spooked all day because of the racket those metal-building people are making."

"So, they're already getting started. Excellent. Leave them alone, no matter how much noise they make. The sooner they finish, the sooner they'll leave and we can get the ranch back on our usual routine."

"I know."

"Why don't you and Don get away from the ranch while that's going on and track down some horses for us to buy?"

"That's not a bad idea. Jimmy can stay here and mind the ranch. He's nearly deaf anyway, so the noise doesn't bother him so much." He scratched his chin.

"Something else bothering you?"

"What'd you do about Pepper?"

"I deposited Mac's check for sixty thousand this morning."

"Whew. He must have wanted that horse bad."

"I also got him to return Dash to me as part of the deal. I figure we can resell him if Lacey will ride him in Vegas. Or we can keep him to work the ranch."

"How's Lacey feel about the switch?"

"Don't know. I haven't talked to her about it."

Ray looked confused. "What do you mean you haven't talked about it?"

"She's gone." Wil steeled herself against the urge to cry and sob it all out to him. She didn't have time to fall into the pit of despair trying to take her down. Too many people were depending on her.

"Gone? What the hell, Wil. Don't make me drag it out of you."

She rubbed her forehead, wishing they weren't on a video call so he couldn't see her expression. "She loaded her mare into her trailer and left me high and dry in Sweetwater while I was picking up Mac's check. She doesn't even know about me selling Pepper. At least, I don't think so. Brittney might have told her. They apparently had a confrontation right before Lacey disappeared." She massaged her temples. Damn. She didn't need a migraine right now. "It's a long, confusing story, and it isn't really about me and her. It's more about ghosts and trauma from her past showing up to bite her in the butt."

Ray's face softened. "I'm sorry, baby. I know you really like her."

"I'm in love with her, Dad. I feel like a piece of me is missing. I promised Mac that I'd get Brittney comfortable on Pepper before the weekend. Then I'm going to find Lacey if I have to drive to every small campground in Texas."

"Wil. Maybe you should wait and see if she comes back on her own. She will if she loves you the same way."

"No, Dad. You don't know what she's lived through. You don't know how much a really bad childhood damaged her. No one's ever had her back, so she's learned to run to protect herself."

"I like her a lot, too, baby, but she might never stop running when life gets hard, and relationships are definitely hard. What do you plan to do if you find her?"

"Fight for her."

❖

Lacey stared into the flames of her campfire. It was getting dark earlier, which fit her mood. She'd thought time would ease the ache in her chest, but it was Friday—five days since she'd seen, touched, talked to Wil—and she was only sinking deeper into depression. She'd begged off having dinner with Joel and Maggie. They meant well, but she needed to get away from their worried looks.

"Okay if I stare into your fire for a little while, too?"

She raised her head at the soft voice and turned toward her visitor. Andie stood on the edge of the pool of light cast by the flickering fire.

"Maggie said she tried everything but couldn't convince you to stay for dinner. Sam and I were hoping to surprise you."

"What are you doing here? How do you know Joel and Maggie?"

"Well, you talked about them so much, Sam and I decided to give this campground a try. It's close enough to our home to come down for the weekend, and we've sort of fallen in love with your friends."

"Have a seat," Lacey said, pointing to the chair Joel often occupied when he stopped by on his rounds to check on campers. "Why'd they call you?"

"They know, of course, that we're friends because all Sam can talk about is you and Denver and the rodeo." Andie laughed softly. "For her birthday, she asked that we subscribe to the Cowboy Channel after she watched it with Joel on their television. I don't know what I'll do if she asks for a horse next year."

Lacey only nodded. "She's a good kid."

"They let me know you were here because they're worried.

Maggie thinks what's bothering you is more than Denver being injured. Sam, bless her heart, blabbed about Wil being your girlfriend, but Joel and Maggie say you've mentioned her only once since you arrived."

"Nothing to talk about. We had fun. She's busy with her ranch, selling horses, and sleeping with an old girlfriend." She hadn't meant to say that last part, and the confession left her feeling like a suddenly deflated balloon.

Andie let that remark hang in the air while they watched the fire for the next ten minutes. Finally, she spoke. "I find that hard to believe of Wil. She seemed so gone on you that day we met her."

"Brittney showed me a photo of them in bed together."

Andie was quiet for another five minutes. "Does Wil know she did that?"

"Only if Brittney told her. I wasn't about to stick around and be the pathetic castoff. I got the hell out of town."

"So, you left without giving Wil a chance to explain. From what you guys have said about Brittney, she'd stop at nothing to get between you two and corral Wil again. With so many fake websites and social media posts around today, how can you believe Brittney without checking? Show me the photo."

Lacey scowled. "I don't have a copy. It was on Brittney's phone."

"Shit, woman. I know third-graders who can photoshop an image, but there are ways you can detect when an image has been changed. You need to get a copy of that picture."

❖

Wil slammed the case closed on her iPad. Her search was going nowhere without some last names of the people she knew were important to Lacey. She also couldn't remember if she'd ever been told exactly where Andie and Sam or Maggie and Joel lived.

She actually knew very little about Lacey's life. Had it been an illusion that she and Lacey had grown close? Had she built up this relationship in her mind to be more than it really was? She closed her eyes and rested her head on the cabin's kitchen island where she'd been working.

"Is business that bad?" Brittney emerged from her bedroom, barefoot and changed from her Western attire she'd worn to barrel race earlier that day into athletic-themed loungewear. In other circumstances, Wil would have found her beautiful. "Because I was hoping you'd celebrate with me. Today was a success for both of us."

To Wil's surprise, Brittney had applied herself seriously to bonding with Pepper, and as it turned out, the two were a good match. With one more day of competition in Big Spring, they were in first place by nearly a full second ahead of the other leaders in both individual and cumulative scores.

Even better, Brittney had ceased to persistently pursue Wil. With the two of them staying in the same cabin, she'd expected Brittney to pull out her best flirtations. The chair she'd put under her bedroom doorknob to keep Brittney out hadn't been necessary. She'd made few of her usual inappropriate comments and hadn't tried walking around Wil half dressed. The marriage mandate seemed to have shaken a lot of the spoiled princess out of her.

Wil lifted her head when Brittney popped the cork on the bottle of wine she'd taken from the fridge. "Excellent run today," she said. "I have to admit, I had no idea you and Pepper would be such a great team."

Brittney's smile was wide. "She's amazing. When we clear that third barrel, it's like she has a jet pack strapped to her butt." She raised her glass in a salute to Red Pepper. "I think I've finally found the right horse for me."

Wil returned her smile. "Good. Pepper's one of the sweetest mares I've trained. She'll have a good home with you."

Brittney flushed. "You really mean that?"

"I do. I can't explain it, but she seemed to bond with you right away." It was true. After one day, the mare was following Brittney around the pasture without being led and nickering to her when she entered the barn.

"I love her to death already." Brittney toyed with her wineglass for a long moment, then pointed to Wil's iPad. "Catching up on email?"

Wil looked down at the iPad and sighed. "I'm still trying to find Lacey. I'm so fucking stupid." With that admission, her dam seemed to burst, and everything that had been flooding her brain poured out of her mouth. "I don't even know the last names of the people who are her friends. All I know is that Andie has a daughter named Sam and teaches at a small college. I don't know if Andie is short for Andrea or Angela or something else. An older couple named Joel and Maggie owns the place where Lacey camps when she's not working the rodeo circuit. I don't know their last names or the name of the campground. I just know it's small and private, and somewhere outside Austin. I've been searching the internet on every browser I have, but I've turned up nothing. Nada. She's not answering my texts or taking my calls. Hell, my calls go straight to voice mail because she's got her phone turned off most of the time. I have no idea if she's listening to them."

"Are you sure she hasn't blocked your number?"

"Yes. I looked up how to tell if someone does that. My text messages still indicated they've been delivered, and I don't even get one ring before it goes to voice mail, much less a message saying the number is unavailable." Wil drained her wineglass, and Brittney did the same, then refilled both.

"You really like this woman."

Wil looked up, holding Brittney's gaze. "I'm in love with her. She's the one, Britt. I don't care what rumors that Chandler guy spreads about me, even if he manages to hurt the ranch's business. I will never stop searching for her."

"How do you know she feels the same way?"

"I feel it in my heart. She's running because she's scared to let me love her, scared to love me."

"Maybe she's taken off with that Andie woman. I heard she's pretty cute."

"I don't think so. I won't believe that. I need to find her and prove to her that she comes first."

"You'd risk the ranch to hook up with her? Your mother's buried there."

The blow was low, but her tone was clearly a question, not an accusation. Wil touched her chest where her heart beat strong and sure. "Mom's body is in that grave on the ranch, but she *lives* here," Wil said. "I know with absolute certainty that her greatest wish—and Dad's—is that I find happiness with someone like they did. Lacey's that someone."

They were both quiet for a long time, until Wil finally spoke. "I'm going to feed the horses and check Dash and Diamond over to make sure they're good to travel tomorrow." She stood and moved toward the door.

"Wil, wait," Brittney said. "I need to tell you…show you something."

She turned back to Brittney. "Nothing you can tell or show me will change my mind about Lacey."

"I know." Her voice was small, and she spoke to the floor like a guilty child. "But I might have shown Lacey something that maybe changed her mind about you." She tapped her phone a few times and held it out to Wil.

Wordlessly, Wil took it and stared at the selfie Brittney had taken in bed with her. "This is a fake. You must have photoshopped this." Anger and panic mixed into a hard ball in her stomach and pressed against her lungs. She couldn't breathe. "Why? Why would you do this?"

Brittney shrugged. "I was jealous. You looked so happy and may be about to start a wonderful life together, while I'm facing a loveless marriage to live up to my family's expectations. I mean, I love Bart, but I'm not in love with him, or else I wouldn't be wanting to sleep with you again."

"You know that's never going to happen."

"I finally realize that. I guess this was my last-ditch effort to break you two up so maybe you'd reconsider what I was offering."

Wil's jaw dropped, and she stared hard at Brittney. How had she still been clinging to the belief Wil would return to her? "A secret affair while you flounce around on Bart's arm and have his babies to keep your social standing?"

"Oh, I don't care about those socialites, Wil. But I do care about my inheritance, which would be zero if I ran off with you."

"Doesn't matter, because I never expected, never wanted anything long-term with you. Our values are too different. We wouldn't be together even if I hadn't met Lacey."

Brittney had the good sense to look ashamed. "I know that

now. That's why I decided to show you the picture—so she won't
blindside you with it if you do find her."

"You sent her a copy?"

"No. I was afraid she'd look at it too hard and figure out
that you're so deeply asleep you're nearly unconscious. I sort of
insinuated that you'd pretended to have a migraine that night to get
out of calling her while we were together. You never sleep with your
mouth open unless you're drunk or drugged. I was scared she'd
know that if she took a second look."

Wil grabbed Brittney's phone and texted the photo to herself.
"You went too far this time, Brittney." Wil snatched up her iPad and
began gathering the few things she'd strewn around the living area
of the cabin.

"What are you going to do?"

"I'm packing up and leaving now. Jake's at the arena with
Pepper and all set to trailer her to your ranch after tomorrow's final
run. I've fulfilled everything I promised your father. Our business
is done."

"I know you don't believe me, Wil, but I am sorry for the
trouble I've caused. I guess I didn't want to admit how much you
cared for her." She gave Wil a pleading look. "I guess hoping we can
be friends is out of the question?"

"I'm very, very angry with you right now, but I'm not one to
hold a grudge. Give me some months to cool off, and maybe we can
try to be friends. I was starting to like soon-to-be-married Brittney
without her groupies."

❖

"I thought I heard somebody rattling around out here." Jimmy
sauntered into the Double R barn as Wil was turning on the automatic
water bucket in Diamond's stall.

"I put Dash in Pepper's old stall, but he's all set, too." She gave
the old wrangler a hug. "It's good to be home. Dad gone to bed?"

"Nope. He's waiting up, just like I was."

Wil pulled out her phone—ten o'clock. She'd trimmed twenty
minutes off the four-hour trip, but refusing to make a pit stop had
her running for the barn restroom the minute she pulled up.

"You guys didn't have to wait up to watch me brush my teeth and fall into bed. I'm exhausted."

"You might find a second wind when you hear the message Ray has for you."

Her heart soared. "Did Lacey call?"

"Nope, but some friend named Andie did."

"Did she say where Lacey is?"

"You're going to have to ask Ray. I didn't talk to her."

They hurried to the house, and Wil burst into the living room. "Dad! Where are you?"

"Whoa. Slow down. I'm right here." Ray appeared in the doorway to their office. "Damn, Jimmy, you should've put a rope around her before she starts a stampede."

"You've got Andie's number?" Wil couldn't believe her luck after a week of dead ends. "Does she know where Lacey is?"

"Come in here, sit down, and catch your breath," he said.

Wil did feel like she might hyperventilate, so she let him guide her into the big leather chair behind the desk and hand her his cup of coffee.

"Take a few sips," he said. "You sound like a bullfrog."

Her throat was very dry, so she sipped at the steaming cup and grimaced. "Ugh." He liked his coffee black, while she preferred lots of cream and sugar. "Andie's number?" She didn't want to waste another minute.

He sighed. "I was hoping to talk about this first, but here you go." He held out a yellow sticky note.

Wil grabbed her phone rather than the landline. She wanted the number in her contacts from now on. After a few overly nervous misdials, the call went through.

"Hello?"

"Andie, it's Wil."

"Hi, Wil. I was expecting your call. Your father wouldn't give out your cell number, bless his heart, but he was just being protective."

Wil glared at Ray. She could have talked to Andie hours ago while she was on the road. Her father glared back, obviously guessing what Andie must have told her.

"I didn't want you driving all worked up or dragging those

poor horses all the way down to Austin. It was best you stop here first," he said.

Wil dismissed his comment. He was right, but they'd talk about his decision later. "Is Lacey okay?"

"Well, you'd have to define okay," Andie said. "She and Denver arrived at the campground with no problems, and she's parked in her favorite campsite. Denver has a nice five-acre pasture and the company of a donkey and some goats, and Joel and Maggie are pampering both of them."

"Has she said why she disappeared on me?"

"I think you need to talk to her about that, but you've got some explaining to do."

"I love her, Andie. I just found out about that photo Brittney showed her. Do you know about it?"

"Sam and I are at the campground for the weekend, so she told me."

"It's not what you think."

"It never is, is it?" Andie's voice held a new edge. "I'm rooting for you, Wil, because I saw how much you care for each other. But if you'd cheat on my friend, you should stay away. We've got her back, and we're not going to let some cowgirl with a ranch full of fancy horses hurt her."

"I promise I'm not going to hurt her, but she has to stop running and trust me. I'm not perfect, and I know she thinks I've betrayed her twice over, but I haven't. Please, please, tell me where to find her."

"Are you calling from your cell phone?"

"Yes. I'm putting your number in my contacts."

"Send me a text, and I'll text back the website with the map. They're northwest of Austin between two small towns."

"I'm headed down there now."

Ray and Jimmy immediately began yelling "Whoa," and Andie laughed. "What they said. Don't show up in the middle of the night. You both need to be awake and clearheaded so you say the right things to each other. Maggie starts cooking breakfast at seven in the morning, every morning. I'll tell them to expect you. Sam and I'll have to head home tomorrow afternoon, but we'll see if we can devise a plan to get Lacey out of her camper and up to the house in the morning."

"Andie."

"Yes?"

"Do you—" She had to pause when her throat tightened around her question. "Do you think she'll listen?" She was tired and stressed and unable to hold back the tears that burned her eyes. "Do you think she cares about me enough to try?"

Andie's voice was quiet. "I think she's in love with you, too, Wil. She's just having a hard time letting herself love anybody. She's been taking baby steps, though. She let Joel and Maggie in. They're her home. And it took a lot of careful work, but she's opened up to a friendship with me and Sam. You're the treacherous third barrel she's afraid could tip over on her."

"I have to see her. I'll chase her all over Texas and beyond to prove what she means to me."

"You're so sweet and exactly what she needs...somebody who'll be there for her."

CHAPTER TWENTY-TWO

A few people had Wil's back as well. Ray and Jimmy had already hatched a plan "to rope Wil's filly and bring her back to the ranch." While their plan needed a new description, their intentions and strategy were all good.

Ray and Don had to drive to Lubbock for an appointment to make a deal on a couple of potential cutting horses, so it was decided that Jimmy would drive Wil down to the J&M Family Campground. Wil protested at first, but Ray pointed out that Jimmy had a camper that fit on the back of his pickup when he took off to go fishing. It would be good cover when they entered the campground, and if all went well, Wil could ride back to the ranch with Lacey. If Wil bombed and Lacey threw her out, then Jimmy would bring her back to the Double R without risking her being in a wreck because she was upset.

When they gathered in front of the ranch house at three that morning, the sun was hours from rising.

Ray pulled Wil into his arms and hugged her close. "I'm rooting for you, baby girl. And I feel like your mother is, too. Your girl might be a hurt puppy, but we've got all the love she and her horse need for them to heal right here."

"Thanks, Dad."

"Did you get any sleep after your shower?"

"I did drift off for an hour or two. Don't bother with the mess in my room. I dumped out my suitcase to repack clean clothes."

"Don't you worry about that. I've never done your laundry and don't plan to start touching your girlie things now." They laughed as he released her. "Now get in that truck, or Jimmy's going to drive off without you. He's all excited about the pond that website said had good fishing."

❖

"You nervous?" Jimmy asked.

"More like scared out of my skin. What if she refuses to listen? What if she doesn't feel the same as I do?"

"Now, don't go digging up more snakes than you can kill. If you want her to trust you, then you have to show some faith in her."

They drove through the gate under the large sign that touted the J&M Family Campground and followed the gravel drive to a modest house painted dark brown with green shutters to blend with the surrounding woods. An older man of average height, a wiry build, and with a shock of wild gray hair escaping from under his ballcap met them on the porch and extended his hand to Jimmy first.

"Howdy. I'm Joel, and you must be Jimmy. I'll show you down to your campsite after breakfast." He took Wil's hand in both of his rough ones. "And you have to be Wil. You're way prettier in person than you are on the television."

"You saw me on television?"

"Just a glimpse when the Cowboy Channel was showing the barrel racing yesterday. They showed you talking to that Brittney woman right before she got her turn at the barrels. Gave your ranch a pretty good plug for training the horse she was riding." Joel might have looked like he'd never made it off the chicken farm, but he obviously wasn't dumb. "Come on in. Maggie's starting breakfast, and Andie has gone down to roust Lacey. She doesn't always eat with us, and she's been staying at her camper more and more every day. Maggie thinks she's depressed."

They wiped their feet and walked through the living room, which was set up as an office and lounge area with a desk, several sofas, and lots of pamphlets about things to do in the area. The large kitchen had lots of counter space and a big pine dining table with a long bench on one side and chairs on the other. A fat pit bull watched them from her bed by the back door. The aroma of bacon and muffins fresh from the oven completed the warm, welcoming room. A rather large woman, who stood at the six-burner gas stove in a flowery dress, tennis shoes, and permanently stained apron, turned to greet them.

"Oh, good. You're here. I'm Maggie. Y'all just make yourself at home." She grabbed a basket draped in cloth napkins and began to fill it with fresh blueberry muffins. "Joel, put these muffins on the table for people to munch on, and make sure everybody has something to drink."

"I'm on it," he said, moving quickly to place the basket, along with sugar and creamer containers, on the table. "Everybody want coffee? We've got a variety of teas if you'd rather have that, and orange juice and milk in the fridge."

"Coffee's good for both of us," Wil said. She sat in a chair at the end of the table so she could face the back door she anticipated Lacey would enter. Jimmy slid onto the bench beside her and served muffins for himself, her, and Joel. She took hers but was too nervous to eat.

Maggie added a double-stick butter dish to the table and spoke to Wil. "Now, about when Lacey gets here. Joel set up a little table out on the deck for you two, if you want to talk in private. We butted in as much as we could when she first showed up here, then called Andie to come this weekend to see if she and Sam could cheer her up, but she's been keeping to herself down by the pond the last couple of days."

Joel picked up where Maggie left off. "She does like her space and a good bit of alone time, but we're really worried—with her horse being hurt and all. She's talking about quitting the rodeo."

Wil nodded. "I've got an idea about that." She fidgeted in her chair. "If Andie can't get her to come up here, I'll go find her."

"Oh, she'll come," Joel said, grabbing Jimmy's coffee cup and taking it to the coffee station to refill it from the huge commercial brewer on the sideboard. "Andie's going to tell her something's wrong with Pig, and we need her help." The fat pit bull slapped her tail against the floor several times at the mention of her name.

"She's on her bed in the kitchen," Andie was saying as she came through the back door. And a second later, Lacey stood there, frozen as her gaze met Wil's.

Wil stood. "Hi. You're pretty hard to track down."

Lacey finally found her tongue but ignored Wil. She looked at Andie. "There's nothing wrong with Pig, is there?"

"No, but you need to hear Wil out."

Lacey spun around to leave without answering, but Wil was quick. She pushed past Andie and caught up with Lacey before she was halfway across the deck. She wrapped her arms around Lacey from behind and held on while she struggled to break loose.

"Lacey, stop. Just talk to me. Please. I deserve at least that." Pain shot up her leg when Lacey stomped her heel down onto Wil's foot. "Ow. Fuck. That hurt." She continued to struggle, but Wil was bigger and just as strong. "If you kick me in the knee, we're going to both end up lying on this deck, because I'm not letting go." Lacey stopped struggling, but Wil didn't relax the hug she'd wrapped around her. "I'm not letting go until you hear me out."

"Fine. Then will you leave me alone?"

"I can't promise that. I love you, and I intend to keep pounding that fact into your head until you believe me." Keeping her hold, she lifted Lacey and set her down next to the small bistro table with a red-checkered tablecloth tucked in a sunny corner of the deck. "Please sit."

Andie appeared with Wil's coffee and a second one for Lacey, and a plate with two muffins. She disappeared back into the house just as quickly.

Wil watched Lacey, in case she tried to make a break for the stairs, but she only glared at her.

"Say what you came to say."

Wil took out her phone and pulled up the photo of her and Brittney. "Let's clear this up first."

Lacey glanced at the photo, then looked away, the muscle in her jaw working. "You're going to claim it's photoshopped."

"I didn't see it until yesterday when Brittney confessed she'd shown it to you, but no. It's not photoshopped."

Lacey's head whipped around, her eyes blazing. "So, you were in bed with her? Did you climb into bed with her after we talked every night?"

"No. You know I didn't. Just look at this and listen." She positioned the photo so that it took up the entire screen, then enlarged it to focus on the time stamp. "This is the day I had that bad migraine. I don't have them often…once or twice a year…usually when the ranch next to ours is cleaning their chicken houses and the wind is blowing that crap to wherever I'm working outside."

"She said the migraine was one of your regular excuses when you dump a girl."

"Not true. To begin with, I haven't dated that many women, and the only one I've ever dumped is Brittney. She could definitely trigger a migraine in most people, but I never even used that as an excuse not to see her. The other women I briefly dated ditched me because I work too much, and they weren't interested in ranch life."

"Excuse or not, you were still in bed with her."

Wil shifted the enlargement to her image and handed the phone to Lacey. "Have I ever worn clothes when we sleep together?"

Lacey stared at the photo. "No." She bent to peer at Wil's image. "That's the collar of a T-shirt. The sleeve is pushed up to make you look like you're naked, but you're actually wearing a shirt."

"Brittney probably posed me like that."

Lacey dropped the phone to the table, sat back, and snorted. "Right. And you slept right through it. What about the locks that were on your door?"

"Look at my face in the photo, Lacey."

Lacey appeared skeptical, but she picked up the phone again and studied the shot.

"When have you ever seen me sleep with my mouth open like that?"

Lacey seemed to think this question over, and then her face softened. "That time we played a trivia game where you had to drink if you guessed wrong. You suck at trivia and got pretty drunk and passed out when I managed to get you into bed. You snored half the night until I managed to shove a pillow up under your chin to keep your mouth closed."

"Exactly. I was passed out the night Brittney took that selfie. Not from alcohol, but from pain pills. I don't like to take them unless nothing else is working, because they knock me out for nearly twelve hours and leave me groggy for two days. I was wearing a shirt, and my door wasn't locked because Dad likes to check on me every couple of hours when I have to take them. Brittney admitted to sneaking in after one of his checks, taking off her pajama shirt, and climbing into bed behind me to take that picture. She said I never stirred, and she didn't try to wake me because she was afraid I'd yell for Dad or call the police or something."

Lacey shoved the phone back at Wil and frowned. "Why would she tell you that now?"

"That's another long story, but she's facing her own personal reckoning, and I don't want to talk about her right now. I want to talk about us."

Lacey looked away again.

"I know about that Chandler guy. Whether he's your biological father or not has no bearing on us or the ranch. The Double R's reputation is solid. I've never flaunted my sexual orientation, but I've never, ever hidden it either. Wealthy Texans tend to put their personal judgments and religious leanings aside when it comes to securing a horse that's going to beat their competition."

"He was saying crude things about you to any cowboy in that bar who would listen."

Wil wanted to kiss her when Lacey's lips poked out in an indignant pout. Instead, she slowly reached for Lacey's hand and held it in hers when she didn't pull away. "He apparently made the mistake of saying things about Brittney, too. She told me that Mac sent a couple of his oil-rig roughnecks to help Mr. Chandler leave town. She said he woke up the next day in a crappy motel south of the border with a case of tequila on the table and no passport to get back into the country. She thinks they're hoping he'll drink himself to death."

"You seem to have spent a lot of time talking with Brittney lately."

"Again, we'll discuss her later. All I'll say now is that she and Pepper are a surprisingly good match. They're going to be hard to beat, but I'm telling you that because we have one more thing to clear up." She squeezed Lacey's hand and held her gaze. "Before I get into that, are we okay? Do you believe me…about the photo?"

Lacey took a moment, then nodded. "Yes."

"Thank God." Relief flooded Wil, and her eyes filled with tears. "Because I don't know what I'd do if you didn't. I love you, Lacey Bishop. I'm in love with you. I'd kill myself before I knowingly hurt you."

Lacey's eyes filled, too. She looked down but didn't try to brush her tears away. "Nobody's ever loved me before. It scares me."

Wil left her chair and knelt next to Lacey's, taking her face in her hands. "I know, sweetheart, and I'm trying not to do that, but we're meant to be together. I feel it in my bones. Since the moment I met you, something that's been missing in my life has clicked into place. If you feel the same, please don't run from me again."

"I might need some space sometimes—for a few hours or even a few days."

"I don't have a problem with that, as long as I know where you are and that you're safe and not planning to stay away."

Finally, Lacey reached for Wil's face and brushed her lips against Wil's. Their kiss deepened until they heard Sam in the kitchen exclaim, "They're kissing, you guys. They're kissing."

They pulled back from each other and chuckled.

"I guess we don't have to tell everyone we've made up," Wil said. "The town crier has taken care of that."

"I'm hungry," Lacey said. "I sort of skipped a few meals yesterday."

"Want to have Andie serve us out here, or go inside with the others?"

"Let's go inside so you can get to know Joel and Maggie. They're sort of family to me."

"Great. I brought someone I want you to meet, too. Jimmy's been a fixture on the ranch since I was a kid. He's kind of like one of those men you grow up calling uncle but isn't really related."

Even though Wil and Lacey had mostly settled their misunderstanding and fears, their touches were tentative when they left their friends and retreated to Lacey's camper for some well-needed privacy.

Wil undressed first, wanting to give Lacey a sense of control instead of being preyed on. Once she'd peeled down to her underwear and bra, Lacey stepped in and took over.

"I never thought I'd get to touch you again," she said with quiet reverence.

"I'm yours, sweetheart, to touch anytime you need to…for reassurance, for passion, for belonging. You are my heart. I will always be here for you."

Wil groaned as Lacey sucked at her taut nipple, then slid down to remove Wil's briefs. She kissed along Wil's legs and swiped her tongue along Wil's sex on her way back up. Wil gasped. "I'm going to need to lie down. And I want you naked beside me. I need to feel your skin on mine, to know you're truly here with me. I was so scared when I couldn't find you."

"Shush. I'm here with you now, Wil. I'm here, and I won't run from you again." She bit down on Wil's shoulder as she began to undress. "I'm claiming you as mine. Those other women can gnash their teeth and bare their breasts at you all they want. You're mine."

"I'm yours," Wil said.

They made love until both had climaxed several times, but the stress and lack of sleep over the past week finally demanded that they rest. Wil spooned her long body against Lacey's, and Lacey tugged Wil's arm forward to cradle it between her breasts.

"Wil?"

"Hmm."

"You said we needed to discuss one more thing, but we never did."

"Oh." Wil blinked, trying to stave off sleep so she could explain. "I sold Pepper to Mac Abbott for sixty thousand and Dash."

"You got Dash back?"

"Yes. Brittney never really matched up with him. He's a better horse than she was getting out of him. The best Mac could do was use him as a ranch horse or sell him to someone lower in the ranks for much less than he paid for him."

"Remind me to never negotiate anything with you. You're pretty good at it."

"The point is, I got Dash back because I think you could ride him better than Brittney…in the national finals."

"Seriously?"

"Yes. He's waiting for you at the ranch. You already have the points to enter, and we have a month for you two to get acquainted. If you want, we can hit one of the rodeos in Lubbock or Amarillo before the nationals, but I don't think Dash really needs the exposure. I don't intend to resell him."

Lacey sat up. "Really?"

"Yes. Dad also said for you to bring Denver to the ranch to rehab." Wil felt suddenly shy. "If you aren't comfortable staying with me, we have a guest room, or we can hook up your camper outside the barn."

"You still have those double locks on your bedroom door?"

"Well, yeah, but I can take them off."

Lacey smacked her hand down on Wil's bare rump. "You better not. The last thing I want is Ray Rivers walking into your room while I'm molesting his daughter."

Wil laughed and pulled her back down to spoon again. "Good point."

Lacey snuggled against her. "I love you, Wil Rivers."

"I love you, Lacey Bishop."

CHAPTER TWENTY-THREE

Lacey stood in her stirrups and leaned far over the neck of Dash of Charm as they raced past Wil, who stood by the imaginary finish line and clicked her stopwatch. Wil looked at the time and smiled, but her eyes told a different story.

"Fourteen-oh-five," she said when Lacey and Dash returned to her. She shrugged. "You're getting better. That's seven-hundredths of a second faster than last time."

"Brittney is consistently running Pepper under fourteen seconds, and several racers hit well below fourteen in last year's national final."

"Times are always faster at nationals. Those arenas have the best footing and most accurate equipment."

Lacey looked down at Wil. "We have to admit that Dash isn't the horse Pepper is. I know it, and you know it. We need to look realistically at whether I can place high enough with him so that the prize money isn't less than our expenses."

Wil looked doubtful, so Lacey softened her words. "I've been doing this a long time. Not just racing, but figuring out whether I needed to walk away from an event because the money didn't make sense. If you're not looking to sell Dash, I don't see the purpose in taking him to nationals."

"But you've had your heart set on it."

"With Denver, yes. But we both know she's done. We should be looking for a stallion to breed her instead."

Wil stared at the ground and fidgeted with the silver necklace she always wore. Lacey had come to recognize this was Wil's thinking mode, so she waited. "I've got another horse," she finally said. "Faster, but raw. His turns need a lot of work."

"Then let's give him a try."

❖

"Fourteen-point-three-five," Wil said, holding up the stopwatch. "I think he's getting it."

Lacey struggled to settle Flash as he pranced in place, clearly eager to go again. "It seems contradictory to stand up in the stirrups when I approach the third barrel, because that's what jockeys do to slow the horses after they reach the finish line."

"I know we don't have much time to train, but I still prefer you don't do that. It's dangerous for you to go into that turn standing up. If you're off a fraction of a second dropping back into the saddle when he flips around, you'll go flying headfirst."

"Nope. I'd go sideways and need to protect my shoulder more than my head. Besides, if I don't stand up, I end up fighting to get him to make that last turn. He wants to keep running straight ahead."

Wil frowned and placed her hand on Lacey's thigh. "Maybe this was a bad idea. I don't want you to get hurt."

Lacey bent down and lifted Wil's hand to her lips. "I know, babe. I'm being careful. Trust me on this?" She had initially chafed at Wil's tendency to be overprotective, reading it as controlling. But Ray had explained the riding accident that took the life of his wife, Wil's mother, to help her understand Wil's concern. So, she tried to be patient with Wil's need to keep her safe. And after some discussion, Wil was trying to lighten up.

"You're right. You know what you're doing."

"Thank you. Now, this big boy wants to go again, so let's do it."

❖

"Thirteen-point-nine-five for Lacey Bishop. That keeps her in the money but leaves the order of the top leaders in place as this year's Wrangler National Finals Rodeo Barrel Racing wraps up."

Wil met Lacey and Flash as they exited the arena. "Great job. That's a personal best for Flash."

Lacey laughed. "You mean a personal best for me. I finally managed to nail that weird third barrel turn."

Wil nodded. "I always said that until I ride perfectly, I can't expect my horse to work perfectly."

"Yeah, well, I have to agree. We're still going to retrain him on turns so I don't break my neck before we find a buyer for him next year."

"Glad to hear that," Wil said, smiling up at her.

Amanda Greene approached. "Hey, guys. Looking good, Lacey, with our Saddle Up logo on your shirt. Everybody is talking about your unique style taking those turns, and that means they're noticing our clothing line."

"Well, you're paying me enough to wear your stuff. I wish I could have placed higher for you, though."

"There's always next year," Amanda said. "We'd like to sponsor you again. Your photo shoot in our clothes has been a big hit."

"Thanks for giving me another chance after I lost my ride for a bit this year."

"It wasn't charity, just a good marketing move," Amanda said. "People have responded to the story that went with your photo spread. Reading about someone starting from the bottom and clawing their way to the top gives hope to a lot of people like you who didn't start out with a lot of resources." She backed away. "Gotta run. I'm catching a plane back to Australia for the holidays. Later this month we'll be sending you a new contract for next year."

They waved their farewell, then smiled at each other.

"That's a pretty good nest egg you're building up with a sponsor and your winnings," Wil said. "Maybe you should think about investing in a few horses to train and sell, too."

"Hmm. I'd need a place to train them."

"I've got an idea about that as well."

"That's some jacked-up turn you did out there," Brittney said, riding up on Pepper. "But it worked."

"Hopefully that's the last time you'll see it," Wil said. "Congratulations on placing fourth."

"It's not first place, but considering the competition, I'm happy with it. I'm pretty sure it's enough for Daddy to back me up when I tell my mother and Nana that I intend to keep racing next year."

"That gives us a year to retrain this guy on turns and give you a race for the big money next year," Lacey said.

"You can try." Brittney's challenge was friendly.

"Going to," Wil quipped.

Lacey didn't hate the woman any longer, after a lot of explaining from Wil about the week she'd spent with Brittney at the dude ranch and a sincere apology from Brittney, along with confirmation that nothing had happened between her and Wil. Still, she couldn't resist one last shot.

"Where are your groupies?"

Brittney pulled a face. "They're putting together a party at my suite to celebrate."

"I thought you were done with all that," Wil said.

"Ha. I wish. Bart and I both are ready for some peace and quiet, so we have a plan. He's having a bunch of the cowboys at his suite, and when everybody gets drunk enough, I'm going to herd my crew over to Bart's rooms. Then he and I will slip away back to mine, put out a Do Not Disturb sign, and lock the door."

Lacey laughed. "Good luck with that."

"What are you guys planning?"

Lacey looked down at Wil and held her gaze. "We'll have a quiet celebration of our own tonight, then head back to the ranch first thing tomorrow."

"You're not going to stay and try your luck in the casinos? After all, you are in Vegas."

Wil reached for Lacey's hand and smiled. "I've already placed my bet and won. We're going home."

EPILOGUE

Two years later

"Everybody here?" Ray stood at the head of the scarred six-place dining table.

"Jimmy and Wil are bringing in the last of the food," Lacey said from the sideboard, where she was fixing coffee for her and Wil. She sat on Ray's right, now her customary spot. Wil would sit next to her. Don took the chair at the other end of the table.

"Here we go." Jimmy placed a large platter of steaming scrambled eggs on the table and took his seat across from Lacey. Then a quiet sixteen-year-old slid in beside him. Jess was Jimmy's nephew, orphaned when his mother died of COVID. Ray had insisted that he come live at the ranch with his uncle, and the boy was shaping up to be an excellent wrangler.

Wil arrived last, delivering a plate of hot biscuits. Lacey tilted her head to accept the customary peck on the lips from Wil as she sat next to her.

Lacey loved their routine. Everyone had risen early to feed the horses and cows, then gathered at the ranch house for a big breakfast before heading out again to take care of the business of the day. She passed dishes of food, filling her plate, and teased Jimmy about the coffee dripping in his mustache. Being here felt comforting and safe. It felt like home. But things were about to change.

"Okay. Everybody keep eating while we get down to business," Ray said. "Jimmy, you go first."

Breakfast today was also the monthly ranch business meeting.

Jimmy sipped his coffee and wiped his mustache. "We birthed a bumper crop of calves last spring and got a good price on the ones we shipped out last week."

Wil interrupted. "According to my calculations, the price is good enough to cover most of our feed bill next year."

Jimmy nodded, then continued. "I kept back five of the heifers to expand the herd a bit since we've got more horses to feed next year. And I kept one calf I think will make a good bull. We need to replace ours soon. He's getting too old to service a herd as large as ours."

"Good plan," Ray said. "Jess, you doing okay in that bunkhouse with Jimmy?"

"Yes sir," the boy said, cracking a shy smile. "He's not very good at video games, but he's a pretty good cook, and he's teaching me to rope. Thank you for letting me have Flash to ride."

Lacey elbowed Wil, who bowed her head at what Lacey knew was coming.

"I told Wil that racehorse would never make a good barrel racer," Ray said.

Flash's second try at the national finals was about the same as his first year, even with his newly taught turns. The cheers of the crowd apparently reminded him too much of the racetrack, and he just wanted to run.

She laughed and elbowed Wil again. "And you were right. He needs a heavier rider, so he's turned out to be a pretty good ranch horse for Jess."

Ray moved on. "Don?"

"You know my report, but I'll share it with everybody. Looks like we'll be starting out the new year in good shape. We should have four cutters and three reining horses ready for sale by the first of the year, and another two cutters and two for reining will be ready by summer. There's more coming up behind them for the next year, so we need Wil to spend more time training the reining horses."

"That's no problem," Wil said. "Lacey and I are narrowing down the rodeos we go to, cutting out a lot of the little ones that aren't producing buyers for us." They had decided during Lacey's first spring at the ranch that she and Wil would act as a marketing team for the ranch, entering events on Double R horses to show them off for sale. The move had worked out so well, they could hardly keep up with the demand for their horses. "Lacey's getting pretty good at showing the reining horses, but I think we need to consider contracting a rider to show our cutters. You and Don could use the help training those horses, too. You guys aren't getting any younger."

Ray narrowed his eyes. "I'll think about it, but I'm waiting on some grandchildren to hand off my job to so I can sit on the porch and smoke cigars all day."

"Not happening soon, old man," Lacey said. "Unless Wil is up to the task."

"You two aren't getting any younger either," Ray said, bringing up their usual good-natured argument.

Neither of them had any desire to be pregnant or tend to the demands of a baby, but they'd tentatively discussed adopting a child five to ten years old, the age that young parents usually overlooked. Yet they weren't ready to share these plans with the rest of the people around the table.

"Since this is our last business meeting of the year, I want to say one more thing." Wil paused, and Lacey slid her hand under the table to rest it on her thigh in a show of support. "I know things are going really well financially, but I want to be careful about buying new horses this year. I don't want to expand so much that we'll find ourselves in a bind if something like the last pandemic shuts things down again."

Ray, Don, and Jimmy all nodded. "I think that's smart," Don said.

"You have something to add, boss lady?" Ray had jokingly labeled Lacey as the little rooster that ran the chicken house, since everyone, including Wil, regularly deferred to her practical approach to things.

"The vet has confirmed that Denver's pregnant with her second Diamond baby. That's the last breeding we negotiated when Wil sold him."

"Good. If we get a colt this time, I want to look at keeping it for stud," Ray said.

Lacey confirmed his proposal with a nod. "Also, I'm happy to report that the crew is finishing the cabin this week, and we'll start moving some furniture in by the weekend." She smiled at Don. "That means you should be able to get your bedroom furniture out of storage the following week and move into Wil's bedroom. It's a lot bigger than the guest room."

Yes, their current arrangement was about to change. Don's wife had succumbed to and didn't survive a second round of COVID. Since the couple never had children, Ray insisted his boyhood friend and fellow horse trainer sell his house and move to the ranch so the two of them could live out their lives in companionship. Neither intended to remarry.

During a short vacation at the dude ranch near Big Spring, Wil had convinced Lacey to build their own log cabin at the ranch, similar to but larger than the one she and Brittney had stayed in. After having no family, Lacey reveled in her growing extended family at the ranch, but they both needed some quiet and privacy, too.

"Good," Ray said, his grin widening. "More room for grand-children."

With that, Wil stood. "Jimmy cooked, so the rest of you men are on dish duty before you head to the barn. Lacey and I took our turn yesterday."

Jess grumbled as he wrapped two jelly-filled biscuits in a napkin and put them aside to eat later, then began gathering plates. "When did the women start being in charge of everything?"

Don laughed. "Son, you've got a lot to learn. The women have always been in charge, ever since Eve told Adam to eat that apple. They just give us enough rein to think we're driving the herd sometimes."

Lacey hooked her arm in Wil's and guided her to the wide porch that ran the length of the ranch house. It'd warm up to near sixty degrees later in the day, but the morning air still held a hint of crispness.

Wil withdrew her arm to wrap it around Lacey's shoulders. "Happy?" she asked.

"Very," Lacey answered, feeling like she would burst with the sensation.

"I know I'll be glad to get in our cabin for some quiet and

privacy. I love Don and Dad, but I'll be really glad to have you alone again."

"Well, you might have to wait for that. We'll barely be moved in when everybody gets here for Christmas," Lacey said.

In just the two holidays she'd been at the ranch, the Christmas she'd never had as a child was becoming her very favorite time of the year. COVID had also claimed Maggie's sister, so she, Joel, and Pig closed the campground for the week surrounding the festive holiday and came to the Double R to celebrate. Andie's widowed mother now had a beau and they liked to travel for the holidays, so Andie and Sam also joined the celebration. This year, Andie hinted that she might bring someone special she'd been recently dating. As much as Lacey valued her private time, she reveled in this upcoming week of family and close friends.

"Good. Then you can put Maggie in charge of decorating." Wil loved picking out a live tree they would plant after the holidays, but she chafed at dragging out all the trinkets needed to turn the house into a winter wonderland. Maggie and Joel, on the other hand, loved the task.

"Absolutely." The fun novelty of decorating was beginning to wear thin on Lacey, too, and they'd have two houses to fill this Christmas.

Wil heaved a big sigh, signaling it was time to end their quiet moment and get to work.

"Hey. I noticed one of the yearlings in the east pasture yesterday is favoring his right hind. Can you come with me to catch him and take a look?"

"Always," Wil said, bending her head to steal a sweet kiss. "I'm always here for you."

About the Author

D. Jackson Leigh grew up barefoot and happy, swimming in farm ponds and riding rude ponies in rural Georgia. She has retired from her career as a journalist but continues her real passion—writing sultry lesbian romances laced with her trademark Southern humor and affection for dogs and horses.

She has published 16 novels and one collection of short stories with Bold Strokes Books, winning five Golden Crown Literary Society awards in paranormal, romance, and fantasy categories. She was also a finalist in the romance category of the 2014 Lambda Literary Awards.

You can friend her at facebook.com/d.jackson.leigh.

Books Available From Bold Strokes Books

Digging for Heaven by Jenna Jarvis. Litz lives for dragons. Kella lives to kill them. The last thing they expect is to find each other attractive. (978-1-63679-453-2)

Forever's Promise by Missouri Vaun. Wesley Holden migrated west disguised as a man for the hope of a better life and with no designs to take a wife, but Charlotte Rose has other ideas. (978-1-63679-221-7)

Here For You by D. Jackson Leigh. A horse trainer must make a difficult business decision that could save her father's ranch from foreclosure but destroy her chance to win the heart of a feisty barrel racer vying for a spot in the National Rodeo Finals. (978-1-63679-299-6)

I Do, I Don't by Joy Argento. Creator of the romance algorithm, Nicole Hart doesn't expect to be starring in her own reality TV dating show, and falling for the show's executive producer Annie Jackson could ruin everything. (978-1-63679-420-4)

It's All in the Details by Dena Blake. Makeup artist Lane Donnelly and wedding planner Helen Trent can't stand each other, but they must set aside their differences to ensure Darcy gets the wedding of her dreams, and make a few of their own dreams come true. (978-1-63679-430-3)

Marigold by Melissa Brayden. Marigold Lavender vows to take down Alexis Wakefield, the harsh food critic who blasts her younger sister's restaurant. If only she wasn't as sexy as she is mean. (978-1-63679-436-5)

A Second Chance at Life by Genevieve McCluer. Vampires Dinah and Rachel reconnect, but a string of vampire killings begin and evidence seems to be pointing at Dinah. They must prove her innocence while finding out if the two of them are still compatible after all these years. (978-1-63679-459-4)

The Town That Built Us by Jesse J. Thoma. When her father dies, Grace Cook returns to her hometown and tries to avoid Bonnie Whitlock, the woman who pulverized her heart, only to discover her father's estate has been left to them jointly. (978-1-63679-439-6)

A Degree to Die For by Karis Walsh. A murder at the University of Washington's Classics Department brings Professor Antigone Weston and Sergeant Adriana Kent together—first as opposing forces and then as allies as they fight together to protect their campus from a killer. (978-1-63679-365-8)

Finders Keepers by Radclyffe. Roman Ashcroft's past, it seems, is not so easily forgotten when fate brings her and Tally Dewilde together— along with an attraction neither welcomes. (978-1-63679-428-0)

Homeland by Kristin Keppler and Allisa Bahney. Dani and Kate have finally found themselves on the same side of the war, but a new threat from the inside jeopardizes the future of the wasteland. (978-1-63679-405-1)

Just One Dance by Jenny Frame. Will Taylor Sparks and her new business to make dating special—the Regency Romance Club—bring sparkle back to Jaq Bailey's lonely world? (978-1-63679-457-0)

On My Way There by Jaycie Morrison. As Max traverses the open road, her journey of impossible love, loss, and courage mirrors her voyage of self-discovery leading to the ultimate question: If she can't have the woman of her dreams, will the woman of real life be enough? (978-1-63679-392-4)

A Talent Within by Suzanne Lenoir. Evelyne, born into nobility, and Annika, a peasant girl with a deadly secret, struggle to change their destinies in Valmora, a medieval world controlled by religion, magic, and men. (978-1-63679-423-5)

Transitioning Home by Heather K O'Malley. An injured soldier realizes they need to transition to really heal. (978-1-63679-424-2)

Truly Enough by J.J. Hale. Chasing the spark of creativity may ignite a burning romance or send a friendship up in flames. (978-1-63679-442-6)

Vintage and Vogue by Kelly and Tana Fireside. When tech whiz Sena Abrigo marches into small-town Owen Station, she turns librarian Hazel Butler's life upside down in the most wonderful of ways, setting off an explosive series of events, threatening their chance at love…and their very lives. (978-1-63679-448-8